CITY OF STORMS

PAUL CAMPBELL

City of Storms
Paul Campbell

This edition Copyright © 2015 by Oxford eBooks Ltd
www.oxford-ebooks.com
Story Copyright © 2014 by Paul Campbell

The right of the author to be identified as the author of this work has been asserted in accordance with the Copyright, Designs and Patents Act 1988.

All rights reserved.
No part of this publication may be reproduced, stored in a retrieval system, or transmitted, in any form or by any means, electronic, mechanical, photocopying, recording or otherwise, without the prior permission of the copyright owners.

ISBN 978-1-908387-99-8 (Paperback)
ISBN 978-1-908387-97-4 (ePUB)
ASIN B00R893CEM (Kindle)

Book design and typesetting by
Oxford eBooks Ltd.
www.oxford-ebooks.com

Oxford eBooks

City of Storms is a work of fiction set against a factual background.

As such, there are real scenes and figures of historical record, as well as some names which reflect actual people whom I choose to salute for their valued personal association over the years I spent in Asia, and beyond.

Yes, there was a Bagyo Cruz, a name I coined for the street waif who reached out to beg pesos from me through the window of an airport bound taxi on Manila's Roxhas Boulevard, one Christmas Day many years ago. His actual words "Me, no Christmas" formed the original working title of this book. His prior, and subsequent adventures, necessarily, spring from imagination.

Paul Campbell
Christmas 2014

Paul Campbell spent four decades as a reporter, editor and foreign correspondent for newspapers, wire services, magazines, radio and television in a dozen countries before turning to books as an editor and author. "In *City of Storms*," he says, "fact is the genesis of fiction."

Prologue

Deep in the Ross Sea a thirty-tonne sperm whale cruises north through icy waters to warmer breeding grounds with his reference point a narrow, mountainous land rising between the Pacific Ocean and the Tasman Sea.

The huge bull is escorted by cows and offspring and the pod moves leisurely over silent days and mysterious nights along the rocky eastern coastline of New Zealand, instinctively following a centuries-old sea-lane.

They occasionally reveal themselves far out on the surface of the sea, venting great misty vapour clouds, the hot breath of life, before surging onwards through the green depths.

The whales skirt serrated eastern fingers of land rounding the northern tip of North Island's Coromandel Peninsula, entering the maelstrom of an eleven-mile wide Colville Channel as the tide begins to move.

Then, with the mainland below the horizon on their left and rugged, isolated Great Barrier Island bearing away to the right, something fails them.

The great bull and his entourage end an ocean traverse by turning east into thrashing confusion on wide, sandy, Okupu beach in Great Barrier Island's aptly-named Blind Bay. It leads nowhere and the senseless touch of land becomes a devil's anvil.

The wide sand beach emerges quickly from the receding tide, stranding the great bull, the cows and calves on baking sands, capped by a cloudless sky and scorching sun. Low water soon seals the trap and the mountains of flesh begin slowly to bake alive.

Has confused navigation turned them too soon to measure the length of the island and emerge northwards into the wide Pacific? Have they broken their pattern to shepherd one of their own from danger?

Islanders who soon gather above the beach say the small calf whale at the highest point on the beach drew in the pod in an attempt to turn the infant back to the sanctuary of the sea.

But the cetacean travellers die on the beach and putrefy while evening sea breezes carry their nightmare stench to blanket the land.

Island residents gather boats to tow the huge rotting carcasses to sea, the whales seared black skins shredding like giant sheets of polythene, obscene under the summer sun.

The grisly task begun, a man steps from the land above the beach, a solitary figure moving towards a great carcass bereft by the tide.

He carries a bow saw to the dead and rotting whale and kneeling at the gaping mouth he begins cutting. His task complete he drags the severed lower jaw across the sand and up to his home above the beach. He takes a spade and begins digging in the sandy clay.

The whale suicide is still being talked about on the island years later when the man, accompanied by a small boy, returns to the area above the beach and with the same spade digs and uncovers the huge jaw.

The child looks on intently, fascinated. The flesh has long been absorbed by earth life, leaving a broad expanse of bone, studded with giant, ivory teeth.

With a chisel the man hacks at the bone and frees one of the smaller protrusions from the huge jaw. From its placing it is the equivalent of a human eye-tooth.

Cutting away the thinner ivory where it was once seated in bone the man takes an awl, makes a hole and takes a waxed cord from his pocket. Making a loop he hangs the tooth round the boy's neck.

Chapter One

Manila, Philippines, 1983

RAIN SWIRLED IN silvery ribbons across battered shop-fronts lining the broken pavement, the road awash from choked gutters overflowing after barely an hour of the tropical downpour.

Lifting the long skirts of her nun's habit with one hand, the other raising her umbrella, Sister Jan stepped into the streaming roadway outside the Caritas office in Tondo, an impoverished suburb of the Philippines capital city, Manila.

Rickety clapboard buildings patched with battered signs advertising soft drinks, beer, cigarettes, foodstuffs and cooking oil lined the street, laced in a cobweb of illegal power lines.

Wary of the ubiquitous jeepneys, originally cobbled together from the remains of US army jeeps after World War Two, and now the adopted style of side street Filipino auto shops, the tall, graceful nun hurried across to a marketplace huddled beneath sagging canvas awnings. A sheltering crowd parted respectfully and the shelter of a rude stall was laced with the pungent aroma of spiky durian fruit.

Smiling, an old woman reached to touch her hand, shouting over the din of the rain, the racket of horns and traffic from the road.

"*Kumusta*. Welcome sister. How are you?" Lined brown parchment face pierced by dark smoky eyes, old with the passage of life. A uniform of the slum, tee-shirt stained and patched, a nondescript wrap-around skirt, gnarled brown feet in battered sandals.

Sister Jan returned the smile. "I'm happy with what the Lord provides, except," she grimaced at the weather in general, "for this." She had Australia's nasal tones and at almost six feet in her tropical habit, head bowed under the low canvas, she towered over the diminutive Filipina.

She nodded at the road where trucks, cars and elaborately decorated jeepneys edged through the rain, her face a bronze cameo in the diffused light, her blue eyes concerned.

"It's going to get worse before it gets better."

Reaching into her robes for a ten-peso banknote she indicated a score of small, almost luminous green fruits on a wooden tray.

"Just some *kalamansi* please."

As she checked the centavos of her change, the rain increased its frenetic drum-roll and she saw the water rising in the road, slow-rolling wheels slapping bow waves into the swollen gutters.

The canvas crackled overhead in the first gust of storm winds hunting the city.

"Looks like the typhoon is definitely heading our way."

"More misery for us," came the stall-keeper's resigned response. "The third this season. We're still repairing the *barrio* school from the last one."

Sister Jan nodded, distracted, as she mentally listed the meagre resources of the Caritas Soriano Centre she had just left; a shelter and soup kitchen with food, blankets and floor space but little else.

By morning her household would swell by several hundred people, the washed-out human scavengers from Smoky Mountain. Manila's giant suburban garbage heap was home to blighted souls scratching a precarious existence from the city's waste; plastic shopping bags washed and recycled, metal collected for scrap, food refuse crammed into hungry mouths as the fossicking went on.

Too often a diseased and hungry death was hidden in the rubbish.

Shaking off images that chipped at her faith, Sister Jan

turned back.

"You should get away to your home while the jeepneys are still running. I must go and see to things at the Centre."

She smiled at the old woman, knowing tonight she would be providing her shelter. Aida would stay grimly at her stall trying to quit her meagre fruit stocks to those who could afford a little extra against the passage of the storm. Fresh supplies could take many days to reach the city.

At a halt in the traffic the nun stepped nimbly back across the road to the Soriano Centre, its stucco exterior imposing its presence on the ramshackle block about it. The downpour left her dripping water into the parquet-floored entrance and slipping off her plastic sandals, she stepped inside.

The house reflected the fall of its former owners under the corrupt regime of the Philippines leader, President Ferdinand Marcos.

Those Filipinos opposed to the dictator in his fortress palace of Malacanyang soon found their fortunes spiralling downwards and the aristocratic family who built the house, whose rural sugar estates were handed down from Spanish colonial ancestors in the days of the treasure galleons, found that shipments disappeared, labour problems hit production, mysterious fires broke out and bank credit became impossible.

Rather than have the town house sold from under him, the former owner deeded the property to the church. But lack of funds for maintenance led to genteel shabbiness as paint lifted in the humid air and bubbled on its walls and the now polished wood of floors and door frames were scarred by mould.

But it was clean and had a secure air, while the smell of food alone gave comfort where a bowl of rice at day's close was too often a luxury on the mean streets of Tondo.

Downstairs a large lounge flowed into a dining hall and three utility rooms opened up to make a kitchen and laundry area. On the upper level of the house were dormitories, some with canvas and cane beds; others with sleeping mats on the floor.

Moving across the hall to the kitchen, intent on a glass of water and a sprinkling of her limes Sister Jan halted abruptly.

Marianne, cook, cleaner and house mother, was seated at the large meal table, her ample frame overflowing her chair, a large brown breast pushing free over the bodice of her blue cotton dress. She suckled an infant.

Before the astonished nun could speak, thunder rolled across the city, punctured by a broadsheet of lightning. The rain thrummed in growing intensity and Sister Jan yelled above the roar on the corrugated iron roof "Marianne - what on earth?"

She moved closer, peering into the tiny face, lifting away the cheap cloth shawl. The child was just a few days old.

"He was left just inside the gate, Sister. I heard him crying when I came downstairs. I've fed my little Anita. Father has also checked the baby. He is healthy. So now I feed him too."

The words spilled out in a rush, her rich brown eyes shining in maternal contentment.

At a sound in the doorway Sister Jan turned to see Father Frederick Stols, German-born, Catholic, a priest who'd made the Philippines a life's mission. Short, stocky and balding, a figure clad in the black robe of the Jesuits, he entered from the small paved courtyard behind the kitchen.

"Yes Sister. Another mouth to feed. A healthy boy, just a day or so old. Another child of Ermita perhaps."

The tawdry tourist belt, an hour-long ride away by jeepney, was concentrated on the red-light street of MH del Pilar. Home to a hundred bars, hotels, restaurants, brothels and boarding houses. The area gave employment, legitimate and otherwise, to twenty thousand souls - bar staff, go-go dancers, prostitutes, drug dealers, money-changers, food vendors, shoe-shine boys, sidewalk pedlars, hustlers and crippled beggars.

From around the world jumbo jets of a dozen airlines landed cash-rich visitors at Manila International Airport, many bent on heady pursuits of the flesh.

Among the thousands of young women who flocked to Manila from an impoverished countryside, were the naïve, the poorly educated and careless and in the Roman Catholic Philippines, abortion was not an option.

Soriano Centre's new infant was likely born in some hovel behind a bar, his mother tended by her street sisters, the squalling infant dumped on the church even as a young mother staggered back to sell herself.

Another kettledrum of thunder collapsed across the city. Sister Jan turned to the old rumbling refrigerator and reached for a plastic bottle of boiled water.

Pouring three glasses, she sliced limes.

"We must try and find out who left him with us," she said. "She must need help." But even as she spoke, hope was dead in her voice.

Marianne rose, adjusting her dress and lifting the infant to her shoulder.

"He can go to sleep with my Anita."

She drained her glass of water and made her ponderous way to the stairs and the small room she shared with her own child under the eaves.

Father Stols finished his own drink then set the glass carefully on the table.

"Thank you Sister. Now I must check with the *barrio* captain to see what emergency measures are being taken. This typhoon promises to be a bad one and we may have a full house by tonight."

Standing slowly, he pressed a hand into the small of his back in unconscious acknowledgement of his years of tropical labour. He took the umbrella propped against the doorway and stepped out into the evening gloom. Flickering lights from the bare bulbs of the still-busy market place sparkled through a curtain of water. The barrio captain, a sort of suburban mayor, lived two doors up the street.

Closing the door to the weather, Sister Jan moved back into the room, opening a large cupboard and its collection of crockery, plastic plates and bowls. Bending, she selected two large aluminium pots from the bottom shelf and filled them with water from the sink to one side. For the hundredth time she thought to get the containers replaced, knowing Father Stols would reject the request for lack of funds.

But, heated on the four-burner bottled gas cooker, the containers would provide a hundred bowls of rice, seasoned with a little fish-paste and a few vegetables. Nourishment for the imminent influx of victims of Typhoon Nora, advancing on the city across the battered rice plains of Luzon province, her breath gusting to 180 kilometres-an-hour.

Chapter Two

TEN THOUSAND FEET over Luzon, a Cathay Pacific Lockheed Tri-Star inbound from Hong Kong arrowed towards Manila International Airport, canned landing music dripping balm for the nervous as the plane descended.

From his business-class seat, Sean Brian looked through the window at the boiling grey clouds rolling below.

The first officer's clipped British tones had warned passengers to beware of turbulence from the fringes of Typhoon Nora, at the same time offering an assurance they'd reach Manila well ahead of the full blast of the storm.

Sean turned back from the window raising his glass. The plane lurched in an updraft and he swung his hand to compensate for the movement. With the other he instinctively reached for the amulet round his neck, touching the ivory, warm from his body heat, lifting it to his lips.

A lean, fit-looking man of 35 years, his deep tan signalled years spent in the tropics. The cut of his light brown hair, clean-shaven regular features, and neatly tailored safari-suit set him apart from many of the flight's other male passengers, jeans-and-T-shirt clad, obviously holiday-bound.

An oil man perhaps, a trader or some other expatriate career professional bringing his expertise to Asia.

Letting the whale's tooth talisman drop Sean mentally rebuked himself for superstition. Years of flying just about every plane that carried passengers should have inured him to white-knuckle syndrome but he'd never be happy carried aloft. A stiff drink was a constant travelling companion.

"*Now,*" he thought, "*I'm flying into a typhoon! Bloody good time to get a job in the Philippines.*"

As the Hong-Kong-based regional foreign correspondent for United Press International, Sean had been telephoned at dawn in his flat near Aberdeen.

Asian bureau chief, Tony Baynes, had been brief and to the point.

"Something's stirring at Malacanyang. Get down there and link up with Rhonda Rollinson in the Manila office."

Lying in bed he'd rolled over to look at the digital clock-radio on the small bedside table, sorting confused memories of the night that had started at the Radio Television Hong Kong club bar in Kowloon.

He and a couple of RTHK journalists and a news crew from TVB, the local commercial television station, had had a few drinks and, primed for entertainment, had taken a taxi over Princess Margaret viaduct through the Cross Harbour tunnel to Wanchai's neon-draped red light district on the island.

First the Popeye Club, then The Wanch Folk Bar and then on to Club Pussycat He found himself talking to a Vietnamese refugee lass who'd made the perilous crossing of the South China Sea to Hong Kong in the early days after the communist takeover. It turned out she had a degree from the Sorbonne in Paris, having been sent to France by her wealthy parents, only to return to Vietnam and a teaching position just as the city fell to the forces of Ho Chi Minh. Now she helped support her family, still in Vietnam, with two jobs; days at the Baptist College in Kowloon and nights in the Pussycat Club, where drink commissions almost matched her daytime salary.

Sean had spent a pleasant hour talking Asian politics in the incongruous setting, buying a couple of over-priced cold teas to save her having to hustle other, bigger-spending customers. Later he'd walked unsteadily out into the hot night and flagged another taxi.

He vaguely recalled the driver warning him a *taifung* was coming. A typhoon signal had been hoisted at the Royal Observatory in Kowloon as a preliminary warning to the colony.

He'd fallen into bed around 4am and the call had woken him three hours later.

He was well aware that over the past week there'd been growing tension in the Philippines.

For two decades, Ferdinand Marcos, self-proclaimed war hero, author and statesman, had ruled the Philippines by presidential decree, supported by the armed forces. Those who opposed him strongly enough had two choices; prison under a martial law provision or exile.

Formerly the governing power in the Philippines, the United States was a favoured destination for émigrés, but Washington turned a Nelsonian blind eye to Marcos's excesses, having been so instrumental in his elevation to the presidential palace.

The White House was also ever conscious that Marcos sanctioned huge US naval and air force bases at Subic Bay and Clarke Field, just north of Manila, U.S. outposts seen as vital links in the defence of the free world.

One of those who chose exile over detention was a long-time Marcos opponent, former provincial governor and senator, Benigno 'Ninoy' Aquino.

In recent months, there'd been a shift in dynamics in his homeland. Marcos was in ill health and as he turned more and more to his attractive and charismatic wife, Imelda, for advice in running the country, rumours spread of a private medical clinic being installed near his bedroom in the presidential palace. A perceived weakening led to opposition becoming bolder.

Aquino was fearful of civil war in his homeland and was soon called upon to come back to link together the opposition forces ranging across the Philippines' political spectrum. His supporters secured assurances from Marcos of his safe passage but ignored warnings from the First Lady that Aquino's enemies were everywhere.

When he ignored the threat and flew home, military officers boarded the Japan Airlines Boeing 747 on the apron outside the Manila terminal building and Aquino was quickly ushered off the aircraft, Journalists travelling with him were ordered to remain seated, 'to enhance security.'

As Aquino stepped away from the boarding steps to be met on the tarmac by an escort of armed soldiers from the Aviation Security Command, he was shot in the back of the head from a .357 Magnum revolver.

He dropped, head shattered, in his first step back onto Philippine soil. The killer, dressed in the uniform of an airport baggage handler, had fallen in turn, under a convenient hail of automatic gunfire from the military escort.

Aquino's body was rushed into the terminal building for futile first aid. A press release from Malacanyang Palace later identified the gunman as a petty criminal who'd somehow evaded 'fool-proof' airport security.

Later in a Manila funeral home a bulletproof vest was stripped from Aquino's body, mute proof that violence had not been unexpected.

But if Marcos and his wife believed opposition to their despotic rule had been eliminated, they'd disastrously misread the national mood.

Millions turned out across the nation to mourn Aquino and street demonstrations against the killing erupted in rioting. Martial law was declared.

A jolt from an air pocket suddenly broke Sean's reverie. He finished his drink and passed the glass to an attractive Filipina stewardess as she bent to check his seatbelt.

Tightening his inadequate lap-strap he swallowed, tasting sourness. An hour from Hong Kong and he was still queasy. The cup of coffee at the airport lounge at Kai Tak had done nothing to quell the fatigue and slight nausea from the previous night's excesses. The two in-flight double whiskeys hadn't helped either.

He leaned back into his seat and moments later the aircraft emerged rocking through the cloud base, banking steeply to line up with the airport runway. Rain smeared the windows and rattled on the thin skin of the fuselage, the sound suddenly drowning under engine noise as the flight deck boosted throttles on final approach.

As the aircraft touched down smoothly Sean relaxed his grip on the arms of his seat and stopped concentrating blindly on the folded tray in front of him, turning to look out over the shimmering silver wing at the rain-slick tarmac. His thoughts drifted to the evening ahead and his spirits lightened in anticipation.

He'd get in touch with Rollinson in the Manila office tomorrow. Tonight he had private business.

Her name was Maria Cipriano, a 23-year-old beauty of mixed parentage, Filipina and Japanese, who'd made something of an impression upon him.

They met on one of Sean's past Philippines assignments and letters and telephone calls over the past few months had added substance and detail to days of whirlwind romance. He'd reached her by phone that morning before leaving for the airport.

Over the years, the Asian beat for UPI had kept him busy and occasional evening entertainment in most of the Asian cities he covered sometimes involved a casual bed-bound relationship. Once married, twice shy, Sean had really settled for superficiality, unwilling to complicate his life with the underlying fear of being hurt again. Then Maria came into his orbit. "A chance meeting in, of all places, a bloody flower shop!" he'd recalled to his drinking companions of the night before.

Picturing Maria in his mind, her eyes were something to swim inside, touching her, electricity shivered through him, breath stopping at the caress of her hands.

His blood surged to his centre and he adjusted himself in

his seat, the big jet's engines roaring in reverse thrust as the plane decelerated abruptly before turning off the runway.

Minutes later the air-bridge hissed in and the forward door cracked open and swung inboard. He stood and slid his overnight bag from the locker overhead and was one of the first passengers out, smiling his thanks to the hostess standing at the exit.

In the narrow tube to the terminal the avgas sting tickled his nose. After the dry cold of the air-conditioned and pressurised Tri-Star, the evening was alive with the smell of kerosene, warm moist air, hot machinery, distant food and the confused sounds of land.

Inside the arrivals island a Filipino guitar band in black slacks and white *barong tagalog* shirts welcomed a China Airlines package tour. Sean hurried onto the moving walkway to Immigration. There, after a glance at his well-thumbed and stamped New Zealand passport and a quick check of the computer terminal below the level of her booth, the officer waved him on.

Customs also obliged with a swift and cursory examination and he threaded his way through shouting taxi touts and porters, their noise swelling through the cavernous vault of the arrival hall. The building's entrance was thronged with hundreds of locals awaiting brothers, sisters, husbands and wives, sons and daughters, uncles and aunts. Hundreds of thousands of Philippine domestic workers employed around the world earned the lifeblood of the national economy and were eagerly greeted as they returned from jobs overseas. The greeting crowd was kept out of the already congested building by an admission ticket system, which few local people could afford.

Outside, Sean pushed his way through to the left of the terminal searching for the Yellow Cabs that approximated some sort of honest service.

Reaching the reserved rank sheltered from the rain by the

elevated sweep of the departures access road he thrust a 100 peso note through the open window of a battered Subaru sedan in payment for the 50 peso trip to town. "Forget the meter, let's go."

He opened the door and threw his bag across the rear seat, crouching to get in and cursing the size of Japanese cars.

Hunched uncomfortably to avoid the roof lining he watched the driver sawing up and down through the gears as the traffic edged towards the airport entrance.

There, opposite the Casino Filipinas, Sean gave directions.

"Pare, friend, head for George's Bar in Ermita."

On the edge of the red light area the bar was Sean's Manila headquarters, acting as a message centre for a number of travelling newsmen.

As his taxi pulled into the four-lane traffic stream on Roxhas Boulevard, heading north skirting the grey, rain-swept waters of Manila Bay, he mused on his destination. *"There's a good story there someday,"* he thought. *"Maybe memoir material."*

The bar was established by a retired Australian gunner on the proceeds of a thriving black market operation in the closing years of the Vietnam war.

In true antipodean fashion the ANZAC soldiers of Australian and New Zealand units had become adept at raiding the American PX installations laid out at Da Nang and other huge sprawling and confused marshalling bases.

These professional soldiers had easily evaded the largely conscripted elements of the US forces and acquired a vast array of misappropriated equipment and liquor, indeed at the end of the day, complete vehicles and stores of supplies which were sold back to the yanks at a profit, as well as to the Vietnamese.

A United States Army Air Corps Iroquois helicopter had even disappeared on otherwise empty Pacific-bound ferry flights, rotor by rotor, motor, piece by piece, instrument by instrument.

Old hands in the services said the pirated fling-wing had since won a US Air Force *concorse d'elegance* competition for allied nations.

George, the only name he allowed, had saved his share of the profits from the enterprise and bought his peace in Ermita.

He ran a straight bar, booze, food, pool, darts, backgammon and yangtze dice. No girls.

The taxi pulled up outside and Sean ducked through the warm heavy rain to the door, pushing it open and stepping down the few inches to the wooden floor inside. Across the smoky room George was seated in his habitual corner. With him Sean recognised the tall figure of Peter 'Pedro' Wright, the chief of the Philippine National Police Bureau. He also noted the *barong*-clad security men at a discreet distance, standing against the panelled walls on three sides of the large room.

George's was a safe-haven when the silver-haired Wright had a drink after work. A target for the Manila underworld, he had a comfort zone in the expatriate bar. Among its clientele local crooks would soon be spotted and removed by his minders.

Sean crossed the room exchanging quick greetings with several regulars.

"Mate, how are you? How long are you back in town?" said George.

"I'm looking at the Marcos situation so I don't know how long. I'll touch base tomorrow. Just wanted to say I'm at the Regent if you get any calls."

He declined a beer, returned Wright's formal hand-shake and edged through the crowd of drinkers, pausing to touch base briefly with John McIvor, an old friend and Manila correspondent of regional news magazine *Asia week*, who was with a group of oil men from the rigs out in the South

China Sea. He left the bar and re-entered the yellow cab.
"Okay *pare*, the Regent. And we'll call it 150 pesos."

Chapter Three

MARIA CIPRIANO STOOD at the window of her walk-up apartment on downtown United Nations Avenue watching the rain as it harried pedestrians crossing the street below.

Music from a *Tagalog* station, the hit song *Anak*, wafted from the mini-stereo on the magazine table beside her. As she absently watched the movement in the street she brushed an emery board across the edges of her nails. The evening was darkening and lights in the apartment building opposite were flicking on, curtains being pulled against the night. The multi-coloured neon sign above Robinson's department store down the block provided an artificial horizon in the murk.

Tall for a Filipina, a lithe figure draped in a towelling robe, Maria was the late-born of a Filipino mother and a Japanese father. As such she was a child of good fortune for unlike many Filipinas left behind with bastard children, her mother had married the Japanese scholar she fell in love with when he returned in search of her several years after the Second World War.

Maria's parents had immersed themselves in a quiet and peaceful life in one of the better suburbs of the city, he an accountant with a successful business handling the complex Philippines tax process for multi-national companies.

Maria's mother retained her maiden name for her children in a land where some stigma still attached to things Japanese and she devoted herself to home and the church, content to ignore the wider world.

Maria grew up with two older brothers in a cloistered world of rosaries and mass; education by nuns at a church-run school. A visit to town would only be made with her mother as chaperone.

But it was a world that fell apart when she was just 20

years old.

Her parents were drowned in the capsize of an overloaded ferry on a holiday weekend trip to the island resort of Puerto Galera, south of Manila.

Maria had stayed at home to cram for university exams. Scarcely out of her teens she was devastated and with her two older brothers soon recalled after the funeral to their provincial army postings, she was left very much alone.

Shocked that such a thing could happen, she took little comfort from the church. 'God's will' was not an answer she wanted to hear from the priests to whom she turned.

The one place she found solace was with an old school-friend, Jaqui Benedict.

The centre of mischief at school and unusually defiant of authority in a society subservient to church rule, Jaqui had forsaken graduation, moved into a small flat on her own and found work as a model in the city of Metro Manila.

There was good money to be earned appearing in lingerie 'fashion shows' which were a favourite lunchtime entertainment for many Filipino businessmen in restaurants and up-market bars and Jaqui's spending ability was soon a strong signal to Maria.

In her shock and despair she turned her back on the programming of her youth with that peculiar acceptance of nature's darker side that marks lapsed religious fervour among those of the Catholic faith. With Jaqui's contacts and encouragement and her own exceptional good looks she was soon on the catwalks in some of Manila's better-known restaurants and hotels.

It was almost inevitable that one day a rich businessman invited the two young women to join his table and from then on she was caught up in an exciting new whirl of flowers, dinner parties and holiday resort weekends. There were sun-soaked, waiter-served, private beaches, parties around swimming pools in the elite suburbs of Manila, weekend sailing expeditions in Manila Bay aboard luxury power-cruisers and helicopter trips to island retreats. Then it had been a short step to Maria's installation in a discreet flat on United Nations Avenue near Manila's Rizal Park.

There were moments of doubt about her new life when she took a Sunday stroll through the park to make a token visit to church, chuckling at the thought that she and her new girlfriends broke church rules but still felt the need to pray.

But in the quiet of the tree-lined grassy fields, with the ruins of Fort Intramuros crumbling on its seaward side, she would feel cold and alone and would hurry back to the streets outside, the bustle of the city distracting her and filling a void.

Maria had a smart teacher in Jaqui and was strictly faithful to her businessman but a Hollywood movie was being shot in the Philippines and in the cast was a blonde, blue-eyed, 20-year-old starlet.

Maria's sinecure ended after a year, but generously. She was let down gradually with her lover's business associates stepping in and distracting her with a small florist's shop they suggested she could run in Makati business district. Before she had too much time to think she had been settled with ownership of the shop as her boyfriend faded into the background.

It was a challenge and Maria had become pragmatic enough to realise that love had never entered into the equation. She threw her energies into the flower shop and with her looks, personality and a flair for design, she built it into a flourishing small enterprise, buying in flowers from markets at the fringe of the city and doubling the price to cater for the busy commercial centre.

Now of independent means Maria's life was full but a little lonely away from the event-filled existence that had carried her through the dark days of her bereavement.

The deaths of her parents left her disdainful of the

sanctimonious rhythms of the conventional church but she was not blind to the crying need of the huge street population of the city, especially of the children who peddled single cigarettes, a newspaper recovered from a trash bin, or merely begged from the gutter.

Her shop was running smoothly and she almost unconsciously cast about for a way to reach some sort of compromise with her past.

One day a tall white-garbed figure entered her shop. The Roman Catholic nun proffered a collection box and Maria, opening the till for change, began a conversation. Noting the heat and traffic fumes in the busy street she invited her visitor to have a cold drink in the rear of the shop and so a friendship was born.

By the time Sister Jan left the shop she'd drawn from Maria details of her excellent convent education and had received Maria's offer to help teach some of the abandoned street children who appeared daily at Tondo's Soriano Centre, more for a free meal than self-improvement.

Two afternoons a week, Tuesdays and Thursdays, Maria made the journey from the upmarket Makati District to the impoverished streets of Tondo to help out. Her initial friendship with the sister formed into a strong bond.

The Australian nun made no effort to restore Maria's lost faith. Instead she questioned her often about the material world she'd entered.

At times Maria wondered if Sister Jan had a little of her own cynicism but dared not broach the thought. So Maria's life had become stable and comfortable, purposeful too with her commitment to help the urchins.

Now Maria glanced at the gold Patek Philippe watch on her wrist, a gift from her former admirer, and felt a rush of pleasure. Sean's plane would be landing.

Some months ago, a soft-spoken stranger with enigmatic eyes walked into her life. They met while Sean was in the

Philippines to do a story on the poisoning of coral reefs by fishermen who used diluted acid solutions to stun exotic tropical fish which were then resuscitated in shipboard oxygenated tanks and flown live to the restaurants of Hong Kong and Taiwan.

The practice devastated the fragile coral reefs for years to come. World conservation bodies were concerned but it was a lucrative freight trade for Philippine Airlines and therefore the self-interest of the Philippines government so it was allowed to continue with local protests effectively silenced. A live reef fish could command a hundred US dollars from diners in many a Hong Kong or Taiwanese restaurant.

When one vociferous group from Palawan Island in the southern Philippines complained the practice was destroying their main tourist attraction, President Marcos simply threatened to suspend the island's air services altogether.

Like Sister Jan, Sean had simply walked into Maria's shop one sunny afternoon and had asked to wire some flowers to New Zealand.

As they chatted she had been impressed by his knowledge of *Tagalog*, the *lingua franca* of the Philippines and the business transaction soon turned into an invitation to dinner. On impulse she had accepted.

The following day he'd called and having spent most of the evening before over dinner at one of the seafood restaurants on Roxhas Boulevard, telling her about his assignment in some detail, he asked if she'd like to act as his guide to the Tubbatahas Reef in the Sulu Sea. Recognising the guide excuse as an open door to a relationship, she was drawn to Sean's quiet good nature, his green-grey eyes so marked a contrast to her own hazel and to the gentle way in which he approached her.

She accepted, deputising Jaqui Benedict to manage her shop and her two young staff.

The ensuing week was one of excitement, adventure and

the pure bliss of falling in love.

They'd sailed to Tubbatahas Reef deep in the pirate-infested Sulu Sea in a 60-foot Philippine Coast Guard *banca*, a long narrow-waisted craft with outrigger stabilisers, gaily painted hulls streaked with red, blue and yellow, and with a two-man armed escort. They chastely shared a small roofed area that served as a cabin while their crew and escort bedded down at night on the deck around them.

The 30-kilometre reef, 11 hours by fast banca from the nearest land, was another dimension, a step into a Gaughan painting, oil on velvet. They snorkelled in a fairytale world of aquamarine seas, in a kaleidoscope of multi-hued fish and coral, the water like warm silk. They sailed past spectral, rusting wrecks, cast by past storms upon the exposed ochre-brown coral rocks of the reef. They thrilled to the mass chorus of alarmed seabirds erupting in confused flight from the rusting hulk of a freighter as the banca engines rent a pristine silence.

They explored an abandoned lighthouse on the south end of the reef and in the north the small island with its comical booby birds, which, undisturbed for years, knew no fear. They drank the fresh milk of green coconuts knocked from palms with sticks; photographed each other against the backdrop of the sea and sand.

Somehow during that time, Sean found time to work, interviewing local coastguard patrols, fishermen and several conservation officials who arrived with Sean's photographer aboard a chartered dive boat for a three-day stay.

Then came an 11-hour trip back to Palawan Island that ended in drinks against a sunset of exotic grandeur on the terrace of a shared hotel room in Puerto Princessa.

Truly alone for the first time in two weeks they'd made love with a burning intensity which still surprised and even shocked her. She'd done with Sean things she'd never done before. "Or would with anyone else" she mused.

That had been two months ago. Maria again glanced again at her wrist and briefly at the ripples of light through the rain in the street then hurried into her bedroom to dress.

Minutes later she let herself out of the apartment and took the single flight of stairs to the concierge's lobby, stepping out under the shelter of the shop verandas along the street. Finding an empty cab in the weather sweeping the city would be impossible and she started walking towards the Regent Hotel, a few blocks away on Roxhas Boulevard.

Chapter Four

Typhoon Nora increased in intensity. Spawned far out in the Pacific Ocean, lifting the sea surface in a swirling pressure dome, she gorged on herself, whipping moisture-heavy air into a juggernaut of furious intent as she began to inundate the Philippines.

Satellite images relayed to Hong Kong's Royal Observatory prompted the raising of a Number Three typhoon signal, warning the colony and nearby regions that terrible devastation was on the move.

Signals flashed to Manila and US airforce weather planes flew from sprawling Clarke Air Base in Angeles City to probe and chart the forces at the heart of the monster, transmitting wind speeds and direction back to civil defence units.

As the airmen's fragile craft tossed in the turbulent air Philippine emergency services chattered to one another by telephone and telex. Typhoon shelters opened in rural barrios, towns and cities in the storm's path.

In Tondo's Soriano Centre, Sister Jan and Marianne helped Father Stols prepare makeshift beds with donated pillows and blankets. In the kitchen, rice simmered along with a mess of vegetables.

Already a young family had sought shelter, their flimsy squatter hut demolished by the heavy rain. The young mother and her two infant children slept in a corner of the upstairs dormitory. The father, a tip scavenger who peddled scrap metal from the city's garbage, dutifully followed Marianne bearing armfuls of bedding.

Outside the streets were streams, grid-locked with stalled traffic. Stormwater drains, fallen into disrepair, were swamped and the waters flowed over the door sills of the high-riding jeepneys.

With the bedding distributed strategically about the Centre, Sister Jan poured coffee for herself and Father Stols at the large kitchen table.

"I guess we're as prepared as we can be," she said. "Now, Father, our new resident, what will we call the little boy?"

The Jesuit priest sighed. "I guess it is really up to us what becomes of him. The government agencies are swamped and they don't have the funding to help. And it's no small responsibility. We'll have him for many years to come. There will be food, clothing, medical care. It's another drain on our already strained budget. I doubt if I can squeeze any more out of Rome. They're faceless men, in a far-away city, they are not knowing what it's like in this place."

His normally excellent English stumbled in his fatigue. A quarter of a century ago the little priest arrived in the Philippines full of enthusiasm and conviction that the Church was a power for change in a country that, somehow, seemed to have missed out on its fair share of fortune. He'd long since learned that attempting momentous change in his national parish was somewhat akin to the self-flagellation practised by more extreme souls of his religious persuasion.

Thus he laid the blame for a lifetime of failing struggle firmly at the doorway of the Vatican, where opulence and plenty mocked the efforts of its missionaries.

Sister Jan was aware the child's future depended upon the resources at hand.

"Father, perhaps there's another way. I keep reading about World Vision and child sponsorship. Isn't that something we could look into?"

The priest looked nonplussed.

"You see Father," Sister Jan continued, "if we could find a sponsor, just as a humanitarian thing, we could provide for the child. It would be more personal too rather than just a kids' photograph and a report from a huge organisation. We'd only need a few hundred pesos a month to give him a really good future. That's what a lot of people spend for a couple of drinks or a meal over in Ermita."

He looked up at her. "Yes, but where do we find this Good Samaritan? Who even knows we're here?"

Sister Jan was silent for a moment and then her eyes lit up.

"What about Maria? Her flower shop is right in the heart of Makati. That's a big business part of town with plenty of people with money. I'm sure she'll help. We could maybe put a notice in her window. Anyway, if she's willing, it wouldn't hurt to try!"

"Perhaps," replied the priest. "At least it'd be direct charity, with everything going to the boy's care. We have our administration already funded, don't we?" He paused in rhetorical thought.

"Yes Sister, the idea has merit. Please ask Maria if she will help."

From the closed doorway came the clanging of a bell in the courtyard outside.

"It begins," he said, getting to his feet. "Sister, you and Marianne had best get the food under way."

Chapter Five

THE PHONE BUZZED urgently outside the steaming shower cubicle in Shaun's hotel room.

Sliding open the glass door he reached for the extension.

"Brian here," he said, leaning away from the stream of hot water.

"Darling, it's me, I'm in the lobby. They won't let me up to your room. They probably think I'm a bar girl." She laughed, a delighted throaty chuckle.

"Maria honey, I'll be right down. Meet me in the house bar, by the Japanese restaurant. I'll be there in a minute."

Sean hung up and pulled the towel from the rail.

Dry, he quickly he dressed in cotton slacks and a *barong tagalog*, the loose-fitting open-necked dress shirt of the Philippines, acceptable formal wear, right up to presidential receptions.

He chuckled at the memory of being turned away from a British-run bar in Hong Kong because *"your shirt isn't tucked in, mush."*

He slipped on comfortable leather shoes, ran a comb through his still-damp hair then grabbed his room key and wallet and headed into the corridor, breaking into a run to catch a lift just disgorging a group of Asian tourists.

Maria was alone in the quietly elegant house bar. His heart tripped. Cobalt hair swung as she turned, rippling in the subdued lighting, a rainbow flickering of oil on water. She wore a white silk blouse buttoned modestly to a mandarin collar and a black leather skirt. Long legs shining in dark nylon were hooked around her barstool. She'd allowed a touch of make-up about her exquisite hazel eyes, which glowed softly beneath coal-drawn eyebrows. Her smile widened. She looked both demure and outrageously sexy at the same time.

"Darling." She put down her drink and threw her arms around his neck. "I've missed you so much."

Their lips met and he closed his eyes, kissing her deeply. At the bar the drinks captain turned his full focus on the glass the he was polishing.

Her skin was warm and sensual through the silk. She smelled of apple shampoo, her hair damp with a spattering of rainwater from her dash across the street to the hotel entrance. Her effect on him was immediately physical and Maria felt it too. Gently disengaging herself, still holding his hands, her eyes sparkling, she hiked herself back onto the stool.

"How are you? How was your flight? Are you hungry?" Sean halted the questions, his fingers on her lips.

"Steady on honey, let me get a drink and sit down." He squeezed her hand.

"Jerry, a couple of San Migs please." The barman looked up in relief.

"Sure Sean. Welcome back. Cold San Miguel coming up."

They took their beers to cane chairs at a small table to the side of the bar. Over the next few minutes they exchange the inconsequential news of lovers and Sean told Maria about his current assignment.

"I could be here for a while my love. These political upheavals seem to take on a life of their own. Can you put up with that?" Her expression answered.

Later at the hotel's Aoki Restaurant with its austere Japanese garden decor, all pebbles, wood and running water, they washed down *tempura* and *sushi* with a couple of bottles of warm *saki*.

Distracting him with the offer of a choice morsel from her chopsticks, with a quick glance around to check privacy, Maria leaned across and slipped a succulent slice of tuna into his mouth through her kiss.

Quickly he caught her mood and called for the check from a *kimono*-clad waitress who bowed, smiling softly at the *gaijin's* unseemly haste.

Upstairs in the expanse of his beige-carpeted room he pulled the floor-to-ceiling window drapes and took a half-bottle of Moet from his mini-bar as Maria undressed. She quickly shed her blouse and skirt, peeling off the black stockings, and stood hipshot, smiling quizzically, clad only in a suspender belt and a black silk G-string.

Sean's breathing all but stopped. He dropped the bottle into a small ice bucket and reached for her. In his embrace she fumbled for his belt, ran her hands inside his loose shirt. In moments he'd stripped of his own clothes. They kissed, tongue seeking tongue.

"God I love you." He eased her gently onto the king-size double bed.

She hooked a finger into her G-string. "Wait," he said softly. "In a little while."

He kissed her soft pulsing throat, lowered his mouth to her already hard and erect nipples, each in its turn. Suckling them, gently nipping, he raised himself on one arm and reached down, gently stroking her inner thigh with his index finger.

Trailing his tongue down across her flat silky stomach he heard her sigh, felt her muscles tense.

"Oh darling, now, please now," she whispered, pulling him by the hair back up the length of her torso, her lips seeking his. Her other hand reached down and he groaned as her nails caressed him.

She parted her thighs and her heels found the small of his back, pressing him in to meet her opening. They gasped together as he slid deep and she thrust upwards and forward, her nails now deepening into the hard flesh of his shoulders.

They became lost in themselves, bodies merging with their souls as outside, the typhoon rolled over the sleeping city and roared through the streets, battering flimsy hillside shelters and shore-front squatter encampments, flinging corrugated iron and wood structures into explosive destruction to merge with the vegetation stripped from trees, rubbish and refuse sucked from the hidden bowels of the metropolis.

Late in the night, as the lovers drifted into cocooned, exhausted sleep, the death toll from the storm began and started to climb.

Many whose inadequate shelters disappeared into the whirling black terror of the night were swept to horrific deaths in debris-swollen, stinking, sewage canals or buried in mudslides from unstable city slopes. In Tondo, an elderly woman was decapitated by a jagged, flying piece of roofing iron; in Quezon City a late night jeepney driver lay crushed to death when a poorly-built brick wall toppled under winds gusting to 150 kilometres an hour.

Beyond the city where the Luzon rice plains swept back to the spiny hills of the island's backbone it was as if a giant child swept a capricious hand from out of bedlam to sweep away structures in some sand-pit from hell.

Whole hillsides slid under the pressure of torrential rains. Mud poured like cold lava into villages below. Homes, many empty as villagers sheltered in more substantial structures, churches and municipal buildings, collapsed like card houses.

Some villagers gambled badly with their lives and those of their children to stay in exposed shacks of bamboo and rattan. They found oblivion of the most terrible kind.

Their screams of terror before being engulfed were lost in the cacophony of the darkness, the sound of wood and metal rending and tearing under impossible strains and above it all the relentless roar of a thousand express trains as Typhoon Nora carved her bloody way across the landscape.

In Ilocos Norte, the provincial governor was swept to his death when a wooden bridge gave way under the onslaught of floodwaters from the hills, his commandeered army jeep and driver disappearing into the torrent.

Casualty departments in hospitals and medical centres in towns and cities across the northern half of the Philippines began dealing with another flood, one of humankind, as children with cuts, broken limbs, lost eyes and a myriad storm traumas, adults dazed and broken and bleeding, staggered in for aid.

In a makeshift medical aid post at a municipal library in Ermita, a harried young doctor washed the encrusted eyes of a child dragged by his older sister from a mudslide that demolished their tin hut.

A nurse hurried past. "Doctor, when you can, please come, a young woman…."

The doctor noted the child's tears completing the task and lifted him into the arms of his sibling. Following the nurse across the room, Dr Nadine Arroya knelt to a body wrapped in a blanket beside the wall. She dragged back the covering and was immediately aware of death, the young woman's sightless eyes staring through her, chilling her heart. She closed the eyelids gently. No stranger to death on this night, she was aware of frigid cold. Death had been master here for some hours.

It was not until near dawn that the flow of injured began to ease and the young doctor took the arm of a passing colleague. "Doctor Rey, if you have a moment. The girl there." She pointed to where the body lay in an anteroom, normally the book returns office.

"Some good souls found her apparently. But I think rigor mortis was becoming evident when that girl was brought in. I thought it strange, a typhoon victim would not be in that state."

Dr Rey moved off to make a further examination. He was back within a few minutes.

"You are quite right doctor. She had been dead for some

hours before the typhoon hit. She was drowned in a stinking canal. Her lungs are choked with filthy water. And I suspect she's a suicide. You see, it's obvious on a brief examination. She'd just given birth to a baby. A canal in the red-light district…" He walked away shaking his head.

* * *

Tondo's Soriano Centre was crowded with refugees from the storm. On the ground floor there was standing room only as the temporarily homeless passed bowls of rice over their heads to newcomers.

Upstairs, the waif Marianne found abandoned suddenly awoke. A shadow flitted across his soul and as the crashing wind shook the building he whimpered.

Marianne reached for the infant, sensing by some primitive alchemy a connection forming briefly between the infant and his birth-right which then faded and expired as his cries of anguish grew. *"Surely not just the storm?"* she thought.

Cooing softly in *Tagalog* she offered comfort. What an entry into the world, she thought, abandoned in the street like a sacrifice to a storm.

"Stormy, that's your future, little one," she whispered. "Perhaps that's a name too. Storm, or *bagyo*, in *Tagalog*."

She thought for a minute and then added her own family name.

"Bagyo Cruz you shall be, little one," she said firmly

As dawn broke over the battered and washed out city of seven million souls, the death toll from Typhoon Nora across the country stood at 153, with thousands injured to a greater or lesser extent. At least 10,000 people were homeless because of the punishing power of the winds, slips and flooding, with livestock losses countless and thousands of hectares of crops destroyed.

As a last gesture before flouncing off into the South China Sea, Nora flicked her skirts at an 8,000-tonne freighter in Manila Bay, driving it hard aground on the foreshore.

Chapter Six

AT 9AM THAT devastated morning Sean entered UPI's offices on the fifth floor of an office building housing a number of international press and television agencies in Intramuros, north of Ermita.

Helping himself to a cup of coffee from the Cona machine in a small kitchen annex Sean continued through to an office where bureau chief, Rhonda Rollinson, was lighting her first cigar of the day. She slouched behind a battered desk, its history carved in coffee stains and cigarette burns.

In her early 50's, her once blonde hair was showing hints of grey and her physique the effects of a good appetite and lack of exercise. Rollinson had had to hold her own with the best in the business at covering the world's hotspots for international media outlets. A cigar-smoking, whisky-swilling career correspondent, originally from Los Angeles, she had spent most of her life in Asia covering first the Vietnam war and later any number of regional conflicts as well as natural disasters and the more mundane assignments in politics and business.

On the wall above her desk hung a photograph of a much slimmer and younger persona astride a motorcycle in mid-air above a humped bridge in Cholon, Saigon, now Ho Chi Minh City.

It was taken by an Associated Press photographer accompanying a Marine rear-guard platoon as Rhonda fled on the 'borrowed' motorcycle from Viet Cong forces advancing into the city in the 1970 Tet offensive. She'd hung on too long to the story instead of falling back with the organised press pool being shepherded by US Army PR flunkies.

Alongside it was another snap, now a photographic news

icon. Photographer Hugh van Es captured the terror, panic and desperation after the Viet Cong victory with a shot of people fighting their way up a ladder to board a helicopter on the roof of a CIA-occupied apartment building in Saigon.

A figure of note in the bars and press clubs of Asia, a woman who'd go anywhere for a good story providing, her peers claimed, the supply of scotch and cigars held out, Rhonda in fact earned their deference, her quick and analytical mind honed sharp in the constant run to deadlines in time zones around the globe.

She'd run the Manila office for four years and had a full handle on the volatile political and military situation in the country and she quickly briefed Sean.

"I'm glad to have you here. We need a front-line man out there in the streets. I've got a whisper there's a march planned on Malacanyang tomorrow and it's bound to break into violence. Marcos has tanks stationed at strategic points around the city and if the way he hit Aquino is any indication he won't be afraid to use them.

"There's a suggestion that Cory Aquino is going to be asked to lead the opposition movement. The Philippines is pretty much a matriarchal society anyway and of course Imelda makes up Ferdy's mind on most things.

"I can handle the political background here with no trouble, I've got a couple of good local boys. But I need someone like you out there to get the mood in the streets on the wire to New York."

Grinning ruefully she waved a second, as yet unlit, cigar. "Too many of these have cut my wind. I can't move around like I did then." She nodded at the photo on the wall.

Sean looked up from his notes. "Is Tina Bell still taking pictures?"

The agency's locally-employed photographer, Tina was determined to make her name in the sometimes-dangerous world of news pictures and once stared through the telephoto lens of her Nikon during a police shoot-out at a bank hold-up as a stray bullet barrelled straight into it. Deflected out through the casing it left her shocked with a very black eye and a reputation as a survivor.

The camera that saved her life now lay in the Nikon museum in Tokyo and the company had presented her with a complete new set of its latest and most expensive photographic gear.

"She sure is," Rhonda says emphatically. "She's over at a sparrow shooting in Makati right now." Sensing Sean's query, she explained.

"They began a few days ago. Sparrow Squads. Marcos's latest campaign against crime. Or maybe I should say his way of getting rid of his enemies. Squads of armed police in plain clothes are shooting people apparently at random - people who, in their wisdom, they decide are criminal elements. The bloody, and I mean bloody man, is mad!"

"Okay if Tina works with me on this?" Sean asked. "Her fish export pictures were great."

"Sure, I'd already thought of it. She'll pick you up at your hotel tomorrow for the demo. Her sister Hanna will drive you. She's a professional and a speedway nut; races regularly out in Quezon City. You'll be in good hands."

* * *

The crowd began to gather early next day as people from all over the city were drawn towards Malacanyang. Stores, offices, factories and government departments all shut up shop.

People from surrounding suburbs packed into and on top of buses and jeepneys or simply walked towards the centre of the city.

Tens became hundreds; hundreds became thousands and tens of thousands until a flood tide of humanity filled the streets. Many carried banners stretched between bamboo poles denoting various sporting and social clubs and trade organisations. Other signs, hurriedly cobbled together in shops and alleyways, clubrooms and offices, demanded that Marcos leave office. 'Go Ferdinand, far away,' read one. 'Marcos Equals Blood,' another

Scrawled in English and in *Tagalog* they also served as focal points to keep groups together in the melee.

The sea of people flowed over the roadways, eddying around the shoals of houses and buildings with the susurration of countless voices. By midday more than a million people were on the move.

But as the leading elements of the huge crowd neared Malacanyang, orders were radioed from Marcos' beleaguered presidential palace and the tanks began to roll. But about a mile from the palace they were called to guard, the great green-painted tanks were stopped.

A group of Filipina Catholic nuns linked arms and barred the road leading to the dictator's stronghold, staring up and defying the throbbing metal monsters and their youthful conscript crews.

Moving forward from the back of the column, an officer politely asked the sisters to let them through.

When the nuns stood resolute the officer, a captain, bluntly warned them to leave or be run over and killed. They stood their ground. He ordered his men to move forward but the young lieutenant commanding the leading vehicle shook his head.

"Sir, I'm sorry, but they are nuns, sir!"

"That fact had not escaped me. They'll move. Roll forward!"

"No sir. Look!"

Behind the nuns the road had filled with demonstrators who began squatting in the path of the tanks, soon forming a solid mass and choking the road all the way to the palace gates.

"I can't kill my own people!" the soldier cried.

The captain, bluff well-called, took his point and stood vaguely shaking his head.

"No, I suppose not." He suddenly climbed onto the tank, took a packet of cigarettes from his tunic and offered one to the lieutenant. "Looks like we'll sit this one out," he grinned.

At the tall wrought-iron gates of the palace members of the hand-picked presidential guard faced the crowd. Soldiers who enjoyed special benefits including housing, schooling and medical care for their families for protecting their master, they nervously fingered the safety catches on their automatic weapons as the mass of humanity before them chanted in deafening chorus "Marcos out! Marcos out!"

The atmosphere was tense and ugly, only a spark away from a massacre.

Then rising above the awesome roar of the crowd came the distinctive thudding flail of an Iroquois helicopter. The aircraft emerged from the low cloud base and settled noisily into the compound behind the gates. Those in the front ranks of the crowd outside could see the U.S. airforce markings.

"It's Blue Label One. It's the American ambassador," shouted a reporter standing atop a low wall, clutching a traffic light stanchion.

The word quickly spread that the U.S. ambassador had arrived and the news seemed to have a calming effect on the crowd. As the Philippines former colonial master the Americans were still admired by many despite some opposition to their presence at Clarke Air Base and neighbouring naval facility at Subic Bay.

Blue label, Filipino slang for anything American, came from the blue strip used to seal packs of imported cigarettes - vastly preferred over local tobacco.

Those at the forefront of the crowd watched as two palace officers escort the lumbering form of the U.S. diplomat toward the palace portals.

His arrival signalled loud and clear that events had aroused the full attention of Washington.

The event was caught on film by Tina who climbed with her camera to a vantage point atop the Malacanyang wall.

"I've got it," she yelled excitedly over the tumult of the crowd. Sean looked up and stretched out his arms for her to jump.

"Let's take off and file the story and picture. We can leave the local guys to watch things. They'll call us if anything starts happening."

They hustled their way along the fringe of the crowd for almost a kilometre and reached a group of shops and the entrance to a garage. Making their way through a small showroom they stepped out the back door into a service lane where Hanna waited, leaning across the bonnet of a late-model Toyota Corona GTR, engrossed in a motoring magazine.

Seeing them she flashed a smile. "Ready to go guys?"

Hanna drove with panache, a fine balance between haste and caution. Threading their way through largely deserted roads to the waterfront they sped on Roxhas Boulevard towards UPI's offices in Intramuros.

Chapter Seven

At the Soriano Centre the last of the storm refugees were leaving, clasping Father Stols' hands in thanks as he farewelled them at the doorway, like parishioners after one of his services.

Twenty-four hours after Nora blew herself out on the coast of South China near Hong Kong, the roads were almost cleared of slips and debris and enough jeepney services had resumed for storm victims to make their way to what remained of their homes.

Marianne and Sister Jan were gathering up the bedding and mats spread through the building.

"Well Father, that went pretty well." Sister Jan stepped through the doorway to glance at the clear, sunny sky.

"Now we have this cleaned up, I think we deserve a bit of spoiling. Perhaps we can have lunch at Shakey's Pizza?" Father Stols nodded in agreement.

"That I think is a very good idea. Marianne can keep an eye on things here. We'll bring her food back."

Outside, the sun was becoming oppressive, beating down and rapidly drying the street in wavering pillars of steam.

But they noticed a strangely deserted air. The normal frantic life of the barrio appeared to have evaporated like the rainwater. Stopping one of the few passersby, a neighbour, the priest asked: "What's everything so quiet for. I though everyone would be out and about after the storm?"

"Father, haven't you heard? The people are marching on Malacanyang. They're demanding that Marcos get out. It's revolution!"

Father Stols stood stunned for a moment before a broad grin rearranged his craggy features.

"They're finally telling him they've had enough!" he cried,

slapping his informant heartily on the shoulder. "That's great news indeed my friend."

Sister Jan too had difficulty suppressing a smile. By some strange charisma Marcos had long managed to convince many Filipinos that he was a very fine fellow, whilst at the same time ripping off the country and consigning millions to poverty and indeed some to starvation and death.

Sister Jan well knew that in the impoverished sugar-growing province of Negros the collapse of commodity prices consigned whole families to scratching in the dust for kernels of grain, roadside plants and anything else they could use to quell aching stomachs and barely stay alive. Many, mostly children, did not.

International relief efforts were a sham, with monetary aid sent home by expatriate Filipino's diminishing drastically as it passed through inept government agencies on its journey to those in need.

If the people have finally had enough, good news indeed!

Sister Jan and Father Stols turned the street corner, arriving at Shakey's, a franchise operation serving piping hot pizza - the equivalent of a five-star restaurant to the impoverished locals.

Taking seats at one of the pink-topped tables inside, returning smiles and waves from the few neighbourhood people at adjacent tables, they looked up to see Maria Cipriano following them in.

"Sister Jan, Father. Are you okay?" she called as she hurried across to join them.

"I thought I'd come down and see if you needed some help after the typhoon. I just missed you at the Centre."

Sister Jan pulled another chair to the table. "Here, sit. We're fine. No damage and the storm passed quickly." The three discussed the typhoon and then the more momentous news of the demonstration against Marcos.

"It's going to be the end for him," said Maria with an

insiders' certainty.

"My friend Sean is down from Hong Kong to cover the story and he says the Americans will give Marcos asylum to get him out of the country without any bloodshed. Sean's over at the palace now."

"It'll be a fine thing if Marcos goes," said Father Stols.

A huge pizza-with-everything was placed before the group with a smile from the waiter. "The boss says it's on the house. His cousin had to shelter in the Centre last night when he couldn't get home. He says thanks."

The three smiled in acknowledgement and fell to the food. The fragrance of grilled cheese, tomatoes, salami and anchovies triggered appetites unwontedly suppressed and conversation died.

At last, wiping his lips with a paper napkin, Father Stols leaned back from the table and sighed.

"There is something to be said for a more worldly existence I suppose," he quipped.

"Now Maria. There's something else. We have a child." Maria looked at him quizzically as Sister Jan continued.

"Maria, some poor woman has abandoned her baby at the Centre. Marianne has christened him Bagyo for the typhoon. We were hoping you might help us."

Sister Jan quickly outlined her idea of finding a sponsor prepared to pay a few hundred pesos a month to feed and clothe the foundling with a little set aside for his later education.

Maria responded quickly.

"I think that's a fine idea. I'll give it some thought and I'll certainly put up a notice in the shop. Tell you what, we should have a picture of the wee mite. That always tugs the heartstrings."

The three discussed their plan further and Father Stols undertook to have a friend photograph the infant Bagyo.

Chapter Eight

Dusk fell over Malacanyang Palace, now besieged by a million people, a seventh of the city's population.

Inside the grounds, guards hurried from building to building, toting boxes and wheeling laden trolleys. Six army helicopters came clattering overhead, red strobe lights flashing in the growing darkness. As they muttered down into the compound a roar went up from the crowd at the gates.

One man clutching a transistor radio to his ear screamed confirmation.

"The President is leaving. The Americans have given him asylum. Marcos is fucking going!"

The deafening roar of delight swelled to a crescendo as the hated leader was spotted in the lights of the palace grounds hurrying towards the helicopters, surrounded by a cluster of beribboned military aides and followed by servants laden with boxes and trunks.

The man who'd ruled a nation for twenty years scuttled along, head bowed.

Then the First Lady, Imelda Marcos, stepped from the main doors of the palace with her head held high. Ignoring the yells of hatred from outside the palace gates she lifted her arm imperiously, more of a salute than a wave and swept ahead of her aides and security men towards the waiting helicopter in which her husband had taken refuge.

It was over in minutes. The lead helicopter lifted, pivoted and soared westward over the palace grounds to gain height before turning back across the crowd. It was followed in quick succession by the other choppers, heading for Clarke Airbase, 70kms to the north, and a waiting US transport aircraft.

The man with the transistor shouted further news.

"The Americans are flying him out. He's going to Hawaii."

The words signalled a change in the mood of the crowd. A surge towards the palace gates began, younger people scaling the wrought iron. The compound was deserted as the remaining guards, their boss gone, melted away through the palace grounds. Those youths first over the gates quickly swung the locks, opening the way for the crowd to follow. With a roar, becoming a mob, thousands surged towards the palace itself.

Stones prised from the courtyard were heaved through windows. The vanguard of the stampede climbed through the shattered casements and heaved open the main doors of the palace.

The rampage became a near riot as the crowd spilled through rooms and corridors, ransacking everything in sight. Pictures were torn from walls, bedding and furnishings stripped, ornaments pocketed or smashed. Then the leaders reached the basement where they halted and stared in astonishment.

Imelda Marcos was well known for her extravagances. Shopping sprees on New York's Fifth Avenue and Hollywood's Rodeo Drive were her choice of retail therapy.

But here in the basement of her former home was evidence of high folly.

Tiers of shelves stretched far into the long fluorescent-lit room and on every shelf, were shoes of every conceivable style and colour, a display to rival any factory showroom.

It was a sight synonymous with the Marcos regime, one of unbridled greed.

Those who reached the basement first moved forward, intent on loot, but even as they grabbed at the footwear a group of serious-faced young men stepped quickly ahead of them.

"No," they shouted. "Leave them, leave them for the world

to see. Let the world judge Marcos and his woman! Don't touch them!"

Despite the confusion raging through Malacanyang, the few people who'd so far reached the basement responded and backed from the room. The young men pulled the door shut and took up position outside.

The rampage in the palace lasted all night. At around midnight, Sean and Tina managed to push their way into the building and, tipped off about the shoes by one of their local staffers, they headed downstairs. The basement discovery had miraculously been kept intact by the group of student militants bent on showing the world what the Marcos's were made of.

Before sunrise, Tina's picture and Sean's report on the tumultuous events and sidebar on the 'Marcos Shoe Emporium' was the lead story on radio and TV bulletins and newspaper front pages the world over.

* * *

As dawn broke, a USAF Hercules C130 aircraft carried the deposed and disgraced first family of the Philippines into exile, unwonted guests of the Americans through the offices of President Ronald Reagan, who'd played host to the attractive Imelda in the White House when her star was in ascendancy.

The Marcos clan remained in the headlines for years to come as a revitalised government in their homeland sought repatriation of their billion-dollar plunder through the international courts.

True to Rhonda Rollinson's prediction, Cory Aquino, wife of the slain former senator Benigno, was thrust forward on a wave of popular support and elected to the presidency.

She brought to Malacanyang Palace a new style of leadership, setting up residence in a humble house in the grounds and opening the palace proper as museum and monument to Marcos extravagance.

Corrupt officials were slowly weeded out of their posts and women come to the fore in several key government positions.

Under Aquino's 'housewife's stewardship,' the Philippines entered an era of semi-stability.

Talks were begun with the armed insurgents plaguing the countryside and political opponents of Marcos were swiftly released from prison.

The hunt for the killer of Benigno Aquino was stepped up and it was no surprise to many when a large group of Marcos' loyalist officers were arraigned in court.

On the economic front, things began to improve as western investors saw the Philippines as a safer place for their money than in previous years.

Japan, the wartime aggressor came forward with loans and free-trade zones attracted funds from the Asian economic tigers, Singapore, Hong Kong, Seoul and Taiwan.

Early in her tenure Aquino had to cope with the devastation of a major earthquake which rumbled out of the northern Philippines and devastated the mountain resort city of Baguio, even damaging buildings in Manila itself.

The death toll may never be known, hundreds, perhaps thousands killed as whole mountains slid across rural valley highways, burying roads and traffic under millions of tonnes of earth.

Baguio hotels collapsed and the international rescue effort lasted weeks with specialist teams flying in from around the world to search the rubble for victims.

But natural disasters, typhoons, earthquakes and volcanic eruptions have always been part of the fragile fabric of life in the Philippine nation and, spared from the human cancer that drained the country under Marcos, the Philippines began hesitantly to move forward in a new atmosphere of national identity.

* * *

At the Soriano Centre in Tondo the foundling Bagyo Cruz grew along with his country.

Learning the rites of childhood with his first steps clutching tightly to the hands of Sister Jan, he was becoming a robust child, his stature suggesting a physical strength inherited from a European father.

At three years old he already had a good command of *Tagalog* dialect from the faithful Marianne and of English learned at Sister Jan's knee as she read to him from donated storybooks.

As Marianne tended her own child, Sister Jan found herself more and more a surrogate mother to the little boy.

His grey-green eyes sparkled with excitement at the sight of a new toy. It might be a poor broken thing left in a church charity bin but, for the child of Ermita, a one-armed, one-eyed teddy bear was the stuff of unbridled joy.

Funds for the child's upbringing were especially easy to find. Maria Cipriano simply mentioned the infant's plight to Sean.

"You need 500 pesos a month for the kid?" he asked when Maria raised the subject over lunch in Josephine's, a popular bayside seafood restaurant.

"Hell that's... let me think... about 25 US dollars at the black market rate. It's peanuts. Hell, I'll sponsor the little guy myself! Twenty-five bucks would buy me about five beers in Hong Kong and they'd be on expenses! With a little creativity - so can this. You have yourself a deal Maria. I'll send the money in US dollars to the Centre and they can change it on the street. They'll get a better rate on the black market. Consider it done. I'll set it up when I get home."

As the source of Sean's bounty, Maria also found herself

drawn into the circle forming around the child. Sometimes she'd take Bagyo for an outing in Rizal Park, with Jaqui Benedict or Sister Jan. Bagyo also provided Maria with a distraction as Sean rotated between Hong Kong, the Philippines and other countries in the region as the Asian story continued to unfold.

In her contentment she dared make plans for the future. Perhaps she'd have her own child one day. Looking at her young charge, delirious over an ice-cream cone from a passing vendor, she found herself thinking of Sean as a father.

At the Soriano Centre, Maria began to spend time in the overgrown garden in the rear of the building, hauling up weeds and replacing them with simple vegetables, and here and there, flower plants to bring a show of colour.

One drizzly day, muddy and unkempt in a pair of old jeans and a T-shirt, she was planting a selection of seeds in the cleared soil when an idea slipped forward from her subconscious. It had a force that made her gasp.

Chapter Nine

"Father, Sister Jan. It's simple. My goodness it's simple! Flowers. Now where do I get my flowers for the shop in Makati? I buy them from growers on the edge of the city. They plant them in tubs and boxes and in pots, along the edge of canals, around rice paddy fields – just about everywhere. And some of the best prices I get are from restaurants and hotels and corporate offices wanting plants in pots that they can put in reception areas, or at their workstations in the office."

Impulsively she took Father Stols by the arm and moved to the window at the front of the Centre, overlooking the busy street.

Glancing up at the veranda roof stretching back from either side of the marketplace opposite, supported by the sagging shopfronts and rickety poles, she asked: "What do you see?"

Father Stols and Sister Jan looked across and there in the bright afternoon sunshine, a patch of brilliant red and green nestled below a window in the the second storey.

"They're geraniums. They're pot plants someone has decorated their home with. They're flowers and they're growing beautifully there," Maria said.

"All it takes to grow them is time and a little care. One pot of geraniums. Ten to 20 pesos from the shop to decorate an office in Makati. And other plants, pot plants. Don't you see? I don't have to travel half-a-day down to the south of the city to buy stock. The people can grow them here! They can grow palms, spider plants, African violets, *monstera deliciosa*...?" Her voice trailed away as she studied their faces. Sister Jan had her hands to her cheeks, her eyes suddenly shining, while Father Stols turned to her and asked: "Monster what?"

"*Monstera deliciosa*, it's called; window plant, a big pot plant for the corner of the room. Maybe a hundred pesos a time. Oh Father. Think of it. The people here have no jobs and lots of time. The climate is like a greenhouse. If we can procure seeds and seedlings, some compost and fertiliser...?" She began tickling off requirements on her fingers.

"The thing is, we can propagate from our own plants. See those geraniums. In a matter of weeks I could have that whole roof covered with pots of geraniums. They can sell in the shop, heavens, to other shops as well if we grow enough. We could sell at stalls in the marketplace in the city itself."

Maria sank into a tattered over-stuffed chair, still looking excitedly out the window. Father Stols picked up her enthusiasm.

"Self-help. Self-help. There's a self-help budget I can use for projects which create work opportunities in the community. This is one. Sister Jan, what do you think?"

"Well, sure. But I'm not a gardener Father. Well, I had a patch in the vegetable garden when I was a kid, but this..." as Maria jumped up.

"Father, Sister, I have the expertise. I have been dealing with the growers for a couple of years. I've watched hundreds of varieties propagated and grown, as I've had to keep up with customer demands and also be a little trend setting along the way. And anything I'm not sure about, well there's the municipal library isn't there. Hundreds of books about horticulture."

Within a few more minutes the idea of a plant nursery in the slums took hold and Father Stols went to the door and sent a local boy scurrying to find the *barrio* captain. He turned back to Maria. "Will you have the time to oversee the work?"

"Certainly Father. It's something the people will have to do themselves, that is, the actual work and all. I can print up general notes on the computer and distribute them with the plants we provide, if we can provide them? After all, seeds will cost very little."

As the *barrio* captain was shown into the room, they got down to details. What areas would be available for the plants? What transport to markets? Who best to oversee the work of individual growers? Who would take part in the nursery project tucked away in the slums?

In the three weeks following her brain wave, Maria was a whole lot busier than the few minutes a day she'd blithely suggested to Father Stols, but as happy as she'd ever been. Combined with running her Makati shop, the Tondo flower project ate up her days and she dragged herself exhausted to bed each night. But her world was rounding into a completeness she'd never before experienced and each day saw her in Tondo, talking to prospective growers, planning varietal plantings against expected demands and inspecting proposed garden sites. One of the most adventurous, in a slum crying for space, was a salvaged door, cantilevered from the wall of a drainage canal, tended by a gardener standing waist deep in brown liquid.

Because church money was being used to back the project, Father Stols insisted on a level of honesty and aptitude on the part of those taking part and the *barrio* captain was asked to personally vet each applicant.

"We cannot suddenly find a clandestine market springing up with stock we have paid to provide," he affirmed.

Five weeks later the first pot of geraniums was sold in the flower shop in Makati and Maria, waiving her commission, presented Father Stols with the Centre's 50 per cent share of the 20 pesos the pot plant fetched. The ten pesos was formally handed to a beaming mother of three at a small street ceremony outside. Cash money generated at home was a rare sight in the community and word of the flower project began to spread.

One evening a month later, after the sale of plants worth

several hundreds of pesos from Tondo's rooftop nursery, there was a small gathering at the centre and Father Stols presented Maria with a letter of appreciation.

When she looked down at the signature she gasped in surprise. The carefully penned document was signed by Jaime Sin, Cardinal of the Roman Catholic Church in the Philippines.

"Oh Father, Sister Jan. I only had the idea. Everybody else did the work."

"That's not what I hear," came a quiet voice from the doorway. Maria spun round, disbelief etching her features.

"Sean," she cried, rushing to him. "What are you doing here? Look, look. The Cardinal has written to me." Then she flung her arms around his neck as the others in the room burst into spontaneous applause.

"Wonderful darling. Sister Jan told me when I rang from the airport. I thought I might surprise you."

"Well you have, you have." She turned as the others fell silent. "We have to go, okay, you don't mind?"

With a broad smile Father waved them from the room "Go, go my children. It's time for our supper."

Outside, Sean's taxi waited and minutes later they pulled up outside Maria's flat, a haven for their time together when Sean was in town. Inside, Maria found fresh prawns, pasta and salad and began building a meal. Sean opened a bottle of shiraz picked up at Kai Tak duty-free and after placing a glass on the bench-top for Maria he flopped on the couch, sipping appreciatively, idly reading the letter of commendation.

He glanced to where Maria stopped to taste the wine and silently lifted his own in salute. *'There are hidden depths here'* he thought. The flower project in Tondo had been adopted in at least two other church welfare centres. He placed his half-empty glass on the coffee table and padded quietly in his socks to the kitchen annex, placing his arms around Maria nuzzling her neck.

"I love you honey," he whispered.

She chuckled throatily. "Food first," she smiled. "And get me some more wine… please?"

Chapter Ten

Puerto Galera, Philippines: April 1986

THEIR COURTSHIP SETTLED into highs of union and gulfs of separation when Sean was elsewhere on his Asian news beat and time passed swiftly in the tumultuous days of emerging Asian economic and political power.

When they were together the long-term future was always skirted around, raised fleetingly and by some mutual chemistry allowed to subside in the happiness of their current moment.

Maria was aware Sean had been parted from his former wife for several years and sensed a caution whenever he was reminded of her. The closeness in their relationship prevented it becoming an issue; each, content just being together and Maria remained cautious, with a feminine understanding that trauma lay thinly buried in her man.

Then, one Easter weekend, Sean arrived in Manila from Hong Kong with the news that his correspondent's beat had been changed.

"Honey, I've been posted to Singapore," he told her next day as they lay on the beach at Sabang, in the beach resort complex of Puerto Galera on Oriental Mindoro Island.

Maria paused, her hands in fists full of hot, fine white sand she was trickling over Sean's sun-bronzed torso.

"We don't cover the PI from there," he added. "It'll be India, up into Thailand, Burma and Laos and west to Pakistan and Afghanistan. No more Manila on a regular basis, so you and I are going to have to make some decisions."

He saw the anguish in her eyes as she became still, almost frozen, before one hand reached clutching for his. Before she could speak he placed a finger to her lips.

"Maria, you're the most special thing that has ever happened to me. You know I was married in New Zealand. Well I've never divorced. But I've asked the lawyers in Hong Kong to get moving and contact my ex-wife so we can get the paperwork done. Yes, I'm going to push through the divorce."

Then he said simply, "Will you marry me?"

Maria collapsed in his arms in delight, inadvertently flicking sand over his face and into his eyes. Sean's solemn question was lost in her momentary panic.

"Sorry, oh sorry," she cried, trying to brush the grains away.

Reaching for the bottle of mineral water from his bag Sean rinsed his face, grinning hugely. Maria knelt and clutched his hands.

"Oh Sean, do you really mean it? Do you?"

"Of course honey. I want to be with you. I can't go on raising hell around Asia forever. I want you with me."

"Yes, oh yes," Maria cried.

Oblivious of the sunbathing tourists attracted by their animation, they kissed hungrily.

"Now come up," said Sean, grabbing his towel and bag. "Let's go get a beer and talk this through. I'll have to go to Singapore and set up the bureau and the divorce will take a little while. You can't get a visa for Singapore until we're married but we'll get there."

They wandered up the beach, arms wrapped around each other, to the open-air Sunset Bar, near their hired beach cottage, and began making plans for the future.

As the sun settled into the sea they sipped cold San Migs and ate delicious grilled king prawns from bamboo skewers, caught by the local fishermen, cooked by their wives and peddled from bar to bar by their children.

In a moment of shared excitement Sean even bought a couple of *baloute*, the fertilised duck eggs that were a national delicacy.

Fortified with a celebratory shot of native Tanduhay rum, with the barman's best wishes for their engagement, and encouraged by other patrons joining the impromptu celebration, he sucked the yellow-green liquid from around the embryo, but drew the line at eating the remainder.

"Tastes like scrambled egg, sort of," he announced.

Later they paddled the shoreline in the warm evening, each immersed in the other with a milestone in their relationship now realised.

Gazing across the oily water of the straits hiding the mainland to the north, Sean allowed himself to remember another time, another marriage and the aching pain and loneliness that followed an unfaithful partner. He recalled the emptiness of betrayal, the whispered gossip in office and pub as his ego refused to accept a visit by his wife to a sick friend could be anything but just that, how he felt in their marriage bed early one morning when her movie date with an alleged girlfriend ended in a night on the town and an empty pillow mocked him.

He held tightly to Maria's hand as she looked up, a slight frown registering concern.

He thrust his thoughts away and smiled. Three years and the dozens of opportunities their lifestyle had offered for fragmentation had seen their partnership grow and flourish. It had to be as good a foundation as any, even if he'd been bitten badly once before.

Out to sea, a sickle moon framed a cluster of stars in an indigo sky, hanging like a fantastic lantern above the horizon still just etched in crimson from the settled sun. Away to the south Sean could see the Southern Cross, the constellation which led early seafarers below the nearby equator to far-off New Zealand.

He made a mental note to write home as soon as he and Maria had settled dates for their future. They retraced their steps along the beach, guided to their cottage by a hurricane lantern hung from the porch by a hut-boy after the village generator shut down.

Beneath the cool curtain of a mosquito net, they made love amid plans for many tomorrows.

Next day they took the catamaran ferry to Batangas City on the mainland, where happiness was briefly shadowed by the rubbish-strewn shantytown slums clinging to the fringes of the port, the listless waifs and adults picking their way through the garbage, like animals grazing.

Beyond the port gates they took an air-conditioned coach to Manila and later that night at the Regent they again sealed their new union with the familiarity of lovers newly bound in a tangible future.

Maria had become an enthusiastic and exploratory sexual partner.

The repressions of her Catholic childhood had been replaced with a willingness to explore her own sensuality and she loved to dominate Sean, tying his wrists behind his back with the belt of her towelling bathrobe and teasing him with her long raven hair, trailing her tresses over his naked body. As he lay voluntarily helpless, she took him intimately into her warm mouth and felt his spasm when he encountered the ice she'd concealed there from her drink by the bedside.

Then she freed his bonds and relinquished the control she enjoyed, submitting excitedly to the passion she'd aroused.

Sean flew back to Hong Kong the following morning, leaving Maria to begin the endless round of government departments, red tape and often small bribes to speed the process of getting a birth certificate, a passport, inoculations and all the things she needed to leave the country. The process would take several months but she was actually thankful for the time. There was the Tondo garden project to delegate more fully, and a good manager to find for the flower shop.

"You own the shop darling. It's an investment, you should hang onto it," was Sean's advice.

But just three weeks later with all the paperwork finally under way and as she and Jaqui began trolling the boutiques and department stores for her trousseau, a doorway opened into terror and despair.

Rhonda Rollinson called her at the United Nations Avenue flat.

"Maria. You'd better sit down." The rest of her words faded into white noise as Maria went into shock. Sean had gone missing while on an assignment in Thailand.

Chapter Eleven

Manila, Philippines: May, 1986.

A CITY BLOCK from the Soriano Centre in Tondo, there was small illegal fireworks factory in a ramshackle shed. A young employee stopped loading black powder into cheap skyrockets and stepped outside during a short meal break. Unable to afford rice from a nearby street vendor he found a few centavos in his ragged jeans and bought a single cigarette from a newspaper seller and begging a light, he sat on the steps and allowed the pungent native tobacco to ease his hunger pangs. He'd be paid this afternoon and tonight he'd treat himself to barbecued chicken legs and giblets along with the routine bowl of rice or noodles.

Dizzy from the cigarette he stumbled slightly as went back inside, flicking the butt behind him through the doorway.

The still-burning cigarette, caught by a sudden puff of breeze, boomeranged back into the factory. It landed on a leaking drum of volatile solvent.

The youth knew no more as the small factory exploded, shredding his young body and turning the dry wooden building into a torch.

Four of his fellow workers were engulfed in seconds, as the fire hungrily took hold of the factory and the shanty next to it, spreading in the growing breeze to a row of sari-sari stores which supplied the daily needs of the residents – including bottled gas for cooking and kerosene for lamps.

Fanned by the wind the fire spread rapidly, sending billows of black smoke over Tondo. In rapid succession three cooking gas cylinders exploded, one rocketing through a wall in flames to spread the holocaust across the street.

Terror-stricken residents ran screaming from homes,

shops and stalls yelling alarm through the neighbourhood.

Father Stols heard the commotion, and ran from the Soriano Centre, feeling the searing heat immediately as flames rolled toward him in a crown-fire of terror.

Running back inside, he screamed: "Fire! Fire! Get out! Get out!"

The Centre staff reeled away from their simple lunch at the kitchen table. Making for the door Sister Jan scooped up three-year-old Bagyo Cruz from where he played with his broken toys in a corner of the room and followed Marianne and four older children into the street.

A dozen buildings were ablaze and smoke began rising from the smouldering upper walls of the Centre itself. Sirens sounded in the distance over the tumult of flames and panic but in Manila's traffic saturation the engines would be lucky to form more than a perimeter around the destruction.

Sister Jan ran with the others as a growing panic-stricken mob poured into the street. The strengthening breeze caressed the horror leaping from tar paper roof to roof.

As she rounded the corner at the end of the street she was suddenly pushed from behind.

The shoulder of a fleeing beggar caught her in the small of her back. The jarring shock drove her sprawling to the ground, her infant charge thrown from her grasp into a shop doorway.

Still jostled by the panic-stricken crowd Sister Jan struggled to her feet only to be struck again.

Confused, the nun reeled into the roadway. Unable to stop, a crowded jeepney hit her a glancing blow, catching her between her right knee and thigh. Her femur snapped in the impact, the shattered bone arcing through the muscle and flesh and she was thrown in unconscious shock into the deep gutter beside the road.

Bagyo Cruz, screaming in panic, blood dripping from his bruised nose, clambered to his feet, unnoticed by the fleeing crowd. Sister Jan was nowhere to be seen. He cowered from the noise, the screams, the sirens, the thinning mob rushing by him. His world was a nightmare more threatening than the bad dreams which had sometimes awoken him in the darkness of the night.

Then someone touched him. A face peered into his. Suddenly he was lifted onto a familiar hip and carried jerkily along with the few people still running from the flames.

Bagyo was desperately clutching the slight form of a pretty, long-haired street girl, named Che, who sometimes came for classes and food at the Centre. Perhaps 12, she was old well beyond her years. Holding tightly to the child, she pounded along with the last of the throng now slowing as they reached relative safety and began turning to witness the destruction of their homes and livelihoods.

At the edge of the crowd a woman suddenly screamed frantically and rushed back towards the holocaust before being chased and seized, pushed to the ground by others, well aware the child she sought would not follow her from the flames.

Chapter Twelve

He awoke whimpering, confused, his nose hurting.

The room was in blackness where normally a night-light burned. He moved and instead of the side of his bed he touched the warmth of another person. Sister Jan? Marianne?

Che stirred from her fitful sleep and sat up, pushing the child away. In the blackness she moved to one side of the tiny structure. She pushed aside a black plastic bag hung as a door curtain and stepped outside to squat and urinate in the mud. The morning smelled of rotting garbage, decay mixed with the residue of the night, food cooking, drifting exhaust fumes, a hint of ozone from Manila Bay.

Some instinct kept the child silent. This was something new, something unknown.

He'd learned before from the loving but firm hand of Marianne that crying would be ignored as way of getting attention.

Outside, in the half-light of dawn Che glanced around at the collection of pitiful shanties perched on a slope leading down to a stormwater canal, which fed into the polluted bay. Turning, she looked back toward the city and the incongruous sight of Roxhas Boulevard just 200 metres away, lined with twinkling lights of hotels, apartment blocks and condominiums.

Here, in the shadow of plenty was poverty the equal of any in Asia. A stone's throw away, tourists and well-found Filipinos alike prepared for hearty breakfasts while the people of the shanties nursed empty bellies.

She stooped back inside her home, a rough-hewn wooden packing case about two metres square, the legend Hyundai stencilled in black alongside shipping symbols on two sides.

Kneeling, she lit a candle and as it flickered, casting

back the shadows, Bagyo Cruz pushed himself into a sitting position and announced: "I'm hungry."

Che snorted, the expression of an impatient adult. On a rudimentary shelf next to the doorway were a few plastic bowls, discarded polystyrene cups, a couple of plastic fast-food utensils she'd picked up from rubbish bins on her 'beat', a short section of Roxhas Boulevard. Pushing them to one side she found a half-empty cardboard carton of soya bean milk and passed it to him.

"You can have this. If we're to eat we must go soon."

Splashing water into her face from a plastic bucket next to the shelf she reached past Bagyo and dried her face on the sheet of heavy cloth, a discarded curtain, that served as their bed draped over a coir mat. The child watched wide-eyed. He remembered running; he was with Sister Jan. He'd fallen. Sister Jan is gone. There's been a fire. Why was he here with Che? The girl had often picked him up at the Centre, carting him around on her hip as she helped out with odd jobs.

"I want to go home," he said, not plaintively, but as a simple matter of fact.

The girl snorted again.

"I think there is no home left," she said.

Rummaging in a cardboard box, she took a T-shirt, and pulled it over her naked torso easing it over her budding breasts, letting it hang outside her baggy shorts, cast-offs from the Soriano Centre charity box.

Bagyo had what he wore, stained brown shorts, the back pocket hanging off, torn in the scramble away from the fire and a T-shirt depicting a 1930's style Mickey Mouse.

"Come on." Che held out her hand and guided him through the opening into the early morning. She had no way of securing her hovel but by the unwritten law of the squatter encampment it would be watched over by neighbours, as she in her turn would stand guard in their absence.

They made their way through huts and shacks as the

tropical sun leaped from Manila Bay. In the growing light the ramshackle settlement stirred, it's residents ever hopeful on a new day.

Reaching a rough track alongside the canal they joined others walking towards the road around the waterfront. Paper, plastic bags and empty soft drink cans littered the ground.

Climbing the steep pathway to the road proper, now in full daylight, the sun already warming the pavement, they gained Roxhas Boulevard where Che turned left towards the Holiday Inn, Regent Hotel and apartment blocks and townhouses in between.

They crossed the four-lane highway at the first set of traffic lights and joined a growing flow of pedestrians. Cigarette and newspaper vendors prowled the footpaths on the lookout for motorists or jeepney passengers wanting their wares.

They passed the concrete block walls of the Chinese Embassy with its high green gates and lion head statues and reached a large open-air food market where crowds were gathering for a breakfast snack on the run.

One of the stallholders tending a smoking charcoal grill, a tall angular woman clad in T-shirt and patched jeans, spied Che and called her over.

"Che, who have you, got here?" she asked.

"He's from the Soriano Centre. We're going to see what happened."

"Child, the centre was burned yesterday. A whole block has been burned down. Ten people killed," the woman said. She'd heard one of the victims was the Soriano Centre's housemother, Marianne Cruz, but did not say so.

"We were there," said Che, pointing proudly to Bagyo: "I rescued him."

The woman looked at the wide-eyed child, taking in his light-coloured skin and grey-green eyes.

'Another child of the night,' she thought, anger compressing

her lips.

It had happened to her when she worked the bars. She was young and had a child while the sailor father went back to the States, promising to send money, to apply for a visa, promises from the bottom of a bottle. The money never came.

Impulsively she picked up two sticks of chicken *satay* from the charcoal burner and dipped them quickly into a pot of bubbling sauce.

"Here, there'll be nothing at the Centre. Where are you going?"

"We must go and see what we can find," said Che. "Perhaps we can find Sister Jan or the Father?"

The stallholder shook her head sadly.

"Child, go, go. If I'm to survive and feed my kids I have to sell this food, not give it away."

The girl and the little boy moved away, gnawing at the tough stringy chicken, savouring the peanut sauce and heading inland through broken-paved streets towards Tondo.

They melted into the noisy human madhouse, two small figures in concrete canyons, dodging along the hot streets, impatient with the steadier adult flow about them. The mid-morning sun was blinding as it bounced from glass-walled office towers then softened through leafy trees around homes of the city's elite.

When they crossed the final intersection into Tondo they found before them blackened devastation.

Smoke still rose in patches from the square kilometre seared open in three short hours. Manila city aides, their occupation emblazoned on reflective ponchos to alert chaotic traffic when they cleaned the streets, joined firemen in poking desultorily through the rubble, putting out hot-spots and salvaging anything that survived the flames. Permeating the air and wiping away the hot fumes of the city traffic was a miasma, a stench of wet ashes and burnt life.

Clutching Bagyo's hand, Che stood across the street in the shadow of the buildings forming the rim of a blackened crater. What was once the Centre was nothing more than a twisting, sagging skeleton. Tears welled and she wiped them away quickly. Where once there was comfort and hope, there was nothing.

With little idea of where to go or what to do she turned, dragging Bagyo with her, and began the long walk back to the waterfront, her young-yet-old mind in turmoil. She had at least shelter, but uppermost in her mind was the daily spectre of hunger.

Three city blocks away she stopped at a Catholic mission house for water and she and the child were given stale bread rolls donated from a nearby bakery. Resting briefly, a little replenished by the water and musty dough, they set off once more toward Manila Bay.

An hour later, back on Roxhas, Che knew what she must do.

Bagyo was exhausted and she carried him the last couple of kilometres. He was asleep when they reached her crude home and she laid him on the mat, covering him before going to the hut next door. Giving a brief account of her charge, she left the old woman within listening for the child to wake and set off into the evening.

Two blocks back from the bayside boulevard she came to Ermita, an area of neon reflections and noise, street life vibrant in shadows cast by intermittent lights.

She passed an open shop-front bar where a pool table attracted several youths intent on winning a handful of pesos that might buy a cheap bottle of wine from the sari-sari store on the corner. Here, big-boned billy-boys, transvestites, gathered in the hope of a five minute assignation in a darkened shop doorway, momentary oral sex that would pay for supper and maybe tomorrow morning's street-stall coffee.

As she emerged from an alley into the bustling and garish tourist strip, music blared from a dozen bars while girls just a couple of years older than Che reached clutching hands at passing servicemen and tourists, male and female, who crowded the footpaths. A knot of US sailors passed her, reeling from bar to lamppost, raucous in their revelry.

Outside a bar on MH del Pilar Street a fat tourist, well the worse for the afternoons' beer drinking, noticed the little girl standing a few feet away, her eyes questioning.

Long black tresses framed the urchin's gamin face. A child's body topped coltish legs as she stood, one hand on her hip, unconsciously coquettish.

A slow leer dragged across his flushed, puffy face and he reached into his pocket, pulling out a handful of notes.

Monopoly money, he thought of the huge wad he'd received for travellers cheques at the airport, but as she reached for the proffered cash he pulled the money back and grabbed her hand in his.

Wise in the ways of the twilight world, Che sighed quietly and walked alongside him. Turning down a side street toward the waterfront they entered a cheap and shabby boarding house.

Without a word the tourist tossed some of the banknotes at the old man in a cubbyhole office behind a paneless window. The aged concierge averted rheumy eyes, pathetically aware of his poverty of spirit and reached behind him to pass a key. With the little girl in tow the tourist mounted the rickety stairs.

* * *

Early in the following morning Bagyo became aware of movement and sound. Turning his head he saw Che in the dim light from the opening in the packing case, sitting beside him sobbing quietly, clutching her knees with one hand, the other pressed between her legs. He sat and reached out to touch her. Distress quivered his lower lip.

Aware he'd woken, Che raised her hand and wiped it across her face, lifting her T-shirt and blowing her nose on the hem.

She managed a wan smile in the daylight brightening the entranceway. "Here" she said.

At her feet was a plastic bag bearing the logo of a supermarket in Robinson's shopping plaza in Ermita. Reaching into it she produced a packet of chocolate-coated biscuits and a carton of milk.

Completely distracted from her unhappiness, Bagyo ripped at the cellophane packet, spilling biscuits as he tore it open in his eagerness, stuffing two of them into his mouth and watching as she opened the milk.

As the child fed ravenously, Che swung the bag onto her shelf and began arranging the contents.

Four more packets of biscuits, a large plastic bottle of Coca-Cola, several tins of fish, a couple of corned beef. There was a bunch of small finger bananas, beginning to turn brown, a loaf of white bread, a bag of cold cooked rice and a carton of eggs.

Reaching under the shelf, she lifted a brick from the floor. Behind it, wedged out of sight in the corner of the packing case was a small jam jar. She unscrewed the lid and reached into her shorts to pull out a small bundle of notes left over from her shopping. The drunken German tourist thrust them at her before she left him snoring on the bed and she began counting them in ten peso notes into the jar. Then she stopped in surprise and shock. For a moment her head spun.

The last two notes, instead of pesos, were US $20 bills. What she held was a fortune!

On the street the two US banknotes would fetch around 800 pesos, a months' wage for a jeepney driver or a watchman at one of the luxury apartments she'd passed on her way home, more money than she'd ever held. But she was streetwise enough to know its value. She'd seen the avarice in her peers' eyes when one of them had picked a tourist pocket of a wallet stuffed with cash.

For the moment, confused and uncertain, she thrust the notes into the jar as fatigue washed over her. She could not think.

Replacing the jar behind the brick she took the eggs and crawled wearily out to the hut next door as Bagyo reached for more biscuits and drank from the carton.

"*La donja*, lady, old one, I want six eggs," she says. "The others are for you. Please cook these for me and take six for yourself."

Speechless at the gift, the toothless crone turned to her most notable possession, a clay pottery charcoal burner. Adding precious charcoal to the meagre flame she put water in a battered aluminium dixie and set the eggs to boil, crouching huddled in a tattered blanket and muttering over her prize.

Back in her own hut, Che curled into a ball on the rude bed. Beside her the child devoured another biscuit, silent, aware that something important had happened but unable to process the thought any further.

His sudden hunger satisfied, Bagyo crept under the cloth and huddled against the girl curled in a foetal position. She made a mewling sound, kittenish in her half-sleep. Minutes later, against the warmth of Che's body, he unconsciously reached for a broken teddy bear that wasn't there and drifted into a half-way world where chocolate biscuits sizzled in bright flames and he flew over the ground, like a bird, in the arms of Sister Jan.

Chapter Thirteen

Sister Jan struggled from darkness, fighting her way towards a pinpoint of light in a sea of agony until the light spread into a white ceiling with a slowly spinning fan.

As consciousness came flooding back she tried to turn her head and a face moved into her line of vision. She glimpsed a hypodermic needle and a white, rubber-gloved hand somewhere above her.

A low groan escaped as she tried to speak, her mouth harsh and dry.

"Shhh, Sister, do not try to talk. I'll get you a sip of water. The anaesthetic has parched you. Wait until the painkiller works. I have just injected it into your drip."

Turning her face to the right, Sister Jan became aware of a small room and beside her bed a stainless steel stand from which hung a flask of saline solution. A thin plastic tube fell from it into her heavily bandaged wrist.

With returning consciousness the pain narrowed to the middle of her body. As she focused, unable to suppress another low moan, it became a white hot vice from her hip to her knee seeming to tighten mercilessly, always increasing in pressure, never relaxing.

The nurse reached for her good hand and in reassurance.

"Just a few minutes Sister and the morphine will begin to work. Just hold my hand."

The gentle singsong Filipino English soothed her as the nurse picked a cool damp flannel from a basin on a bedside cabinet and gently dabbed her patient's brow. Then she reached for a clear plastic water cup and lifted it to Sister Jan's lips, the water like nothing Sister Jan had ever tasted, heaven, trickling across her tongue into the dry cavern of her throat. She finished the drink and lay back on the pillow.

At another movement in the room the nurse turned.

"Doctor? Yes, she is awake," and turning to her charge: !Sister, this is Doctor Parwani."

The young man moved closer and Sister Jan looked up to see a handsome brown face, the nose hooked under dark eyes and a mass of coal-black hair.

"Good evening Sister. I'm Henry Parwani. You are in the American Hospital in Manila. You've had an awful fall and you've been unconscious for two days now." He spoke in the clipped accent of the British Indian *raj*, a distraction for Sister Jan as the morphine began to make itself felt and the incandescent vice on her thigh loosened.

Taking a deep breath and then another, "Doctor," she smiled weakly. "What's wrong with me? How bad is it?"

He lifted a clipboard hanging from the end of the steel-framed bed and took a pair of reading glasses from his white coat pocket.

"Let's see. You have a compound fracture of the femur, Sister. We had to operate when the firemen brought you in. We've inserted a steel plate and five screws to mend the bone."

He nodded at her wrist. "You also broke your wrist in the same accident when you were knocked down. But it's a simple break and will mend quickly."

Sister Jan then became aware of a dull ache in her wrist, a pain until now subordinate to the agony in her leg.

Looking up at the young intern, she asked, "Doctor, what does it mean? My leg, just how bad?"

"Well Sister, I have to be honest, there'll be a slight shortening of your leg and you may be left with a limp. You'll walk well enough but you will always have a slightly unstable gait."

Only then did it occur to her that she had no recollection of the accident. The doctor said she'd been knocked down. But why? She closed her eyes and tried to think. Then suddenly there was noise, screaming, smoke, and fire.

She opened her eyes in fright, panic clutching at her heart.

"There was a fire." As she spoke it struck her like a blow. Bagyo, where was the child?

Impulsively she grasped the doctors' sleeve with her free hand. "There was a child, a babe, about three years old. Is he here? Where is he? Is he hurt?"

He looked at the chart, then back to her and frowned.

"There's no mention of a child. You were brought in alone when the first engines got through to the fire. You were only a matter of metres away from where the flames were stopped by a wide boulevard. You were indeed most lucky to escape with your life Sister."

She lay back, the morphine now delivering blessed relief from the pain and although befuddled by the drug she forced her mind back to the fire. Two days ago? Where was Bagyo?

Now she remembered sweeping him up in her arms and running into the street. Then she' was hit from behind and she dropped him. Then blackness. Nothing. No memory until now, here in the hospital.

But surely, she'd been hit and Bagyo thrust from her grasp outside the perimeter of the fire. She'd escaped the flames and so must he have. Bagyo must be alive!

The effort of remembering was too great and as the morphine seeped through her system, coating the frayed nerve-ends of agony, her eyes closed and she surrendered herself to surreal drug-induced sleep, the face of Bagyo hiding in her mind, elusive and ghostly, floating in a wavering sea of half formed images.

Chapter Fourteen

The Golden Triangle, South East Asia: October 1986.

ONE MOMENT THERE was just the dripping green jungle as Sean strode with a column of Thai soldiers on a narrow track winding into the rolling jungle-covered hills leading to the Golden Triangle on the converging borders of Laos, Burma and Thailand.

The next, shadowy figures stepped from behind cover into shafts of sunlight penetrating the forest canopy, hazy silhouettes that suddenly spat gunfire. Around Sean surprised soldiers fell in the fusillade and the deadly staccato chatter of AK47's was deafening as bullets split the air around Sean's head. Instinctively he fell with his companions.

Then the gunfire stopped and Sean looked up into the face of a grinning Burmese guerrilla, a machete flickering, mercurial in the sunlight as it lifted above him.

Then the blade hissed through the air.

Sean awoke to rattling rain on the split bamboo roof and the contralto of cock greeting the day from the valley below. The image of the machete faded as always when he jerked awake from a troubled sleep, his subconscious mind unable to erase the slaughter which began his capture.

He raised a hand to the scar where the flat of the machete split the skin and flesh at his temple when the razor-edge was deftly turned at the last split-second.

He heaved himself to a sitting position on the narrow army cot and swung his legs over the side to the slatted cane floor. Through the gaps left for ventilation he saw the muddy ground a metre below with stilts keeping the bamboo and rattan hut above the constant dampness and insect pests.

Rubbing his eyes, Sean slipped on rough rubber shoes and

mentally took stock as he had on every awakening of the 172 days of his imprisonment by the opium warlord, Khun San, somewhere in the rugged mountains of the Golden Triangle.

The former general officer carved out his empire after he fled across the border with his dwindling Nationalist army unit in 1949 when the Communists under Mao Tse Tung became ascendant in China.

In the doorway of the hut Sean's night-time guard squatted, a gap-toothed teenager he'd dubbed Macdos, the code-word UPI Bangkok bureau chief, Sandy Macdonald, used as his computer log-on.

Sean used simple mental reminders to keep alive his hope that Macdonald would somehow make a breakthrough and get him out of his jungle prison.

The rain stopped and a patch of weak sunshine slanted into the hut entranceway. Sean pushed himself to his feet, pausing, momentarily giddy.

He'd lost something like five kilos since the Thai government patrol ran straight into the one-sided firefight with an opium caravan heading for the Thai border. The few Thai troops who'd survived the initial attack had been shot out of hand.

Sean as an unarmed Caucasian carrying a reporters' credentials, camera gear and a lap-top computer, had been led with a rope around his neck on a two-day trek into Khun San's camp deep in the jungle amid the granite-peaked highlands of his domain.

The warlord's advisers suggested Sean could be worth more as a hostage than he would be dead.

Khun San evidently agreed. He was also, it turned out, hungry for the opportunity for self-aggrandisement having once been featured in a BBC documentary on the international drug trade. A deteriorating video copy of the programme was still compulsory nightly viewing for his unfortunate officers. Now he had visions of being immortalised in print and to facilitate this ambition Sean was fed reasonably well and allowed whatever exercise he wished, with his captors confident of his security, isolated in the deep jungle. To make doubly sure they took away his boots, which now graced the feet of one of his captors.

Stripped of his computer, his camera and Rolex watch he was left only with his clothing and the whales' tooth talisman. Native superstition apparently prevented the ivory being taken too.

Summoned often to a hut in the village below the hill on which his prison compound was built, for chess games and one-sided conversation, Sean had to listen as the world's premier dope master extolled what he perceived as his personal virtues. Khun San saw himself as an Asian Robin Hood, selling the cash crop of the poppy fields to feed and clothe his people. Sean was careful that their chess games too, were one-sided in the warlord's favour.

First days then weeks dragged by with emissaries from Kun San making contact with UPI in Bangkok only after Sean had been missing for two months and presumed dead by the outside world. Since then messengers made a fortnightly round trip to Bangkok with offer and counter-offer for his release. Today a courier was due back with the latest word from Bangkok.

'Macdos' looked up with a foolish grin as Sean shuffled to the doorway.

"Goo morn," he said proudly. "Goo morn Mister Sean."

Having exhausted his entire command of English he slid sideways on the doorstep to allow Sean to walk to the top of the native ironwood steps leading down to the ground where he paused, using a pencil stub to mark a crude record of days elapsed on the pole supporting a thatched overhang.

He made his way down and across a small muddy yard enclosed by a rickety bamboo fence to a lean-to that served as a crude toilet. A scrawny chicken scuttled away from investigating insects attracted by the ordure of the latrine.

It disappeared in the overgrown remnants of a vegetable patch Sean tried to cultivate, giving up in despair when the few green plants he nurtured were picked by his guards as they changed shifts, departing to the village in the valley below.

Macdos watched disinterestedly as he moved out of sight behind the lean-to. The routine was the same every morning and the *farang* wasn't going anywhere, too much jungle between the prison hut and the outside world. He'd piss and then come back to finish the rice and dried river fish that provided the evening and morning meal, sometimes enlivened with bean paste or straggly chicken. Then Macdos could head down the trail to the village, passing the relief guard on the way up.

He picked dried snot from his nose and studied the broken and filthy nails of feet that had never seen shoes. He was reaching down to tear at a snaggly toenail when a lead-filled plaited leather cosh hit him behind the right ear and his time stopped in darkness.

A figure in green and brown tiger-striped camouflage dragged the inert form of the young guard into the hut and dropped him heavily into the mud through a hole carved with a combat knife through the slatted bamboo floor. Below, a second man crouched and looked up.

"Any more around?"

"Seems the jungle is the prison wall. There's only this guard. The rest are billeted down in the village at least 15 minutes away. Let's get him out of here!"

Moments later Sean emerged from squatting in the lean-to and stopped, stupefied.

Sitting on the wooden porch of his prison hut and casually swinging booted feet over the space below were three very big men all grinning like schoolboys, each with weapons and other equipment slung over jungle uniforms. It was a scene straight out of a Rambo movie.

Now slipping down to face him were two Caucasian and one heavily moustached darker man, each well over six-feet tall. Behind them was Macdos supine in the mud.

After six months of imprisonment, of waiting and hoping, of knowing what might happen if a ransom wasn't paid, Sean rose to the occasion with a little panache of his own, combating his rescuers laconic approach.

"I hope you didn't kill the little bastard," he smiled. "He was a great conversationalist."

Then tears pricked his eyes and he turned away for a moment as realisation set in that here was deliverance.

Typical Macdonald, Sandy had negotiated with one hand while organising a rescue with the other as more and more information was gleaned on Sean's whereabouts. Plenty of ex-special forces soldiers, leftovers from Asian conflicts who could not settle down, hung out in the bars of Bangkok's Soi Cowboy, available for missions they considered honourable as long as the price was right.

The three ex-SAS sergeants surrounded him.

"Swallow these mate," said their apparent leader, his accent spawned in Australia's New South Wales, thrusting a handful of pills at Sean.

"They're pure bloody energy. Chew on them. It's about two clicks to our pickup point. You'll be in a Bangkok brothel tonight mate!"

Then he rummaged in a pack swung from his back and produced socks and a pair of rubberised combat boots, gesturing with them to Sean's feet, clad in rude native clogs made from discarded car tires.

"We need to move it. Get these on quick or we'll have to bloody carry you."

Sean sat on the lower step and brushing the dirt from his feet quickly donned the unaccustomed footwear, looking up in surprise at the comfort.

"Size eight-and-a-half eh?" said his benefactor. "We got two more pairs either side of that in case Macdonald got it wrong." He hoisted Sean to his feet.

"Wait. There's something I have to get."

Clambering up into the hut Sean reached into the thatching at one end. His captors had taken his camera and computer and he'd been left with only a notebook to ostensibly record his host's virtues and the ivory tooth that is his only link to life outside the hut and indeed to home. He pulled these treasures from their hiding place flipping the book open to the picture of Maria taped to the back page. The book also contained a minute shorthand account of the past six months. Thrusting it into his shirt pocket he looped the tooth over his head and with a final glance around, stepped back out of the hut.

"That's it," he said. "I'm outa here!"

The Australian led the way out of the compound and the second of the trio, an American of few words, assisted Sean while the third, who turned out to be a New Zealand Maori, kept well back as rear guard.

The quartet made its way into the jungle following a path the soldiers hacked open during the night and Shaun was now grateful for the freedom of movement and reasonable nutrition during his tenure with Khun San that enabled him to keep up reasonably well with just the odd friendly heave from his companions.

In the latter stages of the hike as the terrain got steeper, the rude path slippery in the ever-present condensation of the jungle, he was more and more given a helping hand.

They made their way steadily up the glowering range overlooking the valley of his captivity. As they paused for a brief moment to let him get his breath there was a single shot from the valley far below.

"They've found I'm not home to visitors," Sean cracked. "The guards only have one bullet to signal with. The fucking general didn't want a threat to his investment."

"Not to bloody worry mate," said the Australian, "We're about there and if they're coming after us from the village they're way behind the fucking eight ball."

A few minutes more of climbing to where a disused rice terrace provided a clearing and about an hour after leaving the compound, now almost exhausted, Sean found himself heaved through the sliding door of a black-painted Squirrel helicopter. The aircraft whined into life and scant moments later lifted them from the jungle. The downdraft from the turbine-powered rotor whipped at the foliage before the craft swooped onto its course down the hill-slope, gaining height over the falling ground and soon scudding south across the rain-forested hills with their viciously naked rocky ridges, towards the Thai border.

His first real taste of freedom came when the lone pilot, who introduced himself as another Kiwi normally flying for an oil company, reached into a cool-box and grabbed a six pack of beer in his huge paw. "Hey pal, your ol' buddy Macdonald said you might like this."

Sean chuckled. The austere Macdonald never called anyone 'buddy' in his life.

He reached for one of the cans, dripping with condensation from the humid air, of New Zealand Steinlager beer. God bless the man. He lifted the can in a silent toast to his rescuers and drank deeply as they opened their own beers.

After a second beer Sean began feeling light-headed and he declined a third. Now he had two main thoughts on his mind, to call New Zealand to say he was free. And then Manila, Maria. Please God she was okay and waiting for him.

Ninety minutes later through the vibrating perspex of the helicopter cockpit the sprawling pall of pollution capping Bangkok flowed over the horizon and then the chopper wound down towards a grassy area surrounded by paddy fields on the banks of the Mekong River on the city's outskirts.

The blades still whirled slowly as Sean was helped from the aircraft and hustled across the ground to a track, which apparently led to the highway into the city. There were several vehicles parked and squinting against the sun-limned backdrop of a plantation of banana palms encroaching on the road Sean became aware of a group of people. Then he spotted Madonald, as always sporting a white shirt and tie despite the climate, leaning against the door of a Toyota Landcruiser. He lifted an arm in salute as light burst from a television sungun and cameras flashed like strobes.

Chapter Fifteen

Manila, Philippines: June-August, 1986

For Maria the days following Sean's disappearance were haunted with unspeakable anguish and pain, despair compounded beyond comprehension by the twin disaster in Tondo.

In a matter of hours Maria's world had collapsed. Sean had gone, Sister Jan, the boy Bagyo, the Centre at Tondo. Every plank of her existence had gone and her mind reeled into some secret darkness of self-preservation.

She was alone in the darkness of her flat, too stunned to move, to cry, as though frozen in time, her blood turning to ice, her world drained, like a plug had been pulled, leaving her emotionally naked, cold, empty.

Dawn after the final blow, the news of the fire in Tondo, found her curled in a chair where merciful sleep had claimed her.

Somehow she dragged herself to her bed where she lay trying to make sense of what had happened. She recalled an earlier tragedy, the loss at sea of her parents, her lonely disillusionment with the Church.

Suddenly she had a focal point for her anguish. The church. The bloody, bloody church taking from her everything she held dear. The tears came then, flooding her soul, alone in the darkened apartment.

Then a drink. Oh God how she wanted to find oblivion. The red wines Sean had collected from his airport duty-free opportunities became a source of escape. A diversion too from gazing too intently at escape out of the open window of her fourth floor apartment to the cold, grey, hard concrete of the road below.

Maria fell into a limbo; her waking hours numbed by wine. Occasional takeaways came from a fast food vendor in the street below when her body signalled the infrequent need for food.

Each day she plagued Rhonda Rollinson at UPI for news. There was none and as those first days ran into weeks her calls became less frequent. The small flat on United Nations Avenue was a cage. Half-eaten food littered the kitchen surfaces. Bottles and glasses spilled from a cane coffee table onto the carpet in the lounge.

When Jaqui Benedict finally used her key to the flat, the front door opened onto darkness. Moving across the lounge she tripped on something and cursed as she snapped open the venetian blinds. She began picking up clothing and makeshift ashtrays, scattered magazines and take-away food cartons. Hell what a mess! In the light of the window she stooped and picked up a pile of torn paper, noticing a crest, gold and red, on the first piece. Glancing through these she recognised one of Maria's treasures, torn from a frame propped on a bookshelf against the wall. Maria's letter of commendation from Cardinal Sin, destroyed and in tatters. Jaqui sighed and dropped the torn missive into a waste-paper basket beside the couch.

Then Maria was in the doorway of the bedroom, wearing jeans and a bra she'd obviously collapsed in the night before.

"Hell's teeth girl," cried Jaqui. "It's noon already. What the hell are you trying to do."

She gestured at the mess in front of them and then looked back at her friend.

"Christ girl, enough is enough." Moving into the bathroom, she picked up towels from the floor and then turned on the shower.

As she had when her parents were killed, Maria fell child-like into Jaqui's care. When some sort of order was returned to the flat, and Jaqui had managed to get her to eat some halfway nourishing food, the day descended into a long sisterly conversation.

Jaqui's approach to her friend's predicament was down to earth in the only way she knew. She'd take her mind off tragedy by getting her out and about and back into the mainstream of her own life.

A month after Sean's disappearance a still wan and troubled Maria finally accepted Jaqui's urging.

"You can't help Sean sitting in a dark apartment starving yourself, you're going to rack and ruin girl! Who'd want you like this? Not Sean! You've got to get on with life. So come on we're going to eat at the Grill and then we're going out on the town. There may yet be news."

That night was followed by another and another. Jaqui had seen to it that the flower shop in Makati was running well in the care of two responsible staff, used to Maria's long absences overseeing her treasured Tondo flower project. Maria needed only to turn up once a week to tally up sales and pay wages.

But a visit to Tondo after Jaqui persuaded her to face the disaster which had spun her life out of control ended in her pulling a mental veil over anything to do with the Soriano Centre, her now destroyed project, Sister Jan, the child Bagyo or Father Stols.

Her thin hold on sanity following Sean's disappearance could not cope with the horror painted by the blackened crater of Tondo and her troubled mind carved those memories from her consciousness.

Six weeks after Sean went missing Maria called the Makati flower shop with instructions every week or so, her staff humouring the erratic calls with the business under stable control. Jaqui had become the effective manager to solve any problems. Finally Maria stopped calling altogether.

She became a creature of the night, getting in at dawn, sleeping through the day and going out again at night, her world a steadily growing round of discos, bars and parties.

She was back in the fast lane, no time to think, fun to be had, memories to forget. There are moneyed men, fast cars and weekend parties at expensive and exclusive beach resorts.

It wasn't long before a tentative flirtation she began with marijuana became more serious.

Then at a late night party in a luxurious home in Manila's elite Forbes Park estate she tried cocaine.

The rapturous feeling from the narcotic finally stunned the pain of multiple loss. For the first time in weeks the ache of being alone faded. The music took over and Maria became a doll.

The smiling drug dealer who provided her cure looked on as the thin, beautiful, raven-haired girl began dancing to a tune only she could hear.

Next morning she awoke beside him, upstairs in the three-storied villa.

With a bilious hangover, the waning effect of the coke and fear nibbling at her stomach, she stared at the sleeping man. She vaguely remembered a night of lovemaking.

Her stomach lurching, she threw back silken sheets looking wildly around. She slipped her feet onto the floor; staggered erect and tottered towards the en-suite on the far side of the room.

She vomited into the toilet bowl, a cold sweat on her brow, her nose streaming mucous.

She felt a towel draped around her and her face wiped with a cool flannel as the man proffered a glass.

"Here, drink this and you'll feel better."

Her mouth dry and raspy, Maria gulped the liquid and staggered to the bed, collapsing on her face. Seconds later the powerful sedative took effect and she passed out.

Smiling to himself, the pusher reached down and opened the bedside cabinet, taking out a hypodermic and holding it to the light streaming through a window.

With this girl's looks he could make a fortune catering to the perversions of his clients, fulfilling the desires of visiting oil-rich Middle Eastern sheiks, outwardly respectable corporate Japanese, Germans and Americans.

First, he had to establish control. This always worked, always.

Maria did not feel the needle sliding into a vein in her arm, the heroin sweeping through her and coating nerve endings with a balm of bliss. She slept on oblivious to the horrors awaiting her.

Leaving the sleeping girl the pusher threw a silk happy-coat over his suntanned frame and left the room for coffee downstairs.

The dose was a big one for a first timer and she'd sleep for at least 12 hours. Then withdrawal would set in and the second dose would be easier ... and then the next. Soon she'd be demanding his services. And then he'd introduce her to her work.

Chapter Sixteen

Manila, Philippines: May-November 1986

FOR THE NEXT six months Bagyo Cruz and Che were a team. From her jealously guarded jam-jar treasure trove, the elfin girl fed them well by street standards where a peso or two bought a chicken leg or a stick of *satay* with rice or noodles. A meal a day came from a Caritas hostel or from the soup kitchen operated by the Little Sisters of the Poor behind the 400-year-old Cathedral of Our Lady of Lourdes on Mabini Street.

Clothes came from the same source. Late model cars periodically arrived at the church, from the matrons of Forbes Park and the wealthy suburbs of Quezon City. Bodyguards and drivers carried cardboard cartons containing cast-off clothing and discarded household items into the church vestry. Charity borne of guilt. Although the Marcos regime had gone there still lingered an aura of corruption in Manila's business and political life. But in an essentially matriarchal society, some of the more affluent felt an obligation to those less fortunate.

Occasionally a sister of the order with nursing qualifications gave the street kids a cursory medical check, dealing to a variety of bruises, grazes and minor infections from a simple first aid kit. Where any serious health problems arose there was limited space at a church hospital in Quezon City. But most street kids regarded the institution with terror and would hide illness to avoid it. Some were found comatose in the street before anything could be done. Some died alone on waste ground or hidden in shrubbery in the city.

Bagyo's inherited constitution and the tropical climate appeared to serve him well and apart from occasional sticking plasters he'd little need of the rudimentary service.

Each day he and Che trekked into the city. Shoeless, Bagyo's feet became calloused and toughened to the hot asphalt of the city streets as he served his beggar's apprenticeship. He'd stand on a street corner outside the Fire House Disco clad in his ragged clothing, eyes pleading, hand outstretched. Always there was an expatriate policeman or public servant on leave from the rich British colony of Hong Kong, an American tourist on his first visit to the fleshpots of Manila, who'd pity the child, press a few pesos into his dirty fingers. With their small reserve and income from begging Che avoided selling herself to the paedophiles haunting the city shadows and as she and the child become familiar on the streets of Ermita they staked out a turf of their own by right of occupation.

They overcame the attempt of a pathetic beggar on crutches who tried to chase them from the block bounded by the Fire House Disco and Bubbles bar on one side, the Spiders' Web and the Pit Stop on the other. His hobbling proved no match for the fleet-footed pair and what began as confrontation settled into uneasy alliance.

Che broke the ice with the offer of ten pesos to the beggar after importuning a particularly generous bar patron. The footless former serviceman unbent to offer his name simply as Rigg. His feet had been blown off by a Muslim guerrilla mine in the south of the country. He'd been a conscript with any hopes of a pension evaporating in the corruption of a dictator's army.

An arrangement of mutual aid emerged as despite his injuries Rigg had an intimidating style. The insipid legacy of army training and developed upper-body strength lifted his profile above most of the ill and half-starved street people around him. Rigg spotted a potential customer down the block and dispatched the children to intercept before the other creatures of the gutter caught on.

The arrangement proved profitable and the trio formed

an alliance of mutual protection and assistance.

But one morning Bagyo awoke alone in the rude hut on the waterfront.

Steady rain was falling so he huddled inside dozing, fretting, sleeping again as he waited for the young girl who was his lifeline. He finally left the hut and set off for the only other world he knew, just another urchin scampering along dodging between the feet of pedestrians.

Rigg was in his usual place in a side street running behind the Spider's Web Bar, in the small corrugated iron shack that housed a crib bed and a wooden fruit box containing his three pieces of spare clothing.

"Che not come home," was Bagyo's opening gambit.

Rigg looked up from where he lay smoking a precious cigarette. He'd been on the street when Che had arrived in the early hours of the morning before. She'd left the sleeping Bagyo for a party in Rizal Park bordering Ermita where many of her peer group slept rough. She'd been given some drink and the raw native rum had its inevitable effect.

Her arrival back in the tourist belt, drunk, was very badly timed.

Ermita's Mayor, Roberto Patrice, was making one of his infrequent responses to demands by the church and some of the more puritan electors of his constituency for the area to be cleaned up. A police task force was sweeping the streets, ignoring the bars themselves from which they earned protection money but picking up any women or girls working the street.

It was a token gesture, which produced arrest figures without actually harming backhanders from the bars and in the sweep Che would have been loaded into a paddy wagon and carted off to a police precinct and a crowded cell with the other flotsam of the night.

With no money for bribes or fines she'd have been handed over to the fledgling social services which had sprung up under the Aquino administration. Now she could be anywhere - in a reformatory or church-run rehabilitation centre. For the moment anyway she'd left Bagyo's life.

Rigg looked up at the child. Without the girl and her street sense the kid was just a liability with nothing to offer Rigg, a man hardened by his own misfortunes with no pity in him.

Reaching down for the crutch by his bed and leaning across the hovel he snagged the edge of the tin door and swung it shut in the child's face.

Chapter Seventeen

Maria opened her eyes wearily then threw up her arms to shield them from the glare in the room, the light hitting her like a physical blow. Shaking her head she tried to think, her brain like cotton wool, thick and yielding. She sat up in bed and almost screamed as pain barrelled through her system. Her nerves on fire, her stomach lurched and tied itself in a knot. It unravelled and re-tied and she lurched from the bed and barely made the bathroom.

Flushing the toilet she clung shivering to the door frame, clad only in a thin nightgown, her feet bare on the cool parquet flooring. Waves of hot and cold flowed through her competing with the tangle in her stomach and her electric nerve ends. She screamed, a drawn out wail of pain and anguish.

Seconds later the door to the bedroom opened and Johan Mel stood there. "Ah my pigeon awakes. Are you not well? Would you like Uncle Johan to make you better?"

Maria looked wildly at him and staggered the few steps to the bed. "You bastard, you bloody bastard, give it me. Give me some more."

She wrung her hands, then pulled wildly at her hair. "Give it me, give it me," she screamed again.

Mel left the room shutting the door behind him and Maria stared in horror. Screaming again she got to her feet, then the door opened and Mel was back with a cloth on a tray. He crossed the room and held the tray in front of the quivering figure who sat back on the bed.

"Uncle Johan as some peace here on the tray. Uncle Johan will make you feel better."

"Please, please," cried Maria, and somehow even the promise of the syringe of heroin began to calm her. She even tried to smile, a ghastly parody of the warmth she once emanated.

Mel smiled. "In a moment or two my pigeon. First you must do something for me. I want you to be pretty for Uncle Johan."

Maria was puzzled. Then the door opened again and a young girl stepped into the room carrying two shopping bags. Maria saw she had her head shaved and was wearing just a towelling robe. The girl closed the door and put the bags on the ground before letting the robe slide from her shoulders. She was naked underneath. Maria gasped as she picked up the bags and glided to the bed. From one of them she took a garment of thin wire filigree. It was a halter, which in a normal fabric would contain a woman's breasts.

Maria recoiled in horror, pulling her feet up under her, crouching, cowering in the corner where the head of her bed met the walls of the room.

"Uncle Johan wants you to wear this," said Mel. "Then uncle Johan will give his little pigeon what she wants."

Maria had been on heroin for almost two weeks and her willpower was gone. The fire in her nerves still waned and peaked. "Oh God," she sobbed, reaching for the garment.

The girl helped her lift off the thin nightgown and she too stood naked by the bed, quivering with tension. Johan Mel picked up the syringe and examined it carefully against the light in the centre of the room, drawing out the moment. Then he lowered the needle and tied a band of surgical rubber around Maria's arm, raised a vein and injected her.

In moments the effect of the narcotic transformed Maria as waves of calm warmth descended on her and she made no objection as the girl lifted the wire garment over her head and lowered in about her breasts. The wire mesh tightened as it fastened at the back.

"Now that's much better," said Mel. He nodded to the girl. "Now the shoes."

The girl took a pair of silver stiletto-heeled shoes from the other bag and knelt beside the bed where Maria now sat with a dreamy expression on her face. She raised one foot and then the other.

"Now stand for me," commanded Mel as he stepped back. "Very nice, just the ticket my dear. Now I think it's time you joined us downstairs for some food. We have roast pork tonight and you need a little feeding I think. And we'll have wine too." He clapped his hands in child-like delight. "Oh yes, you'll do very well you know. You must wear your new outfit to the dinner table."

Maria was still in a dream state, a trance as the heroin flowed through her veins. Suddenly she was hungry, ravenous and longing for a glass of wine. She smiled, this time more convincingly.

"Come down when you are ready," said Mel. "In the meantime, this girl is Carol and she's your friend."

Mel left the room and the young girl stepped forward to Maria and slowly brought her face to meet her own. She kissed Maria softly on the lips and placed her arms about her. The warmth of her body, her softness, struck a chord in the older woman and she suddenly threw her arms about the girl, holding her close, soaking in the human contact and closing her eyes to retreat into a private world.

The submissive girl returned her embrace and whispered. "Soon my mistress, it will be soon."

Chapter Eighteen

Sydney, Australia: November 1986.

THE RETREATING SEA and saturated sand plucked at Sister Jan's heels as she limped out of the surf at Sydney's Bondi Beach, shaking her head to fling the water from her hair, now grown long in her hospitalisation and recovery.

Favouring her injured right leg she made her way to a deck-chair under a beach umbrella and sank gratefully back onto the striped canvas.

Her leg had been out of plaster for a month and a daily swim prescribed by her family doctor was the best physiotherapy she could get.

The ugly scar on her thigh was a permanent reminder of her Manila experience and she'd been warned a gnawing ache would recur whenever the weather took a turn for the worse.

"You'll have a built-in weather vane I'm afraid my dear," old Doc Brockie, the family physician, had said.

Today at least the weather was on her side, a glorious Sydney summer day and while the temperatures hovered around 32 degrees in the concrete and glass city, here on the beach a cooling sea breeze and occasional cloud over the sun brought respite. She wore a one piece black swimsuit which clung rather revealingly to her tall, trim figure.

'If the sisters at Caritas could see me now,' she mused. *'Not the sort of thing one would wear in the Philippines!'*

But this was Australia and despite her vocation, Sister Jan was still a child of the beach, sun and surf, raised in the family home still occupied by her parents a hundred metres from shore.

Sitting comfortably, her leg resting on the handle of

a basket containing a sandwich and a bottle of water she gazed out at the surfboard riders competing for watching girlfriends, speeding in sheets of spray across the face of rolling two-metre waves.

A raft of cloud spread slowly up from the horizon, an errant puff of stratocumulus drifting into the sun. The forecast was for a southerly to spring up and with the harbinger of the weather to come from deep in the southern ocean there came a flash of memory, of a darker day from a past storm.

Her thoughts again returned to Manila and a small boy vanished in the chaos of the fireworks factory blaze.

Almost six months had passed with no word; no hint of where Bagyo Cruz might be or even if he still lived.

Father Stols had escorted her from the American hospital to board her Qantas 747 in Manila when her Sisters of Mercy order decreed that she return home for her convalescence and while promising to do what he could to locate the child, he was pragmatic.

"It may be an impossible task Sister. But yes, of course I'll try. The church will issue a circular with his photograph. It's a good thing we took his picture when we were looking for a sponsor."

A gruff Rhonda Rollinson had telephoned him a few days before the nun's discharge to tell him that Sean, Bagyo's sponsor, was missing. But he decided this news could wait until something more certain was known. Sister Jan was worried enough about the child.

In the ensuing months Father Stols wrote regularly and in his first letter told Sister Jan about Sean. Six weeks later had come the more welcome news that Sean was alive but still in danger, being held hostage in the Golden Triangle. But still no news of the child.

Anxious to get back to the Philippines, Sister Jan had already made plans for her return in another two months, fully recovered and somehow convinced she could succeed in finding Bagyo where Father Stols had so far failed.

Glancing at the sky she saw the sun beginning its drop towards the sea and so gathered up her towel and basket to make her way the short distance home. Her father would rescue the chair and the umbrella.

Reaching the paved footpath skirting the beach Sister Jan walked more confidently on the hard surface and a minute later entered open ranch-slider doors from the garden which overlooked the beach below.

"Is that you dear?" Her mother's voice from the kitchen.

"Hi Mum, had a lovely swim." Her mother bustled in protectively and took her towel and basket.

"I've news for you dear. It's been on the radio this afternoon. That journalist friend of yours has been freed. Sean isn't it? He was interviewed in Bangkok by the ABC."

Chapter Nineteen

Bangkok, Thailand: November 1986

SEAN WAS MAKING serious inroads into a wad of Thai baht drawn from a bank account bulging with six months unspent salary.

In the Crazy Horse Saloon on Bangkok's Patpong Road he and Sandy Macdonald were getting seriously drunk. Four half-naked bar-top dancers draped themselves around the pair, sipping high-priced glasses of soft drink and touching the men intimately until their hands were brushed away.

"Later honey, later," Sean drunkenly admonished a particularly adventurous hostess and nodded to the barman.

"More Mekong, my man," he cried. The raw Thai whiskey would take varnish off a wall but right now Sean seemed intent on depleting the bars' stock.

"Yes mate," said Macdonald. "That's the only thing for it right now. We just have to wait and see."

Normally Macdonald would've declined a drunken night out so early in the week. Bangkok was hard enough on the liver as it was but Sean was having problems.

After a week of good food and rest, interspersed with an extensive debriefing by the Thai military authorities and countless interviews with fellow media men, Sean was pretty much back to his old self.

But not quite. All attempts to reach Maria in Manila had failed. When Sean rang Maria's apartment, a stranger answered.

He'd rented the flat two months before after it'd been vacant for weeks. The landlord was keeping some of her possessions against unpaid rent, a TV, stereo and clothing.

No one knew where she was. The flower shop had

changed hands and the new lessee was only able to tell Sean that Jaqui Benedict had despaired of Maria returning and had dismissed the unpaid staff. She herself had gone with a Chinese boyfriend to Hong Kong with plans to marry. The Soriano Centre had gone in a fire and the church office in Manila had put him in touch with Father Stols, now managing an orphanage in the inland town of Carpos in Tarloc province, but this too became a dead end.

Stols had last heard from Maria after the Tondo fire destroyed her rooftop garden project. The event had hit her hard and with the Centre gone, Marianne dead, Sister Jan invalided home to Australia and the boy Bagui Cruz missing she had withdrawn into herself. Father Stols feared privately that losing Sean at the same time might have been too much for her to bear, but didn't share the thought.

He'd also had a call from Sister Jan to learn she'd lost touch with Maria and learned more details of how the child he'd spontaneously agreed to help was still unaccounted for after he and the nun were separated escaping the blaze.

All of which left Sean carrying a whole lot of emotional baggage he didn't need.

He'd booked a flight out to Manila for the following evening then called Sandy: "I'm going to bloody find her. Right now though, I'm gonna get pissed. Coming?"

Some three hours into the night the pair are on their seventh bar.

"Bloody girl could've bloody waited," said Sean, waving again at the barman, this time motioning him to leave the bottle. He helped himself to another drink, swaying as he reached over the bar. The girl on his left put a small shoulder under his arm to stop him falling from the stool.

Swallowing another mouthful and pushing the girls away from him, he clambered from the stool and staggered toward the door.

As he did so some sober part of his brain asked: *'what the hell is he saying? What's he doing here in this bloody dive?'* The thought of his engagement to Maria had been the only thing keeping him going through the lonely months in the Golden Triangle. She's his lifeline and here he is pissing it up in a girlie bar, imagining the worst.

A very slightly more sober Macdonald put down his glass, recognising the signs. Sean's trademark when aware he'd had enough to drink was just to get up and leave. No good-byes, no social graces, just abrupt departure.

Now Macdonald stepped out of the bar into the neon nightmare of the strip doing a roaring trade with thousands of American sailors on shore leave from the ships of the US Seventh Fleet parked in the Gulf of Thailand off the beach brothels of Pattaya.

He brushed aside a tout seeking an audience for a live sex show and spotted Sean a few feet away, studying the entrance to another bar advertising topless and bottomless dancers. *'Excitement you can touch,'* said the sign.

Reaching him, Macdonald put an arm round his shoulders. "Manila tomorrow old mate, and maybe Maria. Could be she just moved in with a girlfriend when you didn't show up. C'mon mate. Back to the pub. Tomorrow's another day."

With his free hand he signalled a cruising taxi and minutes later they headed for the luxury of the Somerset Maugham wing of the Oriental Hotel on the Mekong riverfront.

Chapter Twenty

Ermita, Manila, Philippines: December 1986

THE PRIVATE CLUB behind locked doors manned by two security guards, both off-duty policemen, was off a side street of Mabini Avenue in Ermita.

Inside throbbing music swelled with a deep sensuous base from Kenwood speakers on each side of a small stage, from where floor rose in tiers of banquette seating curved around small tables. A couple of dozen patrons and hostesses sat with glasses, bottles and bowls of fruit.

The room was darkened with flickering candles in glass holders providing subdued pockets of light.

On a red-sheeted double bed in the centre of the stage a naked woman was tied, spread-eagled. She was European, young, apparently in her teens. Her hands are fastened with crimson silk cords to the top corners of the bed, the tension on her body arching her torso, lifting her pointed breasts, her ankles tied to matching crimson cords.

A spotlight hovered over the girl who lay expectant, her head turning to the heavy red velvet curtain at the rear of the stage. As she did so those watching became aware her head was shaved with only her ears offering relief to the smoothness.

The music swelled as the curtains pared and a masked woman stepped through, her coal-black hair tied back tightly in a bun, fixed by a shining clip, a tight black leather collar studded with silver fastened around her neck.

Black lace gloves reached to her elbows and she was naked save for jet black and silver stiletto-heeled shoes and an open-worked silver wire halter, which shimmered in the spotlight.

The newcomer pirouetted to the music and one wrist drifted into the light. From it swung a black leather quirt, thickly plaited at her wrist and tapering into a foot-long series of tassels.

As the woman turned to face the audience they could see her lips parted, her tongue flickering in a personal and private ecstasy.

The girl on the bed whimpered and rolled her head in fear.

The music swelled and raising the whip the tall woman turned again and the lash descended.

In the darkened, watching room, a minor Middle Eastern trade official flicked his fingers in the direction of a bar in the rear. An attentive club owner he knew as Johan Mel was beside him in obsequious attendance.

"The madam," the berobed Arab said. "I want her to attend me."

Mel shook his head regretfully. "I cannot assist you, the madam is only for the stage, but allow me." He gestured to the back of the room and another woman, European, came forward, dressed in a tight black PVC cat suit with her breasts exposed. She too carried a plaited leather whip. Standing before the customer she caressed his face with the leather. He gasped with pleasure. "Come," she commanded and led him to a heavily curtained doorway at the rear of the club.

When Maria left the bed on the stage, stepping back through the curtain, Johan Mel was there with a towelling robe. "Come, your reward is ready."

Maria and the stoned teenager she performed with shared the joint and a glass of expensive champagne. Mel flicked a forefinger at a plastic syringe and seizing the thin arm he administered another dose of heaven. Number four heroin from a source in Hong Kong, smuggled into the Philippines by fishing boat.

Myopic, Maria felt the now familiar peaceful warm rush

and puppet-like she was wrapped in a gown and led out through a side door to a waiting car.

At the house in Forbes Park, she was hustled inside by a woman clad in the blue uniform of a domestic servant and taken to a bedroom. There, before oblivion came as the lights were extinguished, she rallied briefly. A shadowy figure drifted through her tortured mind, the shape of a man she tried to remember, a man who somehow meant safety. But the fleeting image faded into a strange, uneasy peace.

Chapter Twenty-one

THE RED NEON script over the doorway beckoned through fine drizzle dulling Manila's twilight heat, the soft rain diffusing the garish lights of neighbouring bars and disco-pubs.

Paying off the cab, Sean dashed the few yards to the wrought iron and glass door, stepping thankfully into George's bar, air swirling with tobacco smoke, yeasty but cooled by humming air conditioning.

A wave of chatter all but drowned out the jukebox as patrons crowded the brass-railed teak counter along one wall of the half-lit room, the whole punctuated by the sharper clash of balls from a lone pool table vying for space.

Christmas Eve of holidays celebrated with fervour in Asia's only Christian nation promised expats with an extended session at the bar, many without traditional family in Manila. Most either lived with or were married to local girls who'd be heading home to barrios around the country for serious church-going and family reunions, leaving the half-committed men in their lives to pursuits in the city.

As Sean paused to focus in the dim lights from wall-lamps, conversation melted down to a silence made the more complete as the jukebox died.

"Christ, he's back."

A chorus of cheers followed as Sean grinned good-naturedly and made his way through the throng of regulars. Hands reached to shake his with "Welcome back mate," and "Good on you son."

George pushed through the throng of well-wishers and called for quiet. "Let the bugger be for Christ's sake. He needs a beer, not a mauling."

George led Sean to the corner stool where he held court

as a plump and beaming Filipina barmaid Sean recognised as George's wife, Jeanette, poured an ice-cold beer. He downed half the glass. "Thanks George, I needed that. Merry Christmas."

He turned to the room, which had not fully returned to its normal beery chatter.

"Hi guys, and thanks. I'd love to have a beer with each of you but this'll have to do. Seasons greetings and it's good to be back."

He raised his glass to salute another chorus of well-wishing. Someone slipped another peso into the jukebox.

As *Tie a Yellow Ribbon* boomed into the room Sean slumped onto the stool beside George. "Bloody hell."

"You can't blame these guys mate. You're a bloody hero as far as they're concerned. They'll go home to their wives, girlfriends, every night and maybe their biggest adventure's finding a new sheila in a bar somewhere. Let them have a bit of fun." George passed him a second beer and Sean was aware of someone next to him. He turned to find John McIvor, a sardonic grin lighting his face under its characteristic blond cowlick, blue eyes twinkling.

"Merry Christmas mate. Trust you to take a holiday in the Golden Triangle to make a bit of copy," he says. "The Kiwi mafia strikes again eh!"

They'd both left school in small-town New Zealand 20 years before, each joining one of the two town newspapers as cadet reporters, McIvor on the more racy afternoon broadsheet, Sean the staid morning daily.

Sean's story of capture, incarceration and eventual rescue from the Golden Triangle had hummed across the UPI newswires after his release. The hometown papers gobbled it up.

"Yeah - if I wasn't with a bloody agency I'd have made a fortune," he says. "Now I'll have to do a book to make a quid."

They ordered more beers and Sean broached the subject

tormenting him.

"Mate, do you remember Maria? You met her at that dinner we had at Simon Halley's place when I was doing the revolution story. We actually decided to get hitched just before I was posted."

McIvor nodded. "So I heard. Hell, she's bloody lovely mate!"

"Yeah, well I've damn well lost her. Rhonda lost contact with her about a month after I went bush. I've tried her flat, the Caritas centre in Tondo is gone, and the shop in Makati's closed down. Her landlord had the passport she'd arranged for joining me in Singapore. He'd sold everything else to pay the back rent - the bastard. It's like she's just vanished into thin air. I know that can happen in this fucking country but I can't imagine Maria being involved in anything weird enough to have her dealt to. I just don't know where to look."

McIvor's expression was is sympathetic.

"I've been here a week trying to find out what's happened. What the hell do I do now John?"

McIvor pondered the question as two men in white *barongs* entered the bar, holding the door open as a silver-haired figure stepped in followed by two more bodyguards.

"Shit," said McIvor, "how bloody timely can you get. Why didn't you think of Pedro?"

Sean looked up and the realisation hit him that here was a man with the best intelligence network in the Philippines.

Pedro Wright was head the National Police Bureau responsible for the country's domestic security. "What he doesn't know isn't worth knowing." said McIvor.

Wright became aware of Sean's attention, looked across and grinned broadly, working his way through the crowded bar as customers respectfully made way. Sean stood as they shook hands.

"The man returns," boomed Wright. "Jeanette, a beer please and more for these two."

One of Wright's bodyguards appeared with a stool magically vacated nearby and the Philippines top cop sat between the two journalists. Accepting the pewter tankard he kept behind the bar he raised it. "Welcome back to the world Sean." As another round appeared, he added "Word has it your problems aren't over."

Wright would've been aware of his arrival through airport immigration returns and as with all correspondents in *'his town'*, Sean would've been discreetly shadowed by the network of informants reporting to national police headquarters.

"You've been looking for someone," said Wright. "What's the problem?"

Briefly Sean brought the police chief up to date on his search for Maria.

"I can see why you're concerned. Well, we'd better list her as missing and see what we can turn up. Obviously you can describe her but it's the old story of who's the best looking woman in the Philippines and the answer simply 'the one with the black hair!' Do you have a picture of her?"

Sean reached into the pocket of his safari suit and pulled out the battered notebook he'd filled in the jungle hut on the Burmese border.

Flipping it to the back cover he showed Wright the full-length shot of Maria stepping from a small outrigger canoe onto a beach at Puerto Princessa on Palawan.

"OK, good. That'll crop to head and shoulders and copy up fine with a little computer enhancement," said Wright.

"For a start we'll make a bunch of laser copies and get it circulated. Can I take this now? I'll get it processed first thing tomorrow, Christmas Day or not. One of my people can take it in. We're still staffed at headquarters and it'll give the holiday duty people something to do."

His positive approach put new heart into Sean.

"Pedro, if you can do anything, I will owe you," he said

gratefully.

"Careful, I might keep you up to that." The two men grinned and McIvor punched Sean on the shoulder.

"You see, there are ways and means after all. And I'll get some copies from Pedro and put them around my contacts."

Suddenly Sean felt he had allies and the aching loneliness he'd been living with became a little more bearable.

"Guys, shit, thanks. Well we can't do much until tomorrow, so now it's my round. Hell, McIvor let's shoot some pool tonight and then we'll get a decent steak at the Manila Hotel. I hear it's the only place still importing good food."

Aware of George hovering, obviously with information to impart to his policeman friend, Sean and McIvor moved over to the pool table at the back of the room.

At 3am Sean staggered back into his room at the Regent. He and McIvor wound up on a mild bender in Bubbles bar on the del Pilar strip after a pleasant dinner.

Befuddled by a vast intake of San Miguel beer, he at first did not notice the red message light glowing on the telephone in his room.

But after showering and about to fall into bed, the phone shrilled and he was speaking to the night desk, the message brief and to the point. He's to contact Rhonda Rollinson at home, whatever the hour. He dialled and was connected after several rings. The gravel-voiced bureau chief quickly shook off her sleep.

"Sean, I'm sorry, it's perhaps bad news. Tried to get you at George's but they said you'd shot off on the town. There's a message for you to phone home to Auckland urgently. You'd best do it now - it's about 7am over there."

Swiftly Sean thanked her and with a knot in his belly, flicked the connection closed and dialled the operator.

Chapter Twenty-two

Manila, Philippines: Christmas Day 1986

IN A CORNER of Rizal Park where although he does not make the connection he'd spent many an idyllic Sunday afternoon with Sister Jan and Maria, four-year-old Bagyo Cruz huddled with five other street children.

The sounds of the awakening city, night-filled bladders and daylight hunger stirred the group from a fitful sleep on the scraps of coconut fibre matting and shreds of blankets and cloth of their communal bed on the dried grass of the park.

Lifting his grubby face from a pillowing arm, Bagyo rolled away from the body heat of Calo. Pushing himself to his feet he moved a few yards before hitching up a leg of his shorts to pee against the base of a traveller's palm, rubbing his face with his free hand where sleep had imprinted the coarse pattern of his rude bed. The broad leaves of the palm, running fan-like from east to west like a compass rippled in a light breeze from the sea.

A shaft of the sun lifting over the nearby ruins of Fort Intramuros lit up a slight frame clad in dirty shorts, his body marked by bruises and dirt, hair matted and unkempt.

Completing a minimal toilet he walked more steadily back to the awakening group and rummaged in a collapsing cardboard box finding a plastic soft drink bottle of water.

Beside him, Calo rose, taking the bottle, swallowing warm liquid.

Waking, the other children moved to take a mouthful or repeat Bagyo's morning pee. The one girl among them, a waif of about seven, retreated some distance to squat in the relative privacy of a straggly bunch of park shrubbery that served the park children as a midden.

Outside, the streets were already becoming choked with throbbing lines of traffic, jeepney and taxi drivers clutching rosary beads and medals of St Peter, insurance against the daily commute that was Manila's particular hell.

With all the children awake, 12-year-old Calo called them together. Issuing instructions with the composure of a miniature police sergeant briefing a morning muster he assigned each one to streets outside the park.

Bagyo was pointed towards traffic lights at an intersection on the waterfront Roxhas Boulevard and he wandered off to take up his begging station. The group he fell in with after the disappearance of Che and abrupt dismissal by Rigg needed pesos to buy some bread or rice from one of the ramshackle workers canteens that line the rubbish-strewn seaward side of the road.

Calo had found Bagyo on the del Pilar strip and that he had money, all that remained of the jam-jar treasure. The older boy took him under his wing, first offering to safeguard the remaining pesos. These long spent, he at least offered Bagyo much needed lessons in survival as well as the companionship of his small band.

Bagyo made his way out of the park as half a mile away, outside the Regent Hotel, Sean watched the doorman loading his suitcase into a cab. His face was drawn even more than had become usual.

The telephone in New Zealand had been answered by his sister Adele with news that his mother was ill and while details weren't yet clear he'd better return home and the sooner the better.

A hastily awakened UPI office secretary secured bookings on a Christmas morning Qantas flight to Sydney with a handy connection on Air New Zealand to Auckland. His ticket was at the airport.

Tipping the concierge, Sean got into the back seat of the

cab as it threaded into the southbound river of vehicles on Roxhas.

Failing in an attempt to beat a set of lights the driver pulled up at the red ahead of a line of traffic.

Lost in thought, Sean did not at first hear the tap at his window. The driver's curse in *Tagalog* alerted him and he turned. Looking through the half-open car window was an urchin.

About four or five years old the kid was well made, clad in grubby and torn shorts, his chest heaving from his run across the opposite carriageway.

Mucous from a running nose dried on his upper lip and his hair was matted, a leaf somehow caught above his left ear giving him an immature piratical look.

Then Sean caught the child's eyes with a thrill of recognition like an icy spear.

The grey-green eyes, a mirror of his own, stared back in vacant supplication. There was an instant, a flickering look that traced a pathway through aeons of time, a Celtic memory.

Sean fought to break the spell, the fascination growing within him. The Eurasian kid must be one of millions in Asia, the by-blow of tourism and war, the unwanted interest on a lucrative sex industry. They roamed the dirty streets of a dozen lonely cities and he's long ago given up trying to be a one-man social service. He was about to wind up the window, ignoring the pathetic waif, when the child lifted a hand in supplication and spoke.

Despite himself, still in some kind of thrall, Sean paused with his hand on the window winder. Bagyo Cruz spoke again, more clearly.

"Me, no Christmas!" The small voice tremulous, the spontaneous half-forgotten English words spilling as he gazed at the white man in the cab above him.

Sean felt a frisson sweep through him, nerve-endings

tingling. With the traffic lights shifting to orange he thrust his hand into his shirt pocket and the ten peso notes he kept to tip taxi-drivers and airport porters.

He thrust them through the open window to be seized by a small hand, to a half-smile of stained and filthy teeth, a flash of life that flickered in his eyes. Then wheeling away the child scampered over to the dried grass median strip next to the car.

On an impulse he'll never understand Sean opened his door and stepped out, just as the light turns green.

Ignoring the driver's shouts and the cacophony of horns erupting behind him Sean stepped over to the grass and as the child made to flee he smiled, lifting the cord with its ivory tooth from around his neck and holding it out.

The child reached up to the smooth ivory with his right hand; the left balanced away behind him, to fall back, if need be to scramble to safety.

Angry shouts and horns creating bedlam, Sean hurried back into the taxi and slammed the door.

As the angry driver's foot went down hard down on the accelerator Sean twisted in his seat, the shock of his encounter turning to a belated, half-perceived recognition. It could not be!

The child from Caritas! The ward that Maria brought into her life. The kid he gave beer money to support and educate. No, it could not be! There'd been the fire and he always presumed the kid was either dead or had been spirited away to some other home. In his own preoccupation and anxiety he'd given the foundling barely a thought in the preceding months.

As the taxi cleared the intersection, Sean stared back to see a gang of half-a-dozen street kids converging on the receding figure. Then a bus pulled past the small group and it was lost to sight as the taxi weaved on through the chaotic traffic towards the heat haze and city fumes hiding the airport.

Chapter Twenty-three

Great Barrier Island, New Zealand: February 1988

SPRAY SHATTERED OVER the rocky shoreline halting the south-westerly swell of the Hauraki Gulf and scattered in the gusting wind across the rickety wooden wharf at Okupu on Great Barrier Island.

Across the wide inlet of the Pacific, the sea roiled for the 50 kilometres to the calmer waters of Auckland's land-locked harbour.

Grey clouds scudded through a lowering sky and the light faded rapidly as dusk draped the hills guarding the bay.

Pulling his oilskin parka tightly around him, Sean hurried carefully along treacherous slippery planks to the gravel at the end of the coastal road from Claris on the east coast of the island.

Light spilled from the house set back from the wharf and white sandy strip of beach, glimmering through the dusky drizzle leading the rain still to come. The dark brooding squall line of a front moving across the gulf had driven Sean from Blind Bay and the crayfish pots he'd been dropping off its southern shore.

Kicking off sea boots on the concrete terrace he pulled open the French doors, grabbing one quickly as it threatened to slam against the weatherboards of the house in a swirl of wind.

Firmly closing it from inside the lounge he caught the savoury aroma of roasting meat in the sudden warmth of the house and heard his father clattering about in the kitchen. Now in his seventies, the old man was a dab hand at the stove and the leg of wild pork from the beast Sean had shot the week before had been simmering in the wood-fired oven for five or six hours, liberally basted in rough red wine, the 'chateau du cardboard' the old man kept for such purposes.

"Plus a few cooks' swigs for himself," smiled Sean.

Entering the kitchen, he found Douglas Brian sitting at the kitchen table with, sure enough, a glass ready to hand as he looked up.

"Gidday mate," he said, gesturing to the chair opposite, a bottle of beer beaded in condensation and a glass. The old man had popped the top as the boat's engine shut down at the wharf.

"Going to be a wet one tonight. Did you get all the pots down?"

"Yup," said Sean, pouring a glass and emptying it before he sat and refilled it.

"We've got a dozen laid between Smiths Bay and Allom Bay. I stuck four around the sunken rock under Jack's Point."

The monolithic headland stood sentinel over Blind Bay and its inlets, either named for early settler families or retaining Maori names. It was the landmark around which their cray-fishing territory revolved. Below it, Okupu had been a flourishing Maori settlement in pre-European days and later a base camp for miners and loggers. Now it consisted of their house, several outbuildings and a fish-processing factory.

Relics of earlier residents lined shelves and windowsills in the lounge. Old bottles once holding cheap rum for the miners jostled with half-completed stone tools abandoned eons back by Maori in the stream that ran through the 10-acre property.

"Here's to a good catch," said Douglas, raising his glass. "Dinner will be a half-hour so grab a shower. There's plenty of hot water."

The mainland electricity grid did not reach the island and a diesel generator down in the fish-packing shed provided their lighting. Hot water came from the wood-burning, wetback stove dominating the spacious kitchen, fuelled by a seemingly inexhaustible supply of manuka firewood covering the hills. The bungalow was in sharp contrast to the company apartments and luxury hotels in which Sean had spent so much of his time in Asia, but it was now home, and a hot shower was just what he needed to wash away the salt crystallising from the trip across the white-capped bay.

The past year had been a time of change and upheaval after cancer, swift and inexorable, had taken his mother just weeks after he arrived from Manila.

After the mourning he and the old man had taken stock.

Douglas bought the island property as a retirement option and with both of them at a loss in the world and looking for a new direction they'd decided to sell the family house on the mainland and move to the island.

Sean felt he couldn't leave the old man to fend for himself and his sister had a family of her own to worry about. Asia had lost some of its attraction with still no news of Maria and Sean found he and his father leaning towards each other for mutual support.

Within a couple of months of moving to the island they secured a commercial cray-fishing license and were now making a reasonable living supplying several hotel restaurants on the mainland with the white-fleshed crustacean delicacies. It was an extension of the activity of Sean's youth and long island holidays that revolved around fishing and the charter boat Douglas once operated.

The hard work, fresh air and the bounty of sea and surrounding land had transformed Sean into a lean and fit, younger-looking, version of the world-weary individual who'd stepped from a jetliner at Auckland airport a year before.

It had been a time of healing too with the daily task of surviving and building a new life driving the devils of Asia from his conscious mind.

Many times in the long evenings after the old man had retired he sat staring down the path of the moon to the beach where the whales had been cast up, thinking of Maria and of the boy that was his last real memory of Manila, wondering what'd happened and what'd gone wrong.

In most cases fatigue overtook the painful thoughts and he'd crawl into bed, sleeping soundly until dawn when the daily routine demanded his active attention.

The sound of the oven door clanging jerked him from his reverie and he stepped from the shower and towelled himself down, slipping into clean blue jeans and a sweatshirt.

Douglas carved slices of succulent wild pork onto plates already laden with roast potatoes. Placing the rest of the joint to cool on a bench, he added crisp fresh green beans to the meal.

"Where did these come from?" asks Sean as he fell to the food.

"Old Ernie brought them across. Swapped them for half-a-dozen eggs." The reclusive prospector lived a couple of miles out on the Okupu Road towards the rural post office and manual telephone exchange that was their nearest permanent neighbour on the other coast of the island.

The Great Barrier community thrived on a barter system 'the green dollar' and Douglas's decision to run a dozen hens ensured they could trade for fresh vegetables when those they grew themselves ran short.

Father and son complemented each other in their new venture with Sean's days spent harvesting the sea for fish to bait the crayfish pots, setting them strategically around the neighbouring coastline. The fish-heads baited the pots and the bodies, if there was a good haul on the long-lines, were smoked in wild honey and spices over smouldering manuka sawdust and *pohutakawa* leaves from the surrounding native bush.

The recipe ensured a steady demand from passing boats

and when supplies warranted they also sold at a couple of retail outlets in Auckland.

In his turn, Douglas kept house and cooked, often as not from the day's catch or the results of Sean's Saturday night hunting expeditions with Tom Weeks whose mother ran the post office.

"I wonder what the poor people are doing," quipped Sean as he pushed back his plate, shaking his head at his father's nod towards the still cooling joint on the bench.

"No thanks mate, that hit the spot for sure. But I'll have another coldie and then I think I'll crash. I'm a bit buggered."

Leaving Douglas to clear the remains of the meal and wash up he finished his beer and took down two hurricane lamps from over the stove. Checking the fuel he lit the wicks and carried one through to his father's room. The other he placed on the chest beside his own bed.

Soft pools of light seeped from the kerosene lamps as the generator shut down. With a flurry of windswept rain on the iron roof, sleep claimed them.

Chapter Twenty-four

DAYLIGHT DIFFUSED BY grey cloud and mist wreathing the island's volcanic peaks greeted Sean, a towel round his waist and sipping black coffee, as he regarded the sea of beaten gunmetal beyond the front deck.

Their boat, *Taipan*, named after the James Clavell novel celebrating Hong Kong, swung slowly at its mooring just off the wharf.

Hearing his father stirring he fixed a mug of tea from the kettle permanently steaming on the wood stove as Douglas propped himself on pillows, grimacing from the stiffness he always experienced after a night lying still in sleep.

As a young RAF Blenheim fighter-bomber pilot, he'd been shot down in the Adriatic off the coast of Albania, damaging his back and breaking a leg in the barely controlled ditching.

He'd managed to swim more than a mile to shore only to fall into the hands of the Italian occupying troops where he received rudimentary medical attention before his officer status gained him admission to a military hospital. Years suffering the privations of a prisoner of war in various camps, escape and rough living on the run in wartime Italy had also earned some morning discomfort.

Sean handed him the tea.

"We'll leave the pots down another day and night," he said. "It's Monday anyway and the mail plane will be in provided they can get a break in this weather. I think I'll drive over to the Post Office. There should be a bread delivery at the Claris store too. I'll get a few loaves for the week. Want to come?"

Douglas winced, shifting position.

"I think I'll have a decent lie in. Then I'd better do a roundup for the bloody eggs those chooks are laying."

The free-ranging fowls chose scattered nests around the

fringes of the property, making egg recovery something of a lottery.

"OK," said Sean. "Hang in there and I'll bang some bacon on, then head over the hill."

Breakfast over he donned wet weather gear and headed outside.

The ancient Holden sedan they'd shipped to the island by barge from Auckland started after a couple of attempts and he swung onto the gravel road outside the packing shed and up the hill that led around the edge of the bay toward Claris.

Heavy rain during the night had swollen two streams enroute that normally chuckled through fern-filled gullies to the sea, each crossed by picturesque bridges of island stone built by miners during in a silver rush 90 years earlier.

Driving carefully to negotiate Suicide Point where the roadside fell a hundred metres sheer to the sea, Sean continued over the ridge at the head of the bay and wound his way down past a lonely but imposing kauri tree to the flats leading to the tiny settlement of Claris.

Passing through manuka scrub into patchy farmland, Sean pulled up in front of a roadside dwelling-come-post office. Inside, Betty Weeks - Tom's mother, was sorting mail into pigeonholes.

"Hullo Sean," she smiled. "How's your Dad?"

"He's fine but having a lie-in today. I think the damp is getting to his bones a bit.

"There's a bit of mail for you." Betty proffered several envelopes. "One from the Philippines too."

McIvor, probably, thought Sean, accepting the package bound with a rubber band, thrusting it into his parka pocket to read at leisure in front of the wood stove this afternoon.

"Is Tom around?" he asked. Betty's son had become a hunting partner and sometimes drinking buddy.

With a resident population of only four hundred scattered across the island's rugged terrain and coastline there are few social amenities, and entertainment was home-grown.

Apart from a birthday bash in an isolated farmhouse or a local wedding to offer a weekend of island unity, carousing, fistfights and other assorted diversions, Sean and Tom usually amused themselves by throwing a case of beer onto Tom's truck and heading off with his dogs to hunt wild pigs in the bush-clad valleys.

"He's down at the airfield Sean. A mate of his is flying in from the Waikato. I suspect you'll hear from him sometime as he'll probably want to go fishing if this weather clears."

Sean left and called at Sanderson's farm where an annex onto the homestead stocked the provisions of a small general store as well as the fresh bread flown to the island twice a week by a mainland aero club.

He collected stores and driving back through the house paddock to the road he turned south towards the grass airstrip, the island's main link with the outside world.

Tom was sitting in his old Buick truck, parked back from the runway, with his favourite dog, Blue, prowling the tray.

"Gidday Blue," said Sean. "Give us a smile." The grey dog bared his fangs in a grimace, prompting a chuckle from Sean. The animal seemed almost human in his response to the command. He wrenched open the passenger door, buckled in an encounter with a roadside bank, and climbed up.

"Yeah, gidday," was Tom's laconic greeting as he rolled a cigarette from a pouch of Port Royale tobacco. Burly, bearded, a third generation islander with a passionate dislike for the city. Despite, or perhaps because of vastly dissimilar backgrounds, the two men hit it off well.

"Betty said you were down here and thought I'd catch you about a fish tomorrow. You've got someone coming in?"

In answer, Tom gestured through the windscreen and craning to look up they saw a Cessna 172 overhead, high on a bearing to the airfield radio beacon and beginning it's let-down over the sea to the east. The four-seat aircraft turned on a reciprocal course into the south-westerly wind and lined up over the sand-hills guarding the rude airstrip from the southern ocean that stretched unbroken to South America.

The two men made small talk as the light plane touched down smoothly, a spindly undercarriage fluttering on the rough surface of the paddock. Then Sean pushed open the door with a rusty creak leaving Tom to drive over to the plane and his guest.

"I'll catch up with you tomorrow. Give us a bell if you're into a spot of fishing eh?"

Heading home, he was looking forward to his mail, catching up with news from overseas. He'd kept in touch with McIvor and Sandy Macdonald in Bangkok, who wrote occasionally, envious of his new lifestyle.

Rounding Suicide, out towards Auckland across the Hauraki Gulf, the leaden sky was lighter as the cloud-ceiling rose. The weather was taking a turn for the better.

Reaching the house he found Douglas preparing lunch, a mess of smoked snapper enlivened with sliced hardboiled egg and a tin of sweet corn.

They ate with fresh slices of buttered bread. Then his father set off on his 'bloody Easter eggs hunt,' and Sean stoked the wood stove and settled down with the mail.

Among a bill or two, a letter from his sister to the old man and a couple of circulars from the county council, was a slim envelope in copperplate handwriting with a Philippine post mark. McIvor always communicated by computer printout. Sean slit open the flap, wondering.

Opening the fold inside, he glanced at the sender's address and sat forward in surprise. The letter was from a Catholic medical centre in Pasay City in Metro Manila. The signature confirmed his cautious initial recognition and he began reading.

Dear Sean,

I have managed to track you down through Rhonda Rollinson at United Press International's office here in Manila.

I hope you will forgive me for what may be an intrusion. You have apparently had many things to bear since you left Asia all those months ago. Please accept my condolences on the loss of your mother.

You also left something special in Asia and it is of this that I write.

Since I returned to Manila I have been working with the order in the new Aquino Rehabilitation Clinic in Pasay City. I won't beat about the bush. The clinic provides a haven for women who have been somewhat disadvantaged by life in this city. Indeed many of them are suffering from sexual disease and unfortunately some of those are infected with the Aids virus. Yes, I am being rather blunt and straightforward but as a former journalist in this part of the world you will be no stranger to reality.

Sean: to the point. We have admitted a girl, no a young woman, to our drug addiction unit. She is in recovery from a heroin habit after being picked up by the police in a raid on a thoroughly unpleasant nightclub in the city. I shall not go into details in this letter. Suffice to say this woman is Maria Cipriano, whom we both knew over a year ago when we arranged sponsorship for the little boy who disappeared after the Caritas Centre fire. I am aware of your love for her at the time and it is because of this that I write.

Sean, Maria is but a shadow of the woman you knew. She has been with us now for several weeks. I did not intend to write at first but she is beginning to trust me, and remembers our happier association. Today she mentioned your name through her tears.

I am truly sorry if I am opening old wounds, but Maria seems to be really trying to co-operate with us here. The fact that our paths have crossed again I take as some intervention in our lives from the Almighty. I just felt that perhaps a letter from you might mean something to her, might give her that little extra lever to lift herself back into life.

Forgive me if I am being presumptuous. But even God needs as much help as he can get in this sorry compartment of our world. If you feel you would like to, please write to me at the above address. If you feel you cannot, I, and God I am sure, will understand.

Yours in Christ,

Sister Jan.

Chapter Twenty-five

"So what are you going to do?"

Douglas sat on the foot of Sean's bed in a reversal of morning roles as he handed his son a mug of steaming tea.

Sean stared fuzzily from his pillow. "Christ, my head," he muttered.

"You certainly tied one on last night," said Douglas. "Well, I should talk, I helped a bit."

"Bloody red wine of yours," groaned Sean. "I suppose we saw it all off then?"

"Saw it off! We managed to get through a couple of boxes and if we'd had any more you'd still be going. What the hell were you trying to do?" Sean took an experimental sip and then another.

"Hell dad, I don't know. Put it down to shock I guess."

Douglas leaned forward for Sister Jan's letter from where it had fallen beside the bed after Sean had gone to sleep reading with one focussed eye, for the hundredth time. He realised the generator was still throbbing away. They'd both crashed out with all the lights on.

"What the hell do I do dad?" he asked. As he spoke the bile rose in his throat and he swallowed. His stomach retained the twisted knot that tied his guts the moment he read Maria's name.

"Well, at the end of the day it's up to you. You're the only one who knows your own mind and only you. For one thing, consider the fact that you have managed to, for the most part, get over the girl. I know there has always been a question in your mind. Now at least you know the hard truth. From the letter, she's in a hell of a mess. She went well off the rails and she has just come out of a year on the hard stuff from the sound of it. She'll obviously have a hell of a long row to hoe."

Douglas paused for breath, repeating a discourse of the night before, fearful of his sons intentions.

"I'm well aware of that," said Sean testily. "But now I know she is alive and in trouble, the ghosts are all coming back. If I hadn't wound up in Thailand this wouldn't be happening. But what can I do? I can't go back to Asia and start picking up the pieces there. That part of my life is over now. But Maria…" his voice trailed off as he stared through the bedroom window.

Outside, the sky was clear, the hills at the back of the house washed in fledgling sunlight. In the silence he realised he was simply going over the ground covered *ad nauseum* through wine-fogged minds the night before. Round and round in circles.

"Seems to me you do have two options, to get back in contact - or not. Then take it from there," said Douglas at last. "But I will say this. You'll have a bundle of problems on your hands if you decide to try and pick up from where you left off with the girl. Drugs aren't something to get rid of easily. But one thing's for sure," he gave a lopsided grin, "this is not an environment where she's going to find it easy to find hard drugs." He waved in a sweeping gesture to the bush, the bay, the lack of habitation outside their own.

"Think about it son. Think carefully and follow your head as well as your heart. Now let's get some food down. We have to get those pots in today."

By early-afternoon, Sean had lifted and re-baited their pots, physical effort and the ozone-laden air purging the last vestiges of his hangover.

Twenty crayfish, ranging between one and two kilos joined another two dozen in the holding pot anchored in the shallows by the wharf. Douglas rang de Bretts Hotel in Auckland, and arranged to have the fish put on the evening flight.

Tom Weeks came by and borrowed the boat to take his friend out fishing and Douglas and Sean sat on the terrace overlooking the bay, hot tea and a cold meat sandwich making a late lunch.

Sean stared at the hulk of Jack's Point across the blue water. *Taipan* was anchored below it, too far off to see if the two occupants were having any success.

"Dad, I'm going. I'm out of here tonight."

Douglas looked at him. "I rang Adele while you were out. I suspected as much and she'll meet the plane to pick up the crayfish. I warned her there might be another fish to fry as well."

Without a word Sean went into the house and hauled a light travelling bag out of a closet. In his room, he started to pack. Reaching into his bedside chest he pulled out a leather folder. Inside was Maria's unused passport, collected from her former landlord in Manila over a year before, his only remaining link with the Filipina until now. Gazing at the cold passport photograph, his mind spun with memories, at the same time remaining focused, crystal clear. Adding his own passport to the folder, along with an American Express Gold card, he slipped them into a jacket pocket and crossed the lounge to the ancient hand-cranked telephone mounted on the wall. His one-long-one-short ring was heard in the exchange and Betty connected him to the mainland. Within minutes Sean's Singapore Airlines booking was made. With the four-hour time difference he'd transit in Singapore and be in Manila the following afternoon.

Douglas was already in the packing shed wrapping the crayfish consignment in wet sacking and twenty minutes later they were driving back across the ridge to Claris and the airfield. An hour later, Sean disembarked from the Nomad island shuttle to a hearty hug from his elder sister.

"So you're going," she said, drawing back from the embrace, her eyes searching his.

"Dad said he thought you would. Just be careful, Sean. The airline rang and your seat's confirmed. We'll have plenty of time to make the flight at Mangere so let's go have a drink before you leave. I'll drop the crays off in town afterwards."

They reached the international terminal 30 minutes later along a new motorway extension and spent an hour talking about family and business before Sean's flight was called. Already he could feel the slight adrenaline buzz that always came with the airport and a pending flight. All around them, impeded by carry-on baggage, parcels and coats were other passengers and farewell groups and the lounge bar was a hubbub of anticipation.

Finishing her drink, Adele pecked him on the cheek and left him to make his way to passport control. "I'll have to rush, get these fish in and back to get tea for the kids. Safe trip."

Six hours after the decision to go, Sean was sipping a drink in 747 business class as the aircraft climbed through 20,000 feet over the Tasman Sea.

Chapter Twenty-six

Pasay City, Philippines, May, 1987

THE AQUINO REHAB Clinic was housed in a former army barracks, now shabby and ill kempt, sprawling over a couple of acres in Manila's Pasay City. Sean remembered it as the base from which the deposed President Ferdinand Marcos ordered tanks out against his own people.

The midday heat was like wading in tepid water and his shirt stuck to his skin under the jacket worn on the air-conditioned journey across the Pacific. Fourteen hours of flying broken by scotch-induced naps and a sleepless transit in Singapore left him wrung out and drained and managing pretty much on willpower alone.

Making his way along a concrete path to a former guardhouse now serving as reception area he was greeted by an attractive Filapina as he put down his overnight bag.

"*Como este ca*," he greeted her. "Would it be possible please to see Sister Jan?"

The woman looked up with a smile. "*Kumusta*. Sister Jan? I will see if she is on duty sir, just one moment."

Her singsong English evoked a smiling memory for Sean as she punched a series of numbers. The room was decorated with health posters in English and *Tagalog*, extolling the virtues of cleanliness, diet, safe sex or the danger of drugs, one simply depicting a hypodermic syringe with a red cross scrawled across it.

"Whom shall I say is calling sir?"

Sean identified himself and the woman listened for a moment, stared at her visitor and then replaced the receiver.

"She's coming right this minute sir," she said in surprise. "Sister Jan seems quite shocked!"

"I guess she wouldn't have been expecting me in person and so soon," said Sean.

A few minutes later, the door behind the receptionist opened and a white-clad Sister Jan positively beamed at him and held out her hands. Hesitantly, tears pricking his eyes in his fatigue, Sean reached out and took them in his, suppressing an impulse to put his arms around the nun.

Sensing his need, she squeezed his hands tightly and let go.

"Come," she said. "I think the first thing to do is get you a cup of coffee. You look all in. Come with me Sean."

She led him through the door and across a small patch of brown dry lawn to the first of a serried row of barracks. Inside, the building had been converted into a canteen. A number of nuns and a dozen or so workers were seated at two long tables chatting and drinking tea or coffee.

Sister Jan filled two cups from a steaming stainless steel urn and they sat at a table.

"Well," she said, "you're a surprise to say the least. I hoped you'd write. I certainly didn't expect to see you - at least not just yet."

"Sister, It's really wonderful to see you. Your letter threw me into a bit of a spin but I decided that writing was only putting off the inevitable. I have to see her again. I have to know what happened." The coffee was good and he felt his weariness ease. "How is she?"

A shadow flickered over the nun's tanned features while she looked steadily at Sean.

"Maria," she spoke slowly, searching for the right words, "Maria is on methadone to bring her down from the heroin she's been using. She's malnourished, she's hurting spiritually and she's lost a lot of her will to live. But there's still something there. She still remembers you in a dreamlike way. It's as if you're lost forever but she holds onto your image. It's hard to explain."

She described briefly how Maria was brought to the clinic by social workers called by police who'd raided an expensive private night club and found a number of women in need of help.

"She's gone through the nightmare of withdrawal. At one point we had to restrain her to prevent self-injury. But she is progressing and now that you're here we'll maybe be able to add another dimension to her treatment, have a little bit of a re-think. That'll have to be up to her doctor though. I assume since you are here you want to see her?"

She saw the question was superfluous.

"Well Sean, first I'll have to meet with the doctor, we need to handle this carefully."

Sean nodded. "I'm very much in your hands. I don't know what to expect and all I can say is I have to know for myself how she is and where she's been. It is a case of one step at a time." Jan studied him.

"Well for a start Sean Brian," she put reproof into his full name. "I think you'd better check into wherever you're staying and get some sleep. In the meantime I'll see Doctor Rey who's handling Maria's treatment and see how he wants to handle this. OK? So let's get you a taxi and you can contact me with your number when you get there. I'll set up an appointment with the doctor and call you as soon as I can. I'm sure it won't be long before you can see her but we'll need to give her time to get used to the idea that you're here, alive and well."

She walked Sean back to the reception area where the woman at the desk dispatched an aide to flag down a taxi in the busy thoroughfare outside. Sister Jan gave Sean a quick hug. "Don't worry. I knew I was right to contact you. It won't be long. Get some rest."

Twenty minutes later Sean was downtown, checking in once again to the Regent. He had a quick reviving beer with a surprised and welcoming Jerry in the house bar before going up to his room and ringing the clinic with contact phone and room number. He showered and threw himself on the bed to fall swiftly into an exhausted sleep.

The room was in darkness eight hours later when the phone beside his bed shrilled once, jerking him from a fitful doze.

The message was from Sister Jan. He could meet Maria's doctor at the clinic the following day at noon. Sean then dialled George's bar from memory.

"George, can you line me up a beer and a big plate of your oxtail stew? I'll be round in a few minutes."

He dressed and ordered a cab from the hotel rank. Not long afterwards he had a cold beer in his hand and a steaming plate in front of him.

"Can't bloody keep away then, can you?" said John McIvor stepping back for a moment from his eight-ball pool game.

Before talking, Sean wolfed down the stew the house was famous for, sopping up the gravy with a freshly baked bread roll.

"Well mate," he turned to where McIvor looked downcast at sinking the white off the black and losing his game, "momentous things have happened. I've found her, I've found Maria!"

Before McIvor could react, he went on. "She's in a bad way. She's in drug rehab over in Pasay City. I don't know much yet but I'll find out more tomorrow. Seems she was picked up in a nightclub raid a month or so back with a needle stuck up her bloody arm. What the hell happened I don't know but I had to come back and find out."

"Putting two and two together, this is pretty heavy duty Sean."

McIvor looked pensively at his glass, quiet for a moment as Jeanette poured another San Mig.

"The cops busted one hell of a place in a cul-de-sac off Mabini seven or eight weeks ago," he continued. "Full of

Japs and Arabs, tons of money. Locked doors, high prices and some very heavy live entertainment. There was a hell of a diplomatic scramble with claims of immunity and so on. I filed a piece for Asia week because of the international clients they caught but it didn't appear. Influence in high places I guess."

"Oh Jesus," Sean groans. "Please no."

"There were off-duty cops involved as bouncers. If I were you I'd get hold of Pedro Wright. He'll have the full story. I know after you left he kept making inquiries about Maria but with you in New Zealand it sort of lost impetus I guess. Give him a ring at headquarters tomorrow."

"I'll do that. I'd like to find out who ran the bloody place too."

He finished his drink and stood. "Well, that's enough for me. I need more sleep. I'll call Pedro tomorrow."

He made to leave and McIvor caught his arm. "I'm going down to Zamboanga on Mindoro tomorrow with the air force to do a story on the Moro National Liberation Front. Why don't you call by my place around nine? You can drop me at Defence HQ in Makati and then take my car and driver for a few days. Save you busting your arse chasing taxis."

Sean was about to decline when he realised McIvor wanted to keep his driver occupied instead of plying for hire as an illegal taxi while the boss was out of town, his expenses already paid for by McIvor's employers.

"Hell, that'd be great, mate. Thanks." In the warm night outside, he decided to walk back to the Regent. The streets were busy with bar-hoppers, street walkers and spruikers importuning customers into blaring bars like the Pink Pussy, the Spiders Web, the Palace, Bubbles and dozens of others. Ermita had a tawdry carnival atmosphere but Sean was well aware of seedy back-street clubs, with locked doors, catering to jaded customers with large wallets.

Chapter Twenty-seven

AT 10:30 NEXT morning, Sean was seething with scarcely contained rage over the sordid details of a nightclub, the *Bubbaaero*, the '*Butterfly*.'

Pedro Wright looked up from the case file lying on the polished teakwood desk in his top floor office at the Philippines National Police building.

"Our people tracked a stream of heroin flowing into town from Hong Kong, the Aberdeen fishing port actually," he told Sean.

"We had people under surveillance and one in particular led us to *Bubbaaero's*. It's pretty much as John described to you, catering to businessmen and high-rollers with more money than morals. High priced hookers, dope, whatever you wanted you could get. According to the file, all the girls were handed over to social welfare departments. Looks like the officer in charge decided to bust customers rather than the girls but only a few guys were charged. The rest pulled strings and, let's face it, had the bucks to buy their way out of trouble. We're yet to weed out all of our corrupt cops. Anyway the place is now well and truly shut down. The main man we were after is a..." he looked at the file, "a Johan Mel. He's still being sought." He closed the file.

"Anyway, I didn't make any connection with your Maria. The file only came to me after the event and as I say the officer in charge was happy to let the welfare people take over that particular can of worms. Some of the girls were used on stage doing sex shows Sean. You'd better be prepared for anything. However..." he reopened the file for a few moments, looking thoughtful. "However, perhaps it is time I took a little interest in this Mel chap myself."

He looked up, his policeman's instinct detecting Sean's

anger. "Just leave it with me Sean. I know you're angry but you're essentially a guest in this country. Our law enforcement is none of your business. You just get on with the job of getting Maria back on her feet."

Outside, Sean was picked up by the waiting review car. With an hour before his meeting at the clinic and he directed the driver to the UPI offices a few blocks away. Fifteen minutes later he stepped into the bureau.

"Rhonda, I have to be in Pasay City at noon, but in the meantime can you do me a favour?"

"Whatever you need Sean, just ask."

"Could you get your local staff to search the news files about a big nightclub bust a few weeks back? The local papers go into huge detail in *Tagalog* on this kind of story. If you can get them translated it would help me a lot."

"Consider it done. And after you've seen the doctor at the clinic and hopefully Maria too, come back here. We'll go out for drinks and dinner, hopefully with some translations to digest as well. OK?"

Rollinson's practical approach is just what he needed. Someone solid to lean on a little.

At noon he was seated in a small office at the Aquino Rehabilitation Clinic with Sister Jan and Dr Jesus Rey.

Peering over half-glasses, Rey, a swarthy Filipino of 40 or so with a pronounced American twang, studied the man before him.

"Sean, we have what you might call a double-edged sword here. Maria is definitely in recovery and making progress. She's been through the hell of withdrawal and her medication is being scaled down. She isn't completely detoxified yet but her strength is amazing. She doesn't know you're here and we must move carefully on this. The shock of seeing you could go two ways. There'll be a massive guilt and shame reaction, which could put her into regression. On the other hand, you might prove to be just the tonic she needs."

Sean nodded. "I can see the problem," he says. "But I have to see her."

"Well, what I suggest is this. Sister Jan is as close to Maria as anyone right now. I suggest we let her pave the way." He turned to the nun. "Are you prepared then Sister to gently let Maria know that Sean's alive and well? Let her get used to that idea first, I think we'll keep it from her for the moment that he's actually in Manila. Let's do this slowly and gently."

Sean looked at the doctor. "Can I see her without her seeing me, do you think? Please, I need to."

Somehow he could feel Maria around him. The memory of her face hovering in his consciousness. Dr Rey considered for a moment. "OK. But you must do as I say. Come."

He led the way along a corridor and outside under a canopy connecting the barracks with another identical building behind it.

Inside, he opened a cupboard. "Put these on," he instructed. Sean donned a white gown somewhat too small and then looked questioningly at the surgical mask in his hand.

"That too. You can only look through the glass window of the door to her ward. She's in the second bed on the right."

The small group moved down the corridor to a plain wooden door, a window let into its upper half. Cautiously Sean peered through the glass into a ward with six beds. Only four were occupied and looking to the left his eyes found a figure lying beneath a white cover.

She was asleep.

Sean sucked in his breath, a lump forming in his chest, almost physically painful.

Her hair lay spread around her face on the pillow, deep dark shadows beneath her closed eyes. The white linen bed cover rose and fell with her breathing, which seemed peaceful and measured. Her face was pale but her fine features were as he remembered, thinner, but still with an ethereal beauty and he felt an overpowering urge to rush into the room and hold her, to take her in his arms and pour his energy into her slight frame, to tell her he still loved her.

Then the dam burst and tears welled as he was racked by a sob. He staggered, his knees almost giving way and Sister Jan and Dr Rey grabbed his arms, leading him away to a small couch in the corridor, easing him down onto it. Sean's chest heaved as he tried to get his breath. Slowly he recovered his composure, rubbing his gowned arm across his eyes.

"Oh God. I'm sorry Sister." He took another deep breath. "It's OK. I'm sorry. I'm OK now I think." He looked up.

"So much for the tough foreign correspondent eh?" managing a weak grin, rising to his feet.

"It appears you haven't lost what you felt for this girl," said Dr Rey. "It'll take all the strength of that emotion to help her heal but I'm beginning to believe you just may be what she needs." He helped Sean take off the gown and replaced it in the closet.

"OK, we'll let Sister Jan make the opening moves when she thinks the moment's right. A little more patience Sean and we'll see."

He led the way back to his office. "We have your contact number and I feel pretty sure we will be calling you very soon."

Sister Jan saw Sean out to reception and his waiting driver.

"Have faith. I think I intimated in my letter that this was meant to be. Just take care, I'll call you very soon."

As the car moved off, the heavens open in a tropical downpour.

That night, in a crowded restaurant on Roxhas Boulevard, Sean and Rhonda dined on king prawns from the South China Sea and *pancit canton* a delicious combination of noodles and vegetables, washed with a bottle of iced Australian Chablis.

Over coffee and a superb cognac, Rhonda turned the

subject from the friends and acquaintances they'd been catching up on, the doings of UPI and Sean's new life on the island in New Zealand, reaching for her briefcase under the table.

"You were right, there was plenty of stuff in the *Tagalog* press about the club bust," she said, drawing out a wad of computer paper.

"My secretary's translated everything she could find. There's also an article on a drug kingpin the cops are looking for. One Johan Mel. There's not much fear of libel in the Philippines and they've really gone to town on him. Sounds a nasty prick." She passed across the papers.

"Read them at your leisure. But this Mel character would seem to be the force behind that bloody club. No picture but he's apparently half-Filipino and half-American. According to Bulletin Today, he's believed to be still in business somewhere over in MP Burgos, the new bar district in Makati. But he's a shadowy sort, runs his business through front men."

"I want this bastard," says Sean angrily. "I want him to go down real bloody hard."

"Sean, I know how you feel, but it's not your ball park now. Maria is the important one for you at the moment. Anyway, if I know Pedro Wright, now he's made a personal connection in the case, this guy is going to be one sad shit before he's much older."

She glanced at her watch. "It's getting on. Can you drop me at my place? I'll call it a day and catch up with you tomorrow. Remember the office is there, use it as a base whenever you want."

They parted in front of the restaurant, Sean sending Rhonda home with his driver who'd waited at a nearby sidewalk coffee shop. He walked back to the hotel, to think, to assimilate, to try to get a handle on the turmoil of emotions coursing through him.

A breeze came in from the ocean and the streets were crowded in the warm evening, dinner groups emerging from restaurants to collect cars and tip parking valets.

Watching from the shadows were the street people, ever alert for a small errand, a begged coin, a sold newspaper or cigarette. A group of street children ran raucously past and he was aware that further back from the lights of the avenue, deep in the shadows of palms lining the seafront, more sinister figures lurked. An unwary or intoxicated tourist might choose to walk their way. Some had, before tonight, to end their Manila holiday mugged and beaten or in a couple of cases on a mortuary slab.

Staying on the busy footpath Sean reached the Regent and paused in the house bar for a final drink, a few words with Jerry, then headed for bed.

His sleep was plagued with troubled dreams, twisting images of jungle huts and satin sheets, ti-tree burning in a wood stove and a scruffy street urchin running while Sean waded through pools of glue.

Gratefully awake, gritty-eyed at dawn, he was breakfasting on fresh papaya and coffee in his room when the phone rang.

"I didn't expect to hear from you so soon," he said, surprised.

"Nor I," said Sister Jan. "I spent several hours with Maria last night and it's really amazing. The first thing she did when she woke was to ask about you. It's as if she sensed something. And so I took the bull by the horns and told her you're here. I also gave her a brief idea of what's happened over the past year. I'd have thought it would be a huge shock but she just stared at me and then said: 'I knew he'd come. I knew it. But how? How did I know?'

"All I can say Sean is that you two seem to have an empathy that goes beyond anything I've ever seen. Well, the time has come I suppose. When can you be here?"

Ignoring the coffee, Sean was on his feet heading for the elevator, moments later hurrying out of the hotel to where the car waited.

Chapter Twenty-eight

SHE WAS THIN, so terribly shockingly thin. She'd been moved to a private room where they regarded each other in a sort of numbed wonder.

Sister Jan ushered him into the room, quietly closed the door and left.

Maria was propped up with pillows, her hair brushed out, a hint of makeup over the shadows under her eyes. Her hands rested on the coverlet, the fingers entwined and twisting nervously.

Stepping over the space between them from the door Sean swiftly and gently placed his arms around her, fearful of her fragility. For a terrible moment she was still in his arms, flesh tense under the cotton gown, then she lifted her arms and touched his face with her hands like a blind person feeling for familiarity.

"Sean," she whispered softly, repeating his name over and over. "Sean, oh Sean, Sean..."

The words become sobs. Holding her close he felt as if he was disintegrating, the carefully constructed walls keeping the pain of loss at bay washed away on a tide of warmth and gladness. They wept silently while an energy coursed like heat between them.

At last Sean hooked a chair to the side of the bed and sank into it holding both her hands in his. Their eyes shone, tears flowing freely. A huge aura of calm enveloped them, banishing the need for words. Finally Sean broke the silence.

"Maria, oh my love, Maria." A million questions raced through his mind but he knew instinctively this was not the time. This time was for touching, for holding, for letting demons slip away. A time simply for being.

A tap on the door and Sister Jan appeared pushing a

trolley.

"Tea, you two." Despite her composure her eyes glistened. She felt their need for a human bridge to ease their reunion as she began to pour. Then seating herself on the opposite side of the bed, she looked at Maria.

"You must tell Sean what happened to you." Sean stiffened. The question seemed too blunt and he felt Maria's hands clench in his own.

"Sister..." he began but she raised a finger to her lips to silence him.

"I've been talking with Dr Rey. We have the possibility here of prolonged counselling and some psychological assistance. But Dr Rey thinks if the two of you can confront what's happened and deal with it, Maria can be well on the road to recovery and away from here much sooner than would normally be the case. He thinks your collective strength can overcome what's happened to Maria, no matter what future paths you decide to take. Maria?"

The frail girl on the bed smiled wanly.

"Sean," her voice all but broke, then she seemed to draw on some hidden reservoir of composure.

"Sean, I thought you had gone. I thought you had left me, that you didn't want this *Filipina* any more once you had been posted. I didn't want to believe you had gone missing. I told myself you had changed your mind. Then the centre burned, my garden project was gone, and everything was gone. My faith was ended. I waited for you and then I am afraid I fell apart. I honestly don't remember the details. It is all a blur. At first I was drinking and smoking marijuana. Then something happened and I found myself working for a man. He gave me drugs and after that I wasn't my own person any more. After a while the pain would start and he was the only one who could stop the pain."

Tears rolled down her face. "Dr Rey said I have to acknowledge it. I've done some terrible things Sean. They are only vague memories, but terrible. I can never expect you to forgive that."

She took her hand from his and touched his face. "But my darling believe me, I never stopped loving you. I wanted to die without you and I chose a road to death that was not of my own making. I couldn't physically take a knife and kill myself. I let someone else do it slowly. I lost everything with you."

Sean swallowed. For a moment he remembered a journalist friend in Hong Kong who set out to drink himself to death in the girlie bars of Wanchai after his Cantonese girlfriend ran off with a merchant banker. He'd been found in alcoholic blindness on a bench in Victoria Park one morning, his dirty and torn clothing his last possessions, his ring and wristwatch pawned for cheap Chinese rice spirit and oblivion. The Foreign Correspondents Club had a member's whip-round for a brief detoxification in the Adventist Hospital on the Peak and an airfare home to family in England. Tenuous is our hold on sanity sometimes, he thought.

Neither of them noticed that Sister Jan, having set the ball rolling, had quietly left the room. Maria slipped into a reverie in which she found herself wallowing in the memories, the guilt and the shame. But her mind had become firmer, its own master, urging her to face down the shadows.

She also knew from her long talks with Sister Jan that burying her experiences might sow seeds of destruction within the delicate rebuilding of any life or relationship for her and Sean.

Festering guilt, blame for what she felt at the time was abandonment could erupt and she realised she must face the past, exorcise it truthfully, confess all and risk his inability to accept it, risk losing him again.

Their quiet conversation continued through the long afternoon. Later, after she had all but exhausted herself with talking he told her about his time in the Golden Triangle, of his search for her, of the death of his mother and that loss on top of everything else. He almost brought up his encounter with the child on the morning he left for New Zealand but decided that too was something that could wait.

He picked up a cheap plastic hairbrush from the bedside locker and began drawing it through her hair. As he brushed, each of them registering the smooth, sensual strokes, he began to talk about the island, imagining her bare feet in the sand on the beach, she and Douglas preparing the evening meal, almost smelling the salt on the evening air as he did so.

He knew then they'd be together, both tested in unholy waters.

"It is a heavenly place Maria. It's clean-green stuff, pristine and natural. The scenery is dramatic, magnificent, and life is simple there and satisfying. I want you to see it. I want you to share it with me."

The sun was settling in the western sky when Sister Jan returned. Sean lay beside Maria on the hospital bed, her head pillowed in the crook of his arm. She slept, deeply and peacefully. Sister Jan paused as Sean looked towards the doorway. She smiled softly and motioned him not to move.

She quietly closed the door and hurried away to tell the ward sister to leave room 11 alone. The healing had now truly begun.

* * *

Maria opened her eyes as the door closed softly. Chinks of rich orange light through the loose-fitting curtains told of dusk falling, the sunset rays diffused and discoloured through the cap of polluted air over the city. She stirred, warm in her bed, aware of the form enveloping her almost like a cocoon.

She listened to the steady rhythm of his breathing and lay still. Their long conversations had been a catharsis, a painful past replaced by snapshots of a future as if a mist had lifted and Sean had emerged to take her hands and lead her home.

She turned and studied his face, relaxed in sleep. In minutes she'd let darkness come, warm and gentle sweeping her into a dreamless healing.

Over the following weeks clinic staff were stunned at Maria's recovery. Sean had become almost a resident of the clinic himself and he and Maria found a thousand things a day to talk of. He brought her books on New Zealand from the central library in Manila, even one, *Island on the Skyline* that dealt specifically with Great Barrier Island. They ate meals together in her room, delicacies Sean brought in the seafood market, slices of delicious durian fruit, with Sister Jan firmly closing the door to keep the smell from the corridors.

Six weeks later, Maria was discharged. Dr Rey hovered at reception. He embraced Maria and stood back, his hands on her shoulders, instilling his strength one last time. Maria's lower lip trembled on the precipice of the outside world. Then she hugged him, lifting her head and shoulders with a widening smile and turned to walk to the doors.

At the entrance Dr Rey shook hands with Sean and handed him a packet.

"Maria will need medication for a little while yet," he said.

"The instructions are in here with the medicine along with a letter from me explaining it is for a nervous disorder - for customs." He smiled

"A remarkable recovery has taken place. Have you heard Jennifer Rush sing *'The Power of Love?'* Well every time I hear it I'll remember what's happened here."

Maria and Jan embraced in turn, promising to meet at a quiet dinner Sean had planned for that evening.

In the doorway Maria's hesitated. Sean sensed her fright, firmly taking her around the waist as they stepped into the sunlight to where Rhonda Rollinson waited in a Datsun station wagon. Sean smiled at Hanna behind the wheel.

As they drove towards Manila Bay and the Regent, Maria

was nervous and animated, remarking on the traffic and people in the streets, pointing out remembered landmarks which had changed, a new building here and there she'd not noticed in her twilight year. She was still thin but had begun to gain weight and colour in her face and Sean could sense her becoming once again the vivacious and vibrant girl he remembered. But there was something more emerging, evidence in stance and eye that spoke of adversity overcome, a hint of courage proven and a tempering of spirit.

With Hanna providing a running commentary on their route, Rhonda handed Sean a copy of *Bulletin Today*, the city's most popular newspaper.

"There's a two-column headline halfway down the front page. It didn't take long," she said.

Sean saw the tabloid headline. 'Drug King Hit.'

Chapter Twenty-nine

MP Burgos, Manila, Philippines: June, 1987

MAKATI WAS HOT and sultry with a suffocating pot-pourri of exhaust fumes and city smells hanging heavily in the humid air.

Fragmented music from a dozen bars and nightclubs lining MP Burgos bordering the business district provided a discordant background to the neon night.

Groups of men and the occasional couple, invariably European and *Filipina*, made their way from one bar to another. A shoeshine boy importuned late-night custom from the steps of a closed *sari-sari* store.

In the darkened interior of a shop veranda a shadowy figure stood hip-shot in a doorway. A tight red miniskirt topped black fishnet stockings above high-heeled shoes. A black blouse completed the outfit and a wild mess of black hair obscured the face.

Across the road, two men stopped, weaving slightly, and looked across. "Hey babe, fancy coming for a drink?" called one in an American twang.

His companion reached out to steady him as he seemed about to lurch cross the street.

"Hang on Ralph, if she's on the street and not in a bar she's probably got a dose."

Then he peered closer as the figure stepped out of the doorway into the yellow pool of light from a streetlamp.

"Shit, come on," he muttered and grabbed his companion decisively. "She's too big for a chick. Hell, that's a bloody billy-boy." His bemused companion stepped back onto the footpath.

"A what?"

"A billy-boy, a bloody transvestite. Come on; let's hit the Highway Bar. It's just up here."

They meandered off along the street, Ralph glancing curiously back into the shadows.

As they left, the figure in the doorway reached into a purse and lifted a radio transceiver.

"This is unit three." The voice was masculine. "Subject entered the Club Highway five minutes ago. He's still inside."

The brief crackle of static was silenced as bestockinged narcotics agent Ramon Galman hit the squelch button.

"Acknowledged," came the faint response.

"All units, move up. One, two and three secure the street at the side and the lane at the back of the club. Four, move west opposite the entrance."

Galman stepped from his doorway and thrust the radio back into his copious purse alongside a US Marine issue Colt 45. He minced his way along the footpath to a point opposite the two barflies who were just entering the club. Taking up station on the street corner across the road he leaned provocatively against a lamp-post and lit a cigarette.

Tires screeched on tarmac and first one and then another vehicle swept past Galman's position, braked and mounted the footpath outside the single storey building with its garish neon sign. A third stopped behind them and men clad in white barongs and black slacks spilt from the cars. All were armed with pistols. They waved aside a uniformed club security guard, who immediately took to his heels up the street as the group stormed into the club. Screams erupted interspersed with shouted commands insisting that everyone 'freeze'.

At the rear of the club a door burst open and a lone figure leapt down three steps, slipped on a rubbish-strewn pathway, regained balance, began to run.

The warning came from one of three men spaced at intervals in the shadows ahead of the fugitive. "Stop or we shoot."

Stumbling, the man stopped, raising his hands.

The three agents stepped forward, one moving behind him. Roughly pulling both arms behind the man's back he cuffed him and dragged him back to the door of the club.

It opened and a silver-haired figure was silhouetted against the inside light, flashing a torch in the prisoner's face.

"Johan Mel," said Pedro Wright. "You've been leading us a merry waltz my friend."

Mel swallowed and then spat at Wright's feet.

"Your people will hear about this," he sneered.

"You should know better than to hassle me. There are some people at City Hall and the National Assembly who'll have something to say about this. I've got powerful friends."

"Indeed?" queried Wright, apparently impressed, looking to his men. "I'd like you officers to join the others inside, if you please."

The three policemen glanced at each other uncertainly. "Now!" snapped Wright.

"I'll keep a close eye on our friend here. One of you call HQ for a paddy-wagon. I want this man as well as the staff and the girls taken in. Move it!" The three policemen nodded and filed back into the club.

As the door swung shut leaving their boss alone with his prisoner in the subdued light of a naked bulb above the doorway, Wright, said in a calm voice "So you have friends in high places, eh. Presumably that's what saved you over the *Bubbaaero* business?"

"You bet. You'll be sorry you came down on me. A couple of phone calls and you'll be pounding a beat in Tondo."

Mel knew well who his captor was. The police chief was high profile, his photograph often in the newspapers.

"Is that so?" said Wright. "Surely there is an easier way than calling in your tame politicians." He looked towards the door. "Business seems pretty good in there. Plenty of cash flowing across the bar eh!" Mel was immediately on guard.

"What're you saying? I make more money in a night than you do in a year."

Then he caught the policeman's drift and a quiet sense of relief flooded through him. So that's it! Send the other coppers away, a private talk and a few thousand pesos would probably see an end to the incident.

He lowered his voice conspiratorially.

"OK. We can do business. If you check out my inside coat pocket you might find something interesting."

Wright changed his grip on his Glock pistol and reached forward into Mel's pocket.

He withdrew a thickly packed envelope.

"There's fifty thousand pesos in there," sneered Mel. "A lot of it in US dollars. That'll put your kids through a good academy, hey?"

His confidence grew. Soon he'd have the damned head of the NPB in his pocket.

Wright looked at the money as if to roughly gauge the amount and thrust it into his back pocket.

"OK," he said smiling. "Turn round."

Mel heaved a sigh of relief and turned to let Wright use his master key to unlock the cuffs.

Wright lifted the pistol to the back of Mel's head and squeezed the trigger.

With the muted thump of the shot Mel crumpled to the dirty pathway, a small entrance wound in the back of his head, most of his face missing where a soft-nosed bullet exploded outwards.

Wright replaced the pistol in his shoulder holster and went back into the club. His men were busy taking names and checking the ID cards of those inside. One of them argued with two drunken Americans who were threatening to call the U.S. ambassador if they weren't freed. Wright waved to the officer to let them go.

"Sergeant," he called. A grizzled veteran of thirty years on the metro force hurried over.

"Sir?"

"An unfortunate accident," said Wright. "The prisoner tried to turn and run. I could not risk losing him in the dark. I fired a warning shot. Unfortunately the light was bad. I shot too low and the prisoner is dead."

The sergeant looked at Wright carefully. "Sir?"

"Get someone out, an ambulance, to clean up the mess. I will personally file a report tomorrow on this incident. And sergeant," he added as an afterthought. "Take this."

He handed him the envelope from his back pocket and nodded significantly towards the eight other officers busy with their paperwork.

"Make sure it goes into the appropriate police welfare fund."

"Yes sir!"

"Carry on sergeant."

Wright left the club by the front entrance. Outside he signalled to Galman, still in position across the road. The agent tripped across the road in his high heels.

"There's a body at the back of the club," said Wright, handing him a key, touching him briefly. "Lose the handcuffs, then meet me at the car."

Without questioning the order, Wright's personal assistant and live-in aide hurried up the lane beside the club.

There would be no corrupt politicians or bought judges for Johan Mel.

Chapter Thirty

Great Barrier Island, New Zealand: June 1987

THE PIPER CHEROKEE Six swept in low over the Pacific where the ocean kissed the wide white expanse of Kaitoke Beach and skimming the sand-dunes, settled for landing on the grass airstrip at Claris.

The aircraft turned off the runway, the pilot gunning the engine and taxiing to the green corrugated iron shed.

Douglas was waiting for them as they stepped down off the wing. Clutching Maria's hand tightly, Sean felt like a teenager again as he led Maria hesitantly towards the old man.

Before he could speak Maria bobbed before his father, taking one of his gnarled hands and placing it on her forehead.

The *Filipina* gesture of respect for an elder was greeted in a quiet dignity and understanding by Douglas before he swept the girl into his arms in a fatherly embrace.

"Welcome Maria. Welcome to your new home."

The words were spoken with sincerity and emphasis and for a long moment Maria buried her head in Douglas's shoulder. The two disengaged, Maria's eyes sparkling and then Douglas kissed her heartily on her forehead.

"Good grief girl, now you are a stunner! No wonder that son of mine's been running round in circles over you."

Laughing, Douglas turned to Sean. "Good to have you back mate." Fully aware of the emotion of the moment he gestured at the Landrover parked by the airport shed and changed the subject.

"The old Holden's just about on its last legs so I bought this from a guy in Tryphena. Diesel engine, good and reliable."

As he spoke the pilot brought up their bags and Douglas grabbed them both.

"Thanks Coop, see you next trip." Neil Cooper flew a regular shuttle to the Barrier and sometimes stayed over with Douglas if the weather made him too late to meet civil twilight back on the mainland - or if there should happen to be fresh seafood on the menu.

"Come on you two," Douglas continued. "There's a bottle of bubbly and a couple of crayfish cooling in the fridge and I've made a bloody magnificent salad, even if I do say so myself. It's welcome-home-time, Maria!"

Sean and Maria were swept along "Wow, the old man's in full cry. Sorry honey."

"Oh Sean, he's marvellous. He's wonderful. You didn't tell me he'd be so nice!"

"Wait till you get him in a bad mood. Like when the chooks get into his veggie garden."

Maria looked puzzled and Sean added hastily: "Sorry, chooks - chickens - veggies, that's vegetables. Darlin' there'll be a few new words to learn before you *kin spik Kiwi*." He clipped the last few words in a grotesque parody of the New Zealand accent. Maria learnt fast. "OK... mate," she quipped.

He laughed with her as they hurried over to the Landrover where Douglas gallantly stood at the passenger door.

"You're in front with me, Maria, my dear. Sean, in the back with the baggage where you belong. You've had this lovely lady to yourself plenty long enough."

With a gesture of mock resignation Sean leapt over the tailgate and backing out of the airfield gate, Douglas turned north on the Claris Road.

As they passed the Post Office, Betty Weeks and a small group of locals waved as they passed. *Trust the old man*, Sean thought. *Everyone on the island will know we're back. That means the phone lines are humming and there'll be a hell of a party coming up. All the women'll want to meet the 'girl Sean flew off overseas to bring home.' And the bloody men too, of course!*

Above it all, Sean felt anticipation as a shaft of sunlight swooped from behind a high cloud, lighting the hills and glancing off the emerald swells rolling up the bay as they drove across the island's spine.

At the house overlooking the wharf and the bay beyond, Douglas had excelled himself. On the covered terrace he had set a table complete with a lace cloth and silver cutlery. Looking at his father in silent inquiry while Maria changed inside from her travelling clothes, Douglas glanced sheepishly at the impeccably set table. "Adele sent them over when she heard Maria was coming," he said, "that you and I would have to get our act together if we're going to have a lady in the house. She and Regan are coming over next weekend by the way. Couldn't convince her to stay away any longer."

"That's fine..." Sean broke off, looking over his father's shoulder. "My god. Look at you!"

Maria appeared in the lounge wearing a sky blue silk sheath that clung like a second skin. Her long hair, free to her waist, was tied back with a band of blue ribbon. She held her arms akimbo. "Will I do for the gentlemens?" She smiled.

She'd found the best way to cope with her recent past was by means of a mature mockery of her former self. It worked for them both. The old man, swiftly moved to escort her the few feet to the table.

As the sun fell into the sea with late Indian summer swiftness, they dined on succulent crayfish tails with a butter and lemon sauce and a tossed salad of lettuce, tomatoes and radishes. A bottle of Moet hoarded against just such an occasion was poured and they toasted each other, the island and the future under the warm starlit sky.

Maria made a swift and subtle transition from guest to hostess and when she disappeared into the kitchen, returning with an improvised desert of tinned fruit, ice-cream and a shot of coffee liqueur from the lounge cabinet, Sean and Douglas exchanged glances.

"Have no fear, my son," Douglas said pontifically, expansive with wine, "you have the Brian eye for quality, it seems."

As they finished the meal and settled in with coffee, Douglas regaled the attentive Maria with details of island life, of the disposition of his small empire. The house and gardens were now hers to command and he and Sean would change things however she wished. Sean winced as the old man detailed of the frequency of his laundry habits but Maria simply smiled quietly and listened.

Just when Sean was wondering if the old man had lost his usual sense of impeccable timing Douglas rose a trifle unsteadily and raised his glass.

"Now it's time for my beddy-byes," he announced. "To you two. And wedding bells eh?" He drank and bent to kiss Maria on the cheek. "See you in the morning."

Maria and Sean pulled on sweaters against the cooling night air. Winter was around the corner. They walked to the beach and stood hand in hand for a long while, watching the moon rise higher above the hills at the head of the bay, its light attracting a flickering fantasy from the rippled surface of the water. For once, words were superfluous and they listened to the waters of the Pacific puzzling around the wooden pilings of the wharf. There was an occasional plaintive hoot on the breeze, a morpork native owl signalling its nightly hunt.

Back in the house they undressed and got into bed by the light of a hurricane lantern. Maria nipped the skin of his shoulder with her teeth as her hands reached for the core of him, guiding him to her with a strength and warmth that told him they were well and truly home.

Chapter Thirty-one

BENEATH THE SPREADING branches of a 500-year-old *pohutakawa* tree on the beach in front of the house Sean and Maria were married.

The island's only marriage celebrant, Mike Poole, a retired and somewhat alcoholic magistrate, performed the short and simple ceremony. The quarter-mile of road up to the house was crowded with parked vehicles belonging to what appeared to be entire population of the island, who'd travelled over dusty roads from far-flung farmhouses and holiday homes.

On the rolling lawn, Tom Weeks supervised a traditional Maori *hangi*. A deep pit had been dug with the turf carefully segmented and stacked to one side to later restore the ground surface.

Volcanic stones heated red hot in a blazing ti-tree fire were prodded into the pit and onto these were lowered wire baskets of wild pork, beef, mutton, *kumara* sweet potatoes and other vegetables. On top were laid more baskets containing a bewildering array of seafood; mussels, crayfish, scallops and snapper. *Ponga* fern fronds, an old canvas sail and then a layer of earth covered the whole, and the *hangi* was left to cook for five hours. Whisps of steam issuing from the pit carried a tantalising aroma.

Trestle tables set up nearby held a selection of cakes, puddings and trifles worthy of a royal banquet, all carefully prepared in coal-range kitchens and brought to the wedding by guests.

Overhead in a bowl of blue sky a wedge of *kaka*, the cheeky New Zealand native parrots, slid and skidded in the air and screamed derision at the confusion of human activity below them.

The delighted shrieks of a gaggle of children came from the wharf as they jumped into the warm blue water, swimming around to the boat ramp and repeating the exercise over and over.

Near the fish factory the island's menfolk gathered around another table laden with beer and wine either imported on the barge from the mainland or home-brewed in vats and barrels on the island.

Groups of women flowed to and from the kitchen adding to the already groaning board of desserts.

Maria was radiant. The marriage ceremony barely over, she was whisked away from Sean and swept off with the women. When Sean managed to extricate himself from the camaraderie of Tom and his friends for a few moments he found his bride cradling an infant girl and in animated conversation with a group of young mothers. She passed the child to a young woman and joined him.

"Isn't it wonderful?" She kissed him. "Sean I'm so happy."

A picture in white flowing traditional *kimona*, the distinctive butterfly-sleeved Philippine formal dress, her hair was piled atop her head and held in place by a tortoise-shell *mantilla*. She looked down at herself and then at the casually clad crowd of wedding guests.

"I think perhaps it's time for me to change. I get the feeling that this will turn into a bit of a party before it's over and this is hardly the dress for it."

She smiled. "My darling, thank you so much. This is just wonderful."

Then she hurried off to the house with Adele, who'd served as matron-of-honour, to change.

Sean returned to the beer table and backslapping congratulations. It was clear that he and Maria would be parted until the party was well underway and they could make their escape and head across the bay.

A friend had lent them his holiday home on the other side

of the bay, only be reached by boat and the hideaway would afford them some privacy for a brief honeymoon.

Sean accepted a bottle of home brew with the assurance of its maker that "it's a bloody good drop mate" and drank, making a mental note to pace himself. These guys would love to see him unable to meet his perceived wedding night obligations.

Maria appeared again clad in a denim outfit and was hustled away by Tom to watch the *hangi* being opened.

Carefully, the earth was scraped off the canvas sail which was lifted to reveal the covering *ponga* fronds, now cooked in the steam of the pit. These were tossed aside and a spellbinding scent leapt from the earth, the food, cooked in its own essences, taking in a subtle hint of hot stone and wood smoke.

The various meats combined with the seafood and vegetables into a mouthwatering aroma that drifted swiftly across the gathering.

More than any human command it signified that food was ready and the *hangi* baskets were lifted from the pit to a trestle table and Tom and his helpers began serving. The meat fell from the bone, the vegetables and seafood were firm and succulent.

Soon tinfoil plates were being passed out to the gathering and they ate on their knees and seated on the grass except for Sean and Maria along with Adele and Tom, as best man, who sat at the table on the terrace.

There was a single brief speech. Douglas, resplendent in jacket and tie for the occasion, called for order and raised his glass to the guests strewn across the lawn.

"A toast," he said, his voice thick with wine and emotion, "to the bride and groom. Maria has come from halfway round the world to join us here. For Sean, a wife, for me a daughter," and, catching Adele's look of approval, "for Adele, a sister."

Then, with a meaningful glance at Sean "Our little family is growing and I look forward to it growing even further."

There was a roar of approval from the beer table where the powerful island brews are already taking their toll and giggles and laughter from the women.

Maria blushed but rose to the occasion. She stood and in a strong clear voice announced

"Thanks dad. If those gentlemen over there will stop trying to sabotage my husband, we'll try and make it granddad."

An hour later, the party was well under way. A stereo was wound to full volume in the house with the speakers passed out through the windows. A child arrived up from the wharf wailing and clutching a sprained wrist, to be whisked off to the attentions of the somewhat tipsy district nurse. A forestry worker had a fight with a fisherman from Port Fitzroy, busting him on the nose. Now the pair settled down to get steadily drunk together in the shade of the fish factory. Behind the factory, hidden from the bulk of the guests, a group of young islanders passed a smoke from hand to hand and the pungency of marijuana wafted in and out of the slight breeze from the sea.

Catching an eddy of smoke, Sean looked worriedly across to Maria, only a few feet away. She didn't react to the smell. Then Sean spotted Tom Weeks stalking purposely towards the factory. The young people behind the building suddenly decided to be elsewhere and headed for their cars up the road.

Some of the island women were clearing away the remains of the wedding feast to a relay of dish-washing volunteers in the house as Adele found Sean looking rather blearily at yet another brand of island home brew. She carried a mug of steaming black coffee and exchanged it for the bottle.

"Sean, get this into you. There's only another hour or so of light and I think it's time you and your lady made your escape while you still can."

Fifteen minutes later bride and bridegroom were raucously escorted to the wharf and the waiting *Taipan*.

Sean handed Maria into the boat, started the engine and pulled away as some of the crowd began hurling rice across the short space of water. It scattered on the cabin top, grains falling into the water and attracting a flurry of sprats around the hull.

To the cheers, catcalls and best wishes of the islanders, Sean opened the throttle and *Taipan* carried them across the bay. The noise of the party was drowned by the outboard but the celebrations would doubtless continue into the wee small hours.

On the far side of the bay Sean set the anchor off the beach and they paddled ashore through a glassy warm lagoon left by the receding tide. Maria gave a little cry of delight as Shaun, swept her off her feet and carried her across the sand.

A small black oystercatcher ran ahead of them on orange, drink-straw legs, going to ground beside a piece of driftwood. Sean paused to show Maria where the bird guarded a nest in the sand containing three blue-flecked eggs.

"She's going to be a mummy," smiled Maria and Sean quickly set her on her feet and they ran towards the cabin set in bush above the beach.

Chapter Thirty-two

Eleven months later, Sean and Maria's son came squalling lustily into the world, born at home with Maria tended by the island midwife, a Maori *kuia*, or elder, Carol Te Hana.

Skilled in naturopathy, she'd guided Maria through the latter stages of pregnancy with herbal panaceas for pain and discomfort.

The infant was born in their marriage bed, the midwife assisted by Adele who'd arrived as Douglas flew to the mainland to supervise Adele's twelve-year old twins for as long as necessary.

Sean and Adele's husband Regan huddled nervously in the lounge, the French doors firmly closed against a chill southwesterly sweeping the island.

"You'd better come in," called Adele from the bedroom doorway. "It's time."

Even as Sean moved to her side Maria groaned softly and then with a slithering rush a tiny head and body slipped from her to be quickly picked up by Carol. A lusty wail later, the midwife swiftly swaddled the infant and placed him to Maria's swollen breast.

It was too much for Sean. He swiftly cradled Maria's head in his arms before stumbling to his feet and leaving the room. He opened the lounge doors and stepped into the night to let the wind whip away the tears.

In moments he'd collected himself, helped by a glass of neat whiskey handed over by his brother-in-law. He composed himself and went back into the bedroom, kneeling beside the bed as Maria pushed back the linen wrap from the child's face. His son is pink-faced, eyes firmly closed, a tiny fist clenched to his lips. Sean feels a glow of wonder, of pride.

"A son for you, my darling," said Maria.

As she spoke, the image of a small boy, a dried leaf caught in his hair, an arm reaching in supplication, flitted into his mind. Sean shook himself as the image faded.

Later, as Adele, Carol, Regan and Sean kept a somewhat bibulous vigil in the lounge while Maria and the child slept, Adele raised the inevitable question.

"Okay dad, what are you two going to call the babe?"

Sean looked at his sister.

"Well, for a boy we decided on Peter, after a friend in the Philippines and Douglas as a second name, after Dad. If we'd had a girl we'd have named her Jan.

So I guess Peter Douglas it is. I think there may be a third name. But I'll have to talk to Maria first."

He avoided questions by passing the whisky bottle around. Later he sat alone in the kitchen with a last glass.

In their year on the island neither he nor Maria had dwelt on their twilight time but the swift vision of the little foundling in Manila sometimes flashed into idle moments, times when smooth seas and fair weather out in the bay left his thoughts wandering. For the image to intrude now, at such a time, was disconcerting.

He swallowed the last of his drink and went to where Maria slept peacefully with the baby swathed in clean linen in a bassinet near her arm.

Sean undressed and climbed into a bed his sister made up on a stretcher, gazing in awe at his wife and son before sleep overtook him too. Just before it did he remembered a name. Bagyo, that was it. Bagyo Cruz.

Chapter Thirty-three

Great Barrier Island, November 1991

PETER DOUGLAS BAGYO Brian screamed with delight as fledgling wavelets on the beach chased his tiny steps up the sand. Then as they receded he chased the sea away only to be driven back again and again.

Sean and Maria lay under the *pohutakawa* tree watching the three-year-old in amusement, making sure he was never more than a few metres away.

Between them rested a carry-cot with their daughter Jan, just a year old, sleeping peacefully.

Like her brother she had her mother's jet-black hair and slightly almond-shaped eyes but unlike Maria's glowing brown, the children's eyes had a Celtic green hue from their father. Both children followed Sean's stronger European features and frame, still tempered by their mother's fineness and her olive skin.

Behind them, the house had a new wing and Sean glanced over his shoulder to where his father sat on the terrace watching the small group on the beach. Douglas raised a hand to acknowledge his son's gaze and then went back to a letter he was writing.

Douglas was 76 and more and more kept to the house. His war injuries grew daily more of a hindrance and there'd already been a spell in hospital on the mainland. Sean was sadly aware that the clock was counting down for his father.

Maria had assumed most of Douglas' duties in running the household and the gardens, which had expanded greatly under her re-kindled interest in growing things, as well as tending the children.

Lying alongside *Taipan* in the bay was another boat,

Cheyenne, added to the enterprise when Tom Weeks decided to accept Sean's offer and join the crayfish business. Today, Sunday, was by mutual agreement a time for families.

They were making a good steady income from fishing and outside of his abiding interest in Maria and their children Sean also spent a couple of hours each evening at a word processor set up in the fish factory office, churning out an attempt at a novel based on his days in Asia and specifically the incident in the Golden Triangle. It was a way of keeping in touch with his journalistic past. His old captor, opium warlord Khun San had recently surrendered to Burmese government troops in what Sean suspected was a financially motivated deal with the military regime in Rangoon siphoning off a share of profits from the poppy fields in the hills to the north of the country. John McIvor now posted to India but still keeping a tab on his Southeast Asian beat and corresponding regularly with Sean, shared his suspicions.

The sun sparkled on the water, the cries of seabirds echoing back from Jack's Point across the bay and Sean felt an easy peace. He turned to Maria.

"Look at him," he said proudly. Peter was throwing sticks into the water, chortling to himself as they tumbled ashore on the rippling waves to be picked up and thrown again. "He's getting to be an independent wee thing."

Maria looked fondly at their son. "I still wonder," she said, "about the other one. What age would he be now? About eight or nine I suppose?"

When Sean had finally raised the idea of a third Christian name for their son Maria had been hesitant, a little unwilling to let the past intrude on the happiness she'd found.

But after a day or two mulling it over she'd said to Sean one evening as Peter lay asleep in his crib "Sean, I've decided. Let's give Peter a third name. Let's remember all those forgotten kids. Let's add Bagyo to our son's name. Somehow, maybe, it will keep that other Bagyo safe?"

Sean hugged her close, thankful that she'd thought his suggestion through and made her own decision.

Maria had grown into a strong, purposeful woman and mother in the love and safety she'd found. She'd emerged as a guiding light to many women on the island and even gave counselling sessions to some families who found themselves unable to cope with problems like budgeting, wayward children or spouses.

Now as Sean reflected on how far they'd come in their short years together, Maria rose and called to her son.

"Peter, come here darling. It's time for a drink." The little boy toddled across the sand to his parents and a plastic drink bottle, upending it carelessly and dripping juice down his chin. She scooped him into her arms. "A sleep for you my little man. Watch Jan for me for a little while love."

She made her way off the sand and onto the lawn. Passing her father-in-law on the terrace she noticed he's fallen asleep in the sun. When she'd settled Peter, she made tea and took it to where Douglas sat slumped in his chair. Touching him lightly on the shoulder.

"Dad, it's too hot to sleep in the sun. Have some..." Her voice trailed off. Douglas's eyes were half-open and as she looked closer a cold stream welled within her. She touched him more firmly and his wrist slipped from the armrest of the chair and fell limply to his side.

The fear caught in her throat and her voice cracked as she stepped back, her hand to her mouth.

"Sean, Sean!" Her near-scream shattered her husband's reverie on the beach and he scrambled to his feet. "What the hell? Maria, what the heck is it?"

He saw her standing stricken and began running, stopping and turning back quickly to pick up the carry-cot.

Swiftly but carefully he ran across the lawn and handed the sleeping child to her mother, bending to peer at his father's peaceful face.

"Oh Jesus Christ. Oh bloody hell no," he choked. "Dad, dad?"

His father's head lolled sideways, the half-opened eyes unblinking in the bright sunlight.

Sean didn't have to feel for a pulse. He'd seen casualties of civil strife and war and myriad accident victims in his years as a journalist and reporter. He straightened slowly.

"Darling," he said quietly. "Put Jan to sleep beside Peter please. Then help me get dad inside."

Maria knew from his expression that her father in law had gone and sobbed as she carried her daughter's bassinet with shaking hands to the children's bedroom. Tears cascaded as she and Sean lifted Douglas's spare frame carried him to his room. They lay him gently on his bed and Maria sank to her knees holding one lifeless hand in hers. She began praying softly in *Tagalog*, words half-forgotten in her voluntary separation from the church.

Sean moved quietly from the room and picked up the new touch-tone phone that replaced the old party line and dialled the area code to connect him with Adele in Auckland.

Regan answered, to Sean's sudden relief. They spoke and then Sean disconnected and dialled the island police station, then the new medical clinic.

He rejoined Maria in his father's room, kneeling with one arm around her as he looked at the old man.

At least, he thought, it was quiet and peaceful, in the sun and watching his grandchildren.

He stayed motionless for a few minutes, soothing Maria gently before leaving her to her vigil and returned to the terrace. The letter his father was writing lay unfinished on the table. Sean began reading as he waited for Constable Mason to arrive with the doctor.

Okupu, Sunday, the letter read.

Dear daughter and family,

My cup really does run over. Here it's a beautiful Barrier day. A bunch of brown teal native ducks flew into the stream at the back of the house today. It's good to see them coming back. The Department of Conservation (that has replaced the old Forestry) estimates their numbers have grown to about a thousand after they were nearly wiped out by rats and wild cats.

I'm out on the terrace letting the sun warm these old bones. I'm having to take medication more often now though. It's getting very difficult to sleep. Thank God Sean and Maria and the kids are with me. I really don't have to do too much. Maybe look after the youngsters when they're asleep to let your brother and Maria get over to the shop for an hour now and then.

They're all down on the beach at the moment, and Peter's having a wonderful time.

Those two make a lovely couple and it is so good to see your brother a completely whole person again. Maria has been marvellous for him. When I think of the fear I felt for Sean bringing home an unknown girl with her apparently huge problems it seems like another world.

She could not have been better for him, and perhaps him for her.

The only shadow I sense is in the extra name they chose for Peter Douglas. Bagyo.

There is something in the choice that they have always kept completely to themselves, some sort of link to the past that none of us has been allowed to share. Oh well, they have their own lives of course, and the private things that make it a whole.

Daughter, a quick rest I think. I will..........

The letter ended with a slight scrawl. The Parker fountain pen his father wrote with lay on the flagstone beneath the table.

Sean bent to pick it up, replacing the gold cap with a soft, final click, as he heard the police Toyota Landcruiser changing gear to round Suicide Point.

Chapter Thirty-four

THEY BURIED DOUGLAS high on the hill behind the house where his grave caught the first rays of the morning sun.

The headstone was a rugged piece of stone wrestled from the seashore below Jack's Point. Set into the rock were his father's silver Royal Air Force wings with simply his name, Douglas Robert Brian, etched beneath it. The family balked at listing the dates of birth and death.

"He hasn't gone," Maria told Sean. "He's just in the next room, waiting."

It was six weeks since the funeral when the islanders once again gathered at Okupu, this time on a sombre note, as Mike Poole intoned the words of the burial service over the open grave.

True to Douglas' memory the wake had been a decorously cheerful one. The island's sizeable Maori population insisted in affording Douglas the honour of a *tangi*, a traditional Maori farewell.

Carol Te Hana's *karanga* lament echoed back from the cliffs below Suicide, adding tears of honour for a fallen warrior to the tears of loss.

As the islanders made their final farewells and headed off to their homes, a soft rain had begun to fall. The Maoris took it as a measure of Douglas' mana, his spiritual power. Even the gods had cried.

There were always fresh flowers on the mound covering his father's remains, placed there each day by one or other of them.

As their island lives went on, Sean's work saw him most days out with Tom patrolling the sixty or so crayfish pots that were the mainstay of their enterprise, Great Barrier Marine Products, which was beginning to return a living wage for both their families.

They'd extended the smokehouse at the fish factory and were shipping substantial quantities of highly sought-after smoked snapper and *kahawai* to the mainland.

As the spawning season approached they'd added smoked roe to their produce, a delicacy which also found a ready market.

The children were asleep as Sean and Maria sat down to an evening meal, their Philippines favourite, *pancit canton*, which they ate with fresh fried *terakihi* fish.

After they had eaten, Maria opened a sideboard to one side of the open fire, lit to ease an unseasonal southerly wind chill, and took out a bundle of letters and cards.

"Darling, I think we'd better start replying to these."

She placed them on the table next to their coffee cups. Outside, chill gusts of wind surged through the spreading branches of the tree above the beach. Sean nodded and reached for the stack.

He opened the first few cards, messages of condolence from relatives and friends on the island, in New Zealand and from overseas.

He read a short note from Sandy Macdonald, now promoted to UPI's bureau chief in Hong Kong. He opened one that bore a Philippine postmark.

"This is a surprise." It was from Pedro Wright, recently retired from the National Police Bureau and now standing for the Philippine Senate.

"I remember we wrote and told him about Peter being named after him but how he learned about dad going I'll never know. He's a pretty amazing guy."

"Not really," says Maria. "You rang John McIvor remember. He would've passed the word along to your mates."

She'd become adept at picking up the Kiwi vernacular, and her 'Gidday mate,' or Maori '*Kia ora*' greeting, pronounced in an enchanting Philippine accent, endeared her to everyone on the island.

She was now firm friends with the midwife, Carol, and was fascinated with aspects of Maori culture and tradition that coincided closely with some of those of her own people.

They'd taught each other songs, each in their own tongue and Maria's '*Hoki Mai*' rendition in Maori always prompted demands for Carole to reply in *Tagalog* with the haunting '*Anak*' a popular Philippines equivalent, at island parties.

"Alright then - *mate*," Sean stressed the last word. "I suppose we'd better get down to this."

They busied themselves, each occasionally querying the other as to the source of the condolence message they opened.

Then Sean slit open an envelope containing another card among a few late arrivals.

"Honey, look, it's from Sister Jan!"

Maria reached across. "How good of her. Yes, I did write briefly to tell her what had happened." She scanned the card quickly. "She doesn't have much news, just sends her best and of course she asks after our Jan."

Maria placed it to one side, a thoughtful look in her eye, before bending once again to the task of writing.

A log slumped with a crackle in the fireplace some time later, breaking their quiet concentration. Sean yawned and gathered in the correspondence.

"Coffee?" Maria smiled acceptance, rising and going to turn down their bed. She slipped the note from Sister Jan into her drawer in the bedside table.

Later, their bodies glowing from lovemaking that each time seemed more exciting and adventurous, she stroked Sean into a deep sleep, brushing her hands soothingly over the firm planes of his back, hard and lean from the daily effort of hauling in the crayfish pots.

She listened to the wind play around the eaves, rustling through the native shrubs and plants in the garden outside.

It's time, she thought, *time to write to Sister Jan and maybe even to track down Father Stols.*

Earlier that day she'd picked up a World Vision card from the mantelpiece in Carol's home in Tryphena. It bore the passport photograph of a child, obviously African and querying her friend she learned she was sponsoring the youngster for a few dollars a week. Although she had two delightful daughters of her own, now vivacious teenagers, Carol told Maria she felt a need to succour another. "I'm getting on a little for any more kids of my own," she smiled, "but it's still nice to be needed."

Easing out of bed, Maria stepped through to the children's bedroom, where a small nightlight burned.

Peter and Jan slept beneath their duvets. She kissed each of them, stroking her son's head for a moment longer. She repeated his name softy under her breath. "Peter Douglas Bagyo. Where, I wonder is your namesake tonight?"

Chapter Thirty-five

Manila, Philippines: Christmas Day 1986

THE TAXI WAS gone, hidden in traffic as Bagyo gazed down at the notes in his grimy hand. He had a street-wise appreciation that here was enough to buy anything he wanted. Ice cream, *halo-halo*, the tropical juice and fruit mixture he and his companions loved, chicken legs, satay, chocolate and cola. In his other small fist he clutched the smooth object he'd been given. Unconsciously he wound the waxed cord around his finger, gathering it in.

Thoughts of plenty raced through his head. Calo would be pleased. And the rest of them. His chest swelled with pride, a primeval feeling of a successful hunt leading him to skip in a circle waving the money over his head.

Then suddenly he was grabbed from behind. A hand reached over his shoulder to snatch the notes.

Bagyo was no match for his older and bigger adversary who was backed by another child. His legs were kicked from beneath him and he sprawled, winded on his back on the grass median strip. The two teenagers led a gang of half-a dozen younger children who crowded in to watch Bagyo held down and the money snatched away. Their objective accomplished the thieves broke off and ran.

Tears of anger and frustration welled as Bagyo screamed for help.

"Calo, Calo, Calo," he yelled over and over as he scrambled to his feet in time to see the small gang scampering through the traffic towards the crowded footpath on the inland side of the road. Blinded by tears, he thought of pursuit only to hesitate as they scattered.

Impotent in fury, shame and loss, his screams were

drowned in the roar of traffic.

He stood sobbing disconsolately, broken-hearted at the side of the road.

Calo and his followers found him hour later, a small huddled form at the base of a power pole, his head buried in his arms. Calo nudged him carelessly.

"Hey you, Bagyo. You won't get any money like that. But come on. Riti got twenty pesos. We're going to get food. Come on."

Bagyo raised a tear stained face as the others moved off. He made no attempt to tell them what had happened. Instinctively he knew their wolf pack mentality would regard his loss as weakness.

The girl Riti waited for him to get to his feet. Some maternal seedling made her grasp his small hand in hers and they followed Calo and the others down a path of broken seashells and gravel to a group of rude huts with torn red and white nylon awnings. As they walked, Riti was aware the child held something in his other hand.

Bagyo at first resisted her attempts to pry open his hand then he relaxed his grip and Riti studied her find. For a moment she wanted it. Then she opened the loop of cord and put it over his head to hang around Bagyo's neck, as though dressing a doll she'd never had.

They caught up with the others crowded with other squatter folk into a dusty square of cleared ground scattered with rude tables knocked up from unwanted packing case lumber.

Calo marched up to the first of the illegal canteens fronting onto the makeshift dining room and thrust ten pesos at the proprietor, a middle-aged woman the kids all knew as Mama Loke, a Chinese-Filipina of indeterminate age.

She tucked the money into the bag at her belt and set about feeding the seven children.

They attacked a huge plate of cooked rice with their dirty

hands as she broke stale leftovers of bread, croissants and biscuits she got from her son, a kitchen cleaning hand in one of the hotels on the seafront.

In a rare moment of compassion - life was no easy path for her - she poured a granulated cordial mix into a plastic jug of water and set it before the children.

When they'd eaten, the younger children in the group, Bagyo among them, wandered back to their base in Rizal Park. One rummaged in a communal box for the empty plastic bottle and three of the kids begin an impromptu game of rudimentary soccer. Other urchins soon joined them and their grinding and tenuous hold on life was briefly forgotten in the struggle to kick the container past an imaginary goal line between two rows of dying shrubs.

Calo took the remaining ten pesos in their kitty and walking out to the street he bought two packets of cheap local cigarettes from a footpath vendor, whose offerings included a few sorry-looking bananas and some cartons of soya-bean milk.

Then he began prowling the traffic at a set of lights, calling "One stick cigarette, one stick!" There was always an impoverished jeepney passenger unable to afford a packet who'd part with 50 centavos for a single cigarette to quell hunger or craving.

The markup on a 'stick' enabled him to double his stake money and after an hour Calo had recovered the money spent at breakfast.

Returning to the park he leaned back in the welcome shade of a spreading plane tree where the rest of the band was dozing or talking desultorily as the heat of the day grew.

He noted the sun over Manila Bay and judged the time to be about 11 o'clock.

In another hour he'd lead his small group to the church on United Nations Avenue where a group of volunteers dispensed the children's only regular meal, rice and soup made from spoiled vegetables from nearby hotels and restaurants.

When he led his band into the community hall beside the crumbling 400-year-old Spanish salute to God, they found church volunteers had collected an assortment of donated second-hand clothing to add to a meal of noodles, tinned corned beef and bananas.

It was Christmas Day. Two dozen children were soon seated on wooden forms as a matronly woman led them in singing a compulsory Philippine National Anthem before food was served. The kids parrotted the words; their eyes straying to where steam and smells issued from a small kitchen off the hall.

The song over, they sat on the same forms, balancing plastic plates of food on grubby knees, eating with their fingers, licking each morsel of unaccustomed bullybeef from their hands until dirty skin showed clean.

The bananas also quickly disappeared and then, formed into line by their matronly hostess, the children filed past a trestle table heaped with garments in various states of disrepair. When Bagyo's turn came the woman behind the table looked down and rummaged about in the pile. With a grunt of approval, she held up a small pair of shabby denim pants and looking further, found an almost new T-shirt. Bagyo pulled the pants over his shorts. With the bottoms turned up they fit. The T-shirt, emblazoned with a printed label for Fiji Bitter beer, was several sizes too large and hung to his knees.

It made no matter to the child who joined the others in the hall as they strutted proudly in their new finery, chattering excitedly over their unexpected gifts. This was magnificence indeed!

He joined other children in a game of tag in the yard outside and was pushed hard by an older boy. He recognised one of his attackers of the morning. But he turned away, saying nothing. The instinct for survival was strong and he knew he was no match either in wits or strength for such an opponent.

That evening, Calo dispersed his followers around MH Del Pilar Street and its neon strip of gaudy bars, nightclubs and restaurants. He knew the holiday will have attracted thousands of tourists to the area, many of them from Hong Kong where Christmas was marked by the closure of expatriate and British companies, but not by the Chinese.

There were usually good pickings to be made from befuddled bar patrons, many remembering family and friends in their home countries, made sentimental and more generous with each glass they drained.

With luck they'd beg enough to see them through the rest of the week.

However, though Calo could not know it, the street of bars and brothels providing the twilight children with a precarious income was a dying lifeline.

Chapter Thirty-six

Manila, Philippines: March 1987

"IF I HAD a gun I'd shoot him. I'd kill him."

Lisa Nito, a 19-year-old bar dancer and sometime prostitute nursed a glass of Tanduhay rum and cola in the Firehouse Disco on MH del Pilar on a break from her 30-minute stints on the stage at the end of the room.

Huge speakers belted out the latest hits from the States as bar girls and customers clinched in booths or effected some form of dancing on the metal floor, their faces sickly in the garish lighting. In one booth a tourist was face down, passed out on his table, ignored, with his wallet probably long gone.

Lisa swallowed the rest of her drink, still digesting the news that sparked her threat.

Manila's mayor, an iron-fisted former police general, Alberto Lam, had dispatched a flying squad of officers into the entertainment belt of Ermita with closure notices for bars featuring go-go dancers as a front for prostitution.

Lisa made a reasonable income dancing in a brief bikini for a half-hour break at a time and because of her looks, usually getting 'fined' out of the bar. For five hundred pesos paid to the mama-san, the woman running the escort side of the bar's business, a patron could take her out for the night and whatever arrangement she made for her time outside the bar was negotiable with her escort and hers to keep.

But tomorrow, the doors to the more notorious clubs on the strip were to be boarded up. In one fell swoop a whole section of the city's economy was being shut down. The follow-on effect that meant new poverty, closing restaurants, boarding houses, hotels, shops and so on down the chain to the pittances earned by shoe-shine boys, street pedlars and the beggars including the waifs of the gutter.

For Lisa the closure order spelt a double disaster. She shared a single bed in a tiny room at a nearby hostel with her baby son. Shutting down the Firehouse was likely to cut her entire income and toss them both into the street.

She signalled the barman she'd sometimes sleep with to curry favour and free drinks and he poured and pushed the drink across the bar. Beside Lisa the mama-san made no comment as she too absorbed the shock.

"Mr Lam, he's crazy," Lisa continued. "He's taking our food away and giving us nothing in return. How do we live? I will kill that man if I can get a gun."

The mama-san put her arm around the girl's naked shoulders, consciously caressing the smooth golden skin of her arm.

"There are still the bars over in MP Burgos, girl," she said. "You have lovely looks." She let her gaze fall over the bikini-clad figure, the swelling high breasts. She ran her tongue over drying lips then caught herself. Where she worked she could not play.

"You'd better get dressed and get over there tonight. By tomorrow there'll be a couple of thousand girls looking for work." As an afterthought, she added "If you get a job, you can stay with me for a while because I'm only a block away from the bars there."

Lisa was about to finish her drink and follow her advice when there was a commotion at the door of the bar. A club security guard from the street outside rushed in.

"There's a demonstration," he yelled. "It's led by Lam!"

Patrons and girls rushed out to gather on the footpath, joining hundreds of others up and down the street as, down the centre of the road which has been closed off by police vehicles, strode Alberto Lam at the head of a straggling group of about 100 men and women.

They sang a discordant hymn in *Tagalog* and waved

placards. 'Stop the Aids Spread', was one, 'Send The White Monkeys Home' another and 'Foreigners Out - Feet First If Necessary!' read a third.

The next day, municipal workers arrived in del Pilar in a fleet of trucks, unloading timber boards culled from the demolition of an old house on the edge of Ermita. Without ceremony the boards were slammed across the doors of bars and discos the length of the strip, anchored by six-inch nails driven deep into the door frames. Pinned to one of the baulks across each entrance was a typewritten closure order from the mayor's office.

In a single stroke the lifeblood of the street was sutured off and its heart died. Go-go girls, hookers, bar staff, mamma-sans, food vendors, restaurant owners and all the others who earned a living from the street gathered in the roadway at a loss over the mayor's action.

"I might not be bloody closed," said the Austrian owner of the Heidelburg Restaurant. "But I might just as well be. My customers come in to eat between bars. No bars, no bloody business!"

His companion, the widow of a bar owner, one-time mamma-san and now operator of a dormitory-come-boarding house for bar girls, was sick with despair. "Me too. No bars, no business. Oh what can I do," she wailed.

In Makati, just half-an-hour away, Lisa left the Funky Fox nightclub on MP Burgos Street hugging herself happily. She made her way along the street towards a small house that had survived re-development on the fringe of the central business district and at the doorway she was greeted by the mamma-san from the Firehouse. She cradled Lisa's baby son in her arms and opened the door wider.

"Come in, come in. Did they take you, did you get it?"

"Yes, yes, no problem. They liked me. And I get 100 pesos more because they pool the tips. It's really upmarket. Its blue label, owned by an American."

She took the infant from her friend, and then leaned forward to kiss her softly on the lips.

"You really have saved us you know. I owe you so much. There are hundreds of girls out there now looking from bar to bar for jobs but it's filled up overnight. I'm lucky I started early. Now let me put this little one into his cot and we can have some food."

With the infant soundly asleep, Lisa and the mamma-san sat side-by-side on the double bed in the one bedroom of the house, eating rice and watching a television news replay of the bars being boarded up in Ermita.

"I'm really lucky," said Lisa. "What will happen to all those people? There's no room for them to come here to M.P. Burgos. The local people are already in charge here. It's their own turf."

The mamma-san smiled as she touched the girls bared thigh as she sat cross-legged.

"We are both lucky," she said, getting a warm glance in return.

Chapter Thirty-seven

Manila, July, 1987

As they prowled the darkened streets of Ermita, Calo's band of the lost was growing desperate.

Gone were the busy bars and noisy restaurants and the money changers where they'd waited patiently outside for the odd centavos that had become their staple income.

If it wasn't for the daily meal at the church their situation would be really desperate. As it was when the group huddled together for mutual protection in the dark of Rizal Park, they did so more often than not with empty bellies.

What was once a vibrant, seedy, tawdry money machine with its own life force had become an island of desolation, the loss of crowds and bright lights adding to the sinister cityscape. Increasingly the children were joined by the older homeless as women forced onto the streets by the closure of bars, massage parlours and brothels vied for space in the park and begging places on the filthy pavements.

A few feet away from the patch they jealously guarded under the plane tree an emaciated girl of 18 lay on the footpath beneath a torn red blanket, her hollow cheeks and dying eyes crying Aids to those who hurried past, their faces averted.

The children watched her dispassionately for several days before one morning, she was dead. A Metro Manila aide, employed for a few pesos by the city fathers to sweep the gutters clear of leaves and rubbish finally called a sanitary department van and the lifeless, nameless bundle was carted away to a paupers' morgue somewhere in the city.

With the numbing poverty, crime escalated and the chain reaction set off by the shutdown of Ermita peaked in violence.

A French woman tourist was stabbed to death for the sake of her purse within yards of the brightly-lit oasis of the Midtown Hotel. The few shops that remained open quickly shut down as daylight robberies made them unviable. Increasingly the hotel rooms on Roxhas Boulevard remained empty as the word of mouth tourism telegraph passed the message that Ermita was becoming a no-go zone. Lower echelon employees were laid off to add to the human flotsam that flowed into an urban no-man's land.

Ermita had become a war zone, a nightmarish struggle for survival that saw the street kid's hold on life becoming increasing impossible.

At City Hall, the economic impact of the closure of the red light area was all too apparent. Fledging social services instigated by the Aquino regime were swamped, having hardly touched the surface of the desperate need on the streets.

In a room on the third floor of the mayor's office in United Nation's Avenue a conference was in progress, chaired by deputy mayor Romeo Gonzales to try and map a way out of the mess created by idealism and false hope.

"I was offered an infant child on the street last night for a hundred pesos!" The speaker, a councillor recently elected to his first term with the city.

"A hundred pesos for a human life. This is what we have come to in Ermita and it has got to stop." He slammed the table in front of him for emphasis, raising his voice over the hubbub his comment provoked.

"If we're selling our children we're selling our souls. May the Lord God forgive us for what has been done here!"

The speaker sat burying his face in his hands as Gonzales rapped the table for order.

"Councilor Rey," he said. "You've pointed out what we all know. But what is the solution here? You suggested when you asked for this meeting that you had some ideas."

Dr Jesus Rey looked up from his hands and put on his glasses.

"I have sir," he said.

"I believe the situation we have here equates to a full scale civil emergency. I propose that we seek the release of emergency funds from the government for a start, to provide shelter, food and medical care to those people out there." He gestured to the unseen streets.

"I am at present chief administrator of the Aquino Rehabilitation Clinic. As you probably know we are based at Camp Crame in Pasay City. We are only using four of the two dozen barrack rooms, which were handed over by the armed forces on the departure of Marcos.

"I respectfully suggest that we immediately open these facilities to women and children. That we provide transport to that facility and that a process of documentation is begun to get this nameless horror that has been created into some sort of order. I am reliably informed that Madame President herself will give her support to the project."

He looked round the room at the dozen other councillors and their support staff.

"Unless," he added quietly, "anyone has a better half-way measure?"

Silence in the room. Gonzales stood and shuffled the agenda papers before him.

"I am in full accord with Councillor Rey," he announced. "I ask though for a show of assent." Everyone in the room raised a hand.

"Very well, I will visit the mayor and request that he accompany me forthwith to Malacanyang and the presidential residence. I believe we should act immediately."

The officials filed from the room, hurrying to their various departments to prepare for the virtual evacuation of refugees thrust upon them.

Outside the building Dr Rey got into his small, battered,

Toyota Starlet and joined the slow-moving traffic towards his clinic, his mind running over sources for beds, blankets, medical supplies and food.

With luck, Aquino would sign over funds immediately. He had impressed the need upon her when she visited the clinic bearing her name two days ago.

A mother of three children herself she immediately supported the plan for Ermita, with the admonition that Dr Rey go through official channels.

She'd assured him that she'd act with dispatch once he had.

Chapter Thirty-eight

Manila, August 1993

ON A LARGE parade ground where soldiers once drilled at Camp Crame about a hundred youngsters lined up in ranks of twenty. The Philippine National Anthem died away from loudspeakers on each corner of the ground and they stood fidgeting, with an occasional outbreak of horseplay in the rear ranks.

From a rostrum in front of them a camp prefect read from a clipboard. The slim and pretty girl in her late teens was Che, who had rescued an infant before being picked up in the social services net cast by Mrs Aquino.

"Classes will start as usual at 11 o'clock" she said. "Until then, the following duty roster applies. Del Pilar barracks will conduct the camp cleanup. All papers, rubbish and cuttings from the lawns are to be collected and placed in the dumpster by the main gate.

"Rizal barracks is on laundry duty today and all bedding in this barracks must be aired and the sheets and pillow cases washed in central laundry and hung to dry.

"Mabini barracks is on food preparation duties. Please report to the cookhouse to assist under the instructions of Mr Fely."

Che went on allocating duties for each barrack in the camp then dismissed the children who filed off the parade ground line by line. At the head of the first group a lithe auburn haired boy, slightly taller than his companions, stepped aside and as Che passed he grinned and they slapped raised palms.

Then he turned and led his group of children to a utility area at the rear of the parade ground. From a tin shed by the last barracks he handed out brooms, rakes and sacks to his companions. They ambled away in the hot sun to begin quartering the camp in search of rubbish.

Thirteen-year-old Bagyo Cruz watched until the other children had moved away and checking that he was unobserved he ducked around the corner of the barracks.

Keeping the building between himself and the rest of the camp he strolled towards the fence surrounding the camp, pushed aside a loose board and stepped into the street outside. He crossed the road and entered a small sari-sari store. Inside a time-worn woman reached automatically for a packet of cigarettes, blue-label, Pall-Malls. She knew the boy's taste and he always had money.

Lighting-up, Bagyo walked through to the back door of the small shop and sat on the steps there, puffing the cigarette. Moments later there was a sound behind him and he was joined by another boy about his own age.

"Hey Raoul," he said in greeting, offering the newcomer the smoke.

The boy accepted and hunkered down beside Bagyo.

"Bloody camp, bloody duties, bloody rubbish." It came out as almost a snarl and Bagyo grinned.

"Hey pare, at least it is a place to sleep and a place to eat. As long as we do what we are asked to do, or appear to, we'll do alright."

Raoul nodded reluctantly. "What about tonight?"

"Sure," said Bagyo. "I'll meet you by the shed at about nine, an hour after light's out - the usual time anyway."

The pair finished their cigarette and moved back across the road.

Checking the coast was clear through the loose plank they stepped back into the camp grounds and made their way cautiously to the last barracks, then rounded the corner of the building boldly, on legitimate business again, rejoining their clean-up crew returning equipment to the shed.

Lessons begin at 11 o'clock and Bagyo dozed his way

through the drone of an elderly volunteer teacher with few qualifications putting in a little church-time for the underprivileged. His street-sharpened mind usually earned him a pass mark during tests that were inevitably geared to the lowest common denominator. However, the rudimentary camp schooling had at least given him the skill of reading and with it a more than passing interest in the written word.

For the most part, lessons bored him and he preferred to pick up knowledge of choice from the tattered collection of books and magazines in what passed as the camp library.

But his real heart was on the street where he'd grown up. The camp was a restrictive regime but he was cunning enough to see it served as a good cover, with secure food and shelter.

The bare two hours of schooling he received each weekday were soon over for this day and he joined some of his friends in a game of football on the parade ground before being called to tea by yet another rendition of the national anthem over the loudspeakers.

The simple meal over, the children were left to their own devices. Most watched television in the communal hall near the clinic fenced off from the camp proper.

In the years he'd been at Camp Crame after being picked up with the rest of the street gang from the church on United Nations Avenue, Bagyo had never been near the clinic, stressed as being off limits from the start, only for sick people who might pass their illness on to the urban refugees. It was a place to be avoided.

He'd seen some of the staff coming and going and he'd noticed the white-clad nuns, their faces hooded from the sun, as they hurried between buildings.

The sight vaguely disturbed him but he couldn't decide why and he shied away from the area as a result.

Chapter Thirty-nine

Bagyo watched television until 'lights out' was rung over the camp and he joined the twenty other children and teenagers in his barrack dormitory. Iron cots abandoned by the army were a luxury for children whose first pillows were their forearms, their first beds the pavement or a strip of park grass.

He feigned sleep for an hour before quietly slipping out of his dormitory. As the eldest in the room had the bed nearest the door, screened by a makeshift curtain from his slumbering companions.

At nine o'clock that evening he was waiting for Raoul near the lean-to shed and minutes later they were at the store. Inside they quickly changed from their camp-supplied shorts and T-shirts into tight blue jeans and buttoned cotton shirts. From his neck, Bayo took the talisman and rolling the ivory in its cord, he secured it in his zippered jeans pocket for safekeeping on the busy streets they were bound for.

The raddled old woman owner reached out once to stroke Bagyo's light olive skin. "Give you a year or two boy, and I'll bed you myself," she cackled.

"Piss off Carla," hissed Bagyo. "You'll get your money later. That's all you'll get."

Dressed, the pair left the shop and walked quickly to the end of the ill-lit street to board a slow moving jeepney heading towards the brighter lights of the Makati business district downtown.

At the end of MP Burgos, they stepped down as the vehicle paused in traffic, flipping the driver a peso coin to cover the fare.

They begin patrolling the street, strutting consciously to add stature to their age. MP Burgos had replaced Ermita as

Manila's nightlife strip under the benevolent eye of a Pasay City mayor who lacked the crusading zeal of his Ermita counterpart.

Bars and restaurants jostled for space, garish lighting painting out the daytime squalor of peeling paint, rusting corrugated iron and cracked concrete. The footpaths were busy with tourists and bar-girls moving from night-club to bar to night-club, the tourists bent on sampling the sleaze, the girls hurrying to disco-dancing dates and the whole sub-culture of street vendors, beggars and spruikers adding a confusing and exotic human background.

Thirty minutes later outside the Funky Fox nightclub, one of the more imposing of the street's disco-pubs, Raoul gestured to a figure sitting in a battered Datsun parked across the road.

"There he is." The two boys crossed over and Bagyo's friend Calo got out of the vehicle.

"Hey *pare*," he called.

Bagyo had kept in touch with Calo, who after two years in the camp was, at 16, expected to make his own way in the world and had insisted Bagyo stay in the barracks where he had security and the cunning to come and go.

"Just wait for a while," he'd said. "I'll be in touch, don't worry." He'd been true to his word.

"Look," he said now. "There're two inside the bar. They aren't into the girls. When they come out, mark them."

Bagyo and Raoul lounged against a parked car and waited. Only a few minutes later, two men left the club. They were holding hands and Calo reached through the car window to signal the two boys. He and Raoul swung in front of the tourists.

"Hey mister," said Bagyo, smiling. Raoul stood with hands on hips and pouted at the two men, who exchanged glances and muttered together. One asked in heavily accented English "How much you do a blowing job?"

"One hundred pesos," replied Bagyo.

"Five marks, German," leered one to the other, who nodded, sweaty-faced in the flickering green light of a San Miguel beer sign over a nearby bar.

"Come then," offered Bagyo and he and Raoul lead the way up the street.

After a hundred yards they turned into a poorly lit alley and made their way towards a small down-at-heel hotel frequented by short-time customers seeking brief privacy.

They stepped over a sleeping figure sprawled half-up the hotel steps, an empty rum bottle skittering along the pot-holed footpath as one of the men kicked it aside.

With the two men following they entered and Bagyo took a key from an elderly woman at the desk, heading down a dimly lit corridor, the carpet threadbare and holed in places.

Halfway along he used the key to open a door and entered the room, flicking on a light that also rattled an ancient air conditioner into life.

With the two Europeans inside he shut the door and leaned against it. Raoul moved with practiced casualness to one of the two beds.

One of the men stroked the teenager's face, at the same time reaching for his own belt.

The other sat on the bed and beckoned to Bagyo.

"First the money. Please put it there." Bagyo pointed to a bedside shelf.

The German took two $100 peso notes from a stuffed wallet and placed them there.

He lay back on the bed and unbelted and unzipped his trousers.

Bagyo moved across the room and knelt at the bed, reaching out his hand.

The door crashed open and three men burst into the room almost filling it. Calo was flanked by two other young men. They wore jeans, white *barong tagalog* and dark glasses.

One of them carelessly flicked open a silvered butterfly knife.

"So, a couple of bloody paedophile queers," snarled Calo. "You two get the fuck out of here." He motioned to Bagyo and Raoul who leapt to their feet and ran from the room.

"We should cut your balls off," Calo went on as the tourists fumbled frantically with their clothing and got to their feet, faces bright red in embarrassment, showing shock and the first stages of fear.

"We are volunteer police. We can take you in for questioning. It goes hard with foreigners who exploit our children."

If Calo had gone anywhere near the police he'd have been immediately grilled over any number of minor crimes.

But one of the men immediately grabbed for his wallet.

"Please" he simpered. "Please, here, take this. We didn't mean anything…"

Calo took the wallet and flicked through the notes inside. His face remained stony. "Not enough for your fine." He looked at the other man.

Calo's companion silently tossed the knife in his hand. Malevolence throbbed in the room.

Trembling, the second man produced a wallet and handed it over. It was thick with foreign currency, Hong Kong dollars, Thai Baht and US dollars as well as German marks. Calo emptied it of cash, leaving credit cards and licences, and threw both wallets on the floor.

"Pick them up and get out," he snarled. "If I or any of my people see you in MP Burgos again, you'll get this." He nodded at the knifeman. "Now get the hell out."

The men fled, blocking the door in their haste as they rushed to get out of the room, feet pounding up the corridor.

A few minutes later Bagyo and Raoul reappeared in the doorway, grinning delightedly.

"Another good one," crowed Calo. He and his companions were counting the notes on one of the beds.

"Altogether about 11,000 pesos," he said exultantly.

"Here, He passed 1,000 pesos to the two boys to share and began dividing the rest between himself and his two companions, two notes going in his pile to one in theirs.

"You kids get back to camp. This'll keep us going for a while. No sense in pushing our luck. Let's all lie low for a while and we'll meet up again next Friday night. End of the week's a good time to score 'cos tourists seem to like arriving at the beginning of the weekend. Now get going."

Sean and Raoul left by the back door of the hotel. Calo would take care of the unseeing woman at the desk on the way out front.

Chapter Forty

"Where did this come from? Where? Answer me." Camp director Pauline Ramos was livid with fury.

Bagyo Cruz stood before her desk with Raoul Urbanista, caught climbing through a fence behind the camp in the early hours of the morning by an insomniac staff member on a walk around the grounds.

Each was found with 400 pesos in their pockets.

"Well, am I going to get an answer or am I not?"

Bagyo looked at her defiantly as Raoul shuffled his feet, his eyes downcast.

In the continued silence from the pair, Ramos turned to her assistant, Che. "Take Bagyo out of the room please."

When the door closed, the director moved around the desk and cupped Raoul's chin in her hand.

"You had better tell me right now just what you've been doing."

Without the moral support of his street-wise companion Raoul began to lose what little composure he had and within a few minutes he had broken down to confess.

"We went with some men," he said.

"We take them to the hotel. For sex. But we don't let them. Calo stops it. They take the money. They scare them and send them away." The words spilt over themselves in confusion, and the director stepped back in shock as the full import sank in.

"Oh my God! Che," she yelled through the door, "bring the other one back in here."

Before going back into the office, Che grabbed Bagyo's arm. "Shit you sound like you're for it," she whispered. The two were friends now in a tenuous way, in a world where relationships were always temporary. Both remembered their first days but any substance was blurred by years of simply surviving. Now a woman, Che had found a vocation in helping run the camp and had little other ambition.

"What the hell." Bagyo didn't bother to lower his voice as Che opened the door. "Sooner I'm out of here the bloody better."

An hour later, Bagyo and Raoul were sitting in an examination room in the clinic next door, wrapped in thin blankets, their clothes hanging on hooks.

In the adjoining office, Dr Jesus Rey looked at the director of Camp Crame.

"My dear Pauline," he said. "What can I say. Both boys are perfectly healthy. They have not been sexually used in any way that I can tell. It's a con game where they act as bait. That's all there is to say." He looked at his notes. "They're free of any illness or disease. Medically, there's nothing else to be done. I guess the ball is back in your court."

Ramos stood wearily.

"We have our rules doctor, as you know. I can't have this, this... infection!" she spat the word. "They must go!"

Dr Rey nodded. Under the charter which funded the camp any indiscretion was enough to cut off the meagre government funding it received. The initial official zeal for rehabilitating the children of the night had pretty much evaporated, once they were safely parked out of sight.

Cleansed of its bars and brothels Ermita itself was now a burgeoning business belt controlled largely by Chinese money from Hong Kong and Taiwan.

With the British Crown Colony reverting to the rule of Beijing, political and commercial uncertainty had tipped the once stable coffers and there had been an outpouring of millions of investment dollars.

MH del Pilar was a busy construction site as mid-range hotels rose skyward to service a growing number of Chinese restaurants, designer clothing malls, jeans shops, karaoke joints and up-market pool parlours and social clubs.

Asian package tours from the powerhouse economies of Singapore, Korea, Japan, and Taiwan, enjoying a massive gain in exchange rates, had replaced the boisterous European pleasure seekers. The sex industry had also gone more upmarket, expensive but discreet in the face-saving way of the Chinese.

The people of Ermita who'd been displaced in the transition were, semi-officially, out-of-sight, out-of-mind and Pauline Ramos had no desire to draw attention from government officials who might question the continuing need for her camp - or her job.

With the medical examination the actions of the two boys were now imprinted on official records and this could not be ignored.

That afternoon, Bagyo Cruz and Raoul Urbanista found themselves outside the main gates of Camp Crame.

As they swung shut, Bagyo kicked out at his companion, missing but emphasising the strength of his feelings. "Stop bloody snivelling. Who needs them anyway." He jerked his head at the camp. "I'm going. Come if you want to."

Picking up a plastic shopping bag that contained a few items of clothing, he headed down the street in the direction of the *sari sari* store. Carla would give them a roof for the night and she was holding money for them.

Tomorrow he'd find Calo.

Chapter Forty-one

At Caritas headquarters in the Makati district, Sister Jan sat in a spacious corner office lined with filing cabinets.

She'd aged well but white crows-feet etched the corner of her eyes from years of squinting through the bright tropical sun. She wore a modest business suit in place of the habit of her order. As an assistant administration director of Caritas she'd taken a step back from the front line and a step upwards, now in charge of the organisation's medical clinics in the Philippines.

As such she had daily dealings with government officials and agencies and the order found it more fitting that she dressed appropriately for the endless round of committee meetings she had to endure.

On her desk was the daily report prepared by her staff, detailing events of the previous 24 hours in the various Caritas hostels and clinics around the country.

She read through it and then reached for a stack of files pertinent to the report, which had been placed in her in-tray.

There'd been two deaths the night before. At the Bataangas Clinic a young girl cut her wrists in the showers after the child she had still-borne three days before had been buried.

In a convent rest home in Quezon City an elderly nun passed away quietly of old age and, no doubt, exhaustion after 50 years administering to the needs of the poor.

Sister Jan signed the appropriate forms and placed the files on the other side of her desk to be dealt with by her assistants.

Picking up another, she glanced at the accompanying note from the Aquino Rehabilitation Clinic in Pasay City where she'd been one of the original staff. She smiled in memory. From the signature she saw Dr Rey was still serving the medical needs of the less fortunate.

There were now fewer victims of the red light districts and the clinic's work had expanded to provide general medical services to the local population, recognised as a medical institution and used as a training ground for some of the nurses and doctors churned out by the state schools and universities.

Over the past day some two dozen patients had been treated there with cases ranging from a broken leg in a traffic accident to a domestic stabbing at a shantytown on the nearby canal.

Sister Jan unconsciously rubbed the scar on her thigh. Her own leg injury still gave her a twinge in wet weather.

She ran her pen down the list of cases before signing it off, when suddenly a name sprang out from the page. Her pen moved back and stopped.

A Bagyo Cruz had been one of two boys examined for signs of sexual abuse by Dr Rey the day before. He found no evidence of anything untoward and the child, together with another, was handed back to the jurisdiction of the director at adjacent Camp Crame.

For a moment Sister Jan stared in shock and surprise at the name. Bagyo Cruz. 'Storm' Cruz. It just had to be him! She glanced at the estimated age of the child. It fit with the little boy she lost all those years ago after the Caritas Centre blaze when she'd been nearly crippled fleeing the firestorm.

As the memories came flooding back, she sat back in her chair and uttered a prayer under her breath. Moving quickly she reached to a filing cabinet to remove a brown cardboard folder, opening it to a sheaf of papers and beginning to read. For the most part the file contained lists of children registered in the various church institutions in the Metro Manila area. It also contained form letters from Sister Jan requesting details of a child called Bagyo Cruz.

The Church replies had been always in the negative

with records kept sketchily at best. The file also held copies of correspondence from Sister Jan to Maria Brian, in New Zealand, and Maria's original letters.

The first of these was dated five years before.

Dear Sister Jan,

Happiness, pure happiness, is the only way I can describe my life here on the island. Sean's business is going very well and we have been able to expand the house and add some mod cons to make things more comfortable. The children are thriving and Peter now wants to help his father on the boats. He even goes out occasionally, well wrapped up in a life jacket.

Jan is just starting to walk and is really happy and healthy.

For myself, believe it or not, I am still gardening and I've managed to plant our land out in native trees and shrubs so one day it will look like it did in centuries gone by. But enough of that now.

Last night I sensed in Sean a longing. I don't know whether I told you we have given Peter another Christian name, Bagyo, a reminder to us both of those days so long ago before happiness turned to despair and then happiness again.

I know you have always made your own inquiries about the little boy you rescued and then lost. I have a friend here on the island who is sponsoring a child through World Vision. It occurs to me that your efforts may be assisted a little with some financial help. Therefore I am enclosing a postal order for a small amount. It is from my housekeeping and each month I plan to send what I can to assist you in your search. I know it maybe a hopeless task, but anything I can do will repay you and the clinic for what was done for me. It will also ease my mind that I may be doing something to help where Sean is concerned. He is a wonderful, wonderful husband and father.

Just occasionally though, I notice a faraway look in his face when he uses our Bagyo's name.

Not long after Peter was born he told me he thought he had seen the little boy on Roxhas Boulevard on the Christmas Day he flew home from Manila. Whether he did or not is surely uncertain. But if the child is alive, I think it would mean a lot to him in completing the circle that brought us together.

So there it is Sister. I will continue to send what I can from the housekeeping, in the hope that perhaps someday, we will track Bagyo down.

The letter finished with more details of Maria's new gardening project and an account of daily life with the children.

Sister Jan folded the letter again and stared out the window to where a new office skyscraper was under construction across the road.

Workers scurried through a latticework of bamboo scaffolding, carrying timber, bricks and mortar on their backs. From the street below came the sound of traffic punctuated every few seconds by impatient car horns.

She turned back and picked up her most recent letter to Maria.

My dearest Maria.

Oh how the years have flown by. As you will see from the address I now have a new position. I'm finding it very busy, if not as satisfying as tending to the needs of others on a personal basis. But is a very necessary part of the Order's work here and I undertake it cheerfully.

I thank you for the assistance you have been able to send over the past few years. It has gone a long way to cover the expenses of our search. I am afraid postage and telephone costs have taken up a large part of it but we still have a hundred dollars or so American in our little account.

I will continue as I can but I fear I have perhaps exhausted most avenues of inquiry.

But who knows. There is something in our lives that is unfinished and perhaps we must simply wait for God's hand to appear. My love to Sean and the children and a special hug for your own Jan.

She put down the letter. Had God's hand appeared? She reached for the telephone and consulting the list of numbers taped to the top of her desk, she pressed buttons.

Chapter Forty-two

Bagyo roamed MP Burgos as night fell. He stopped briefly at a pavement stall to buy a cheap snack of fish-balls skewered on a bamboo sliver.

Raoul had stayed behind with Carla, still snivelling and bemoaning the loss of the only home he'd known. Carla seemed delighted, fussing around the teenager who responded to her attention like the lost child he was.

Bagyo dismissed his friend to the ministrations of the hag and hurriedly left the store.

After his snack, he wandered the street and when he reached the Funky Fox, loitered near the doorway. One of the youths who joined Calo's extortion of tourists appeared out of the deepening, oppressively warm night. Bagyo stepped to meet him.

"Calo?" he asked briefly. The youth recognised Bagyo and stopped. "Calo? He's back there at the Casa Rosa."

The cheap workers' canteen and bar was a hundred metres up the street and Bagyo hurried away and soon found his street mentor with a plate of rice and fish, eating hungrily. Calo waved him to a seat opposite and minutes later Bagyo, a plate of food in front of him, poured out his story between mouthfuls.

Calo finished and wiped his mouth on his hand, reaching for a bottle of coke which he emptied in a couple of swallows.

"So young Bagyo has flown the coop eh?," he said. "Well my friend, what are you going to do?"

Bagyo looked surprised. "We can be together again. We can keep doing it," he said hopefully.

Calo studied the boy. He'd filled out from the scrawny urchin taken under his wing those years ago in Rizal Park. He was tall for his age and the legacy of his European forebears was a sturdy frame by comparison with Filipinos of his age.

"I'm going south," he said abruptly. "It's getting too hot here. Someone we dealt to had the guts to go to the cops after we rolled him and they've been hanging around the street. I have a stash and it's time I left town for a while."

Melodrama, from the movies he loved. He paused in thought and then said quickly "Do you want to come?"

Bagyo was startled and leaned forward eagerly. He'd thought often of the world he knew existed outside his small realm. South he knew meant the southern Philippines. His passing interest in geography at his classes has given him a rough picture of the largest of the seven thousand islands that made up his country.

"South," he says. "Where, to Cebu? Mindanao?"

"Mindanao, place called Zamboanga" replied Calo. "I'm sick of this shit anyway. The bloody cops are on the take and the city's full of crap. I hear there's a bunch of rebels down south who're looking for people. They want to change things."

Calo wasn't completely clear about the rebels but he had a glimmer of feeling that here was a chance to change things for himself. To react to the system that had ground him and his kind down for so long.

"I think it's a chance to fight. If you want to, you can come along."

Bagyo's resourcefulness could prove useful and it'd be no bother to have company on the trip. He could always lose the kid if it didn't work out.

Bagyo had little real option. Calo was his only link to life outside of the camp and while he had an innate sense of his own ability to survive he'd become used to the direction of the older youth.

"OK. I'll come," he said, a decision born of no alternative plan.

He'd carried his plastic shopping bag of meagre belongings with him. "When?" he asked.

"You can stay with me tonight," said Calo. "We'll get a ferry tomorrow."

He slept in a storeroom at the back of the hotel where he plied his trade with indiscreet tourists.

The pair sat a while longer, Calo chatting up the girls who stopped by the canteen for a break from the streets. Then he and Bagyo headed for the hotel where Calo spread a foam mattress on the floor for his guest. "So much luxury, eh *pare*?" he said before getting into his own bed raised on a row of boxes.

Sleep did not come quickly for Bagyo. He felt the cool floor pressing at his hip as he rolled onto his side, peering at the crack of light under the door. As Calo slipped into the regular breathing of rest, Bagyo tried to grasp his suddenly changed circumstances.

Life on the streets of Ermita was still with him, as were vague memories of an earlier, very different life, a time without hunger and uncertainty. Then came the overriding camp years, of enough to eat, of a place to sleep, of an awakening curiosity about the world around him.

The milestone of learning to read had pulled aside a curtain to a window of infinite possibility. Excitement and uncertainty tumbled around in his thoughts before he too fell into an uneasy sleep.

Sometime in the early hours of the morning he awoke, cold despite the humid night. With nothing to add to his meagre bed he huddled into a foetal position, clasping his knees to his chest, dozing fitfully through the remaining hours until dawn.

At seven o'clock that morning after a hasty breakfast of fish balls and rice at a street stall the pair took a series of jeepneys across the raucous awakening city. The jolting rides in the open-backed vehicles wandered a passenger-determined route from commercial district to shantytown, paved main street to rutted track. Several hours later, shaken, hot, dusty and tired they eventually climbed stiffly out at their destination on the southern arm of Manila Bay and a stretch of wharves. Dilapidated ferries bought second or third hand from richer ports in Asia made passage here to the other Philippine islands.

After asking around, they were directed to a rusting freighter, converted to carry passengers in sea-borne dormitories, bound for Zamboanga in the far south of the archipelago.

They queued interminably and late in the afternoon, from the money belt fastened tightly beneath his shirt, Calo doled out their fares at a kiosk on the wharf, taking care to conceal the amount of cash he carried from others waiting for tickets. With another two hours to kill before sailing they visited a nearby market set up to supply the travelling public with the obligatory cheap gifts the homeward bound will take to impoverished provinces, as well as food for the journey.

Calo and Bagyo bought *baloute*, fruit, and packets of sticky rice bound in leaves. Calo also stepped into a section at the rear of the market that housed hardware stalls selling cheap clay pottery and kitchen utensils.

From a cutlery vendor he bought a bronze butterfly knife, the metal handle folding in two halves to conceal and protect the blade and which fit unobtrusively in his jeans pocket. As an afterthought, he took a second knife, which he handed to Bagyo.

"You'll have to start looking out for yourself," he warned. "Don't let anyone fuck with you."

Bagyo now and then touched the silky sheen of the metal in his pocket, feeling very much the equal of his friend.

On the deck of the slab-sided, rust-plated ferry they found a slatted wooden bench under a large canvas awning covering the afterdeck.

"It'll be too bloody hot downstairs," said Calo. "If it rains we'll get cover under here."

They ate some of the rice and *baloute*, stashing the remainder in the sports bag in which Calo carried spare clothes. Bagyo's luggage still consisted of two plastic supermarket bags.

Due to sail at five o'clock, it was past seven and dusk when three strident blasts from a siren on the tall angular funnel above the superstructure signalled the first movement of the vessel as it backed into the turgid waters of Manila Bay.

Swinging west to make the entrance to the harbour they passed the sentinel island of Corregidor before entering the slow roller coaster of open water and night threw an obsidian cloak over the sea.

Behind them in the east, the glow of the city pulsed and flickered off the cloud base, here and there a taller building punching a stack of lights high above the electric carpet of Metro Manila.

The ship turned south, her diesels thudding in a soon monotonous rhythm, puffs of rust erupting from cracked deck-plates, scabrous safety rails fencing the deck vibrating in sympathy.

The travellers opened two six-packs of San Miguel beer and gravitated to a small group of other passengers gathered round a youth with a guitar on the afterdeck, keeping a watchful eye on their bench.

As he looked through the ship's railings into the night, memories seeped into Bagyo's thoughts. Waking hungry in a park, running over a hot pavement, a full belly after a meal at a city mission. The rough and tumble in the streets, getting robbed of the handful of pesos from the man in the taxi. Camp Crame, sudden order in his personal chaos. Regular meals, a growing awareness of himself and the wider world around him.

He reached as always without thought to the ivory tooth that hung from his neck, hidden by his singlet and another T-shirt layer against the night breeze of passage.

Suddenly realisation hit him that for the first time in his young life he was in control of his own destiny. It was a quick heady rush, adrenaline unleashed. He was suddenly in charge of himself. He had freedom.

Then he became aware again of the group around the guitar player, voices joining in surprisingly good cover versions of Stateside hits favoured by Manila's rock radio stations.

Emboldened by the unaccustomed beer, Bagyo sang along with the others.

Ahead where the rising moon suddenly illuminated a sharp, dark horizon, knife edging to silver, life held the promise of magnificent adventure.

Chapter Forty-three

THE TELEPHONE HUMMED softly. Dr Rey let it ring several times before putting down a file he was reading to pick up. Sister Jan's greeting brought a smile. Exchanging brief pleasantries, she came quickly to the point.

"Doctor, I have a file on my desk on two of your patients from the camp. Two boys you checked yesterday for sexual abuse?"

Rey quickly recalled the incident. "Yes Sister, how can I help?"

"I'm very anxious to trace the boy called Bagyo Cruz," Sister Jan said tightly. "I believe he may be someone I've been looking for many years now."

Dr Rey leaned back.

"Yes, I remember, a rather striking kid, Eurasian. Green eyes. Brownish hair. Quite tall?"

Sister Jan was silent for a moment.

"It has to be him," she said, her excitement obvious now. "Doctor, I'll try and get over this afternoon. Can you locate him for me?"

Dr Rey paused. It was apparent Sister Jan had more than a passing interest in the child and he spoke carefully.

"Sister, I handed the two boys back to the camp. But I fear from their attitude they were not long for there. A girl collected them. They'd been slipping out of the camp and getting into trouble in town. I believe Pauline Ramos, the director meant to turn them out. She's paranoid about losing her funding. But let me check with her first and I'll call you back."

For the rest of the morning Sister Jan found concentration difficult. Just before she was due for lunch at the convent next door the phone rang.

Briefly, regretfully, Jesus Rey confirmed her fears. The two boys had been unceremoniously ousted from the camp and their whereabouts were no longer known.

"I'm sorry Sister, if I had any idea..." his voice trailed off.

Sister Jan replaced the receiver, staring at the file lying on her desk. With a sigh she closed it to return it to the cabinet.

Hesitating, she reached for the writing pad, looking at the blank sheet of paper for a moment. To write, or not to write?

Then, with another sigh of resignation she pushed it way. It was not for her to raise hopes she could not fulfil. Why write to Maria with such tenuous news when it appeared nothing could immediately be done?

If indeed she'd truly encountered the life of Bagyo Cruz once more she must have faith that it was somehow ordained, that something would cone of it.

Leaving her desk she went down to the street and walked the few metres to the convent. Passing the chapel on her way to the small dining room she stopped and retraced her steps.

Chapter Forty-four

Mindanao, Southern Philippines: November 1998

THE GUERRILLA CAMP high in the Mindanao cordillera was reached only after a tortuous journey on foot through heavily jungled foothills, along narrow winding trails that sometimes disappeared into thickets to emerge from the thick vegetation in another direction.

The tropical rain forest was redolent with life, a backcloth of insect industry splashed with bird-song and the barking cough of monkeys in high branches overhead.

In a narrow clearing, with forest trees almost touching overhead and protected by the ramparts of a bamboo forest was a longhouse, surrounded by a cluster of storehouses, a cooking area and further towards the edge of the surrounding jungle, a makeshift latrine.

A small dusty patch of ground outside the bamboo and rattan longhouse with its steep-sloping thatched roof served as a parade area. From above and just metres away in the surrounding forest the camp was all but invisible.

Smoke curled lazily above the open-sided kitchen to waft into the mist cloaking the rain forest.

In the longhouse, youths and men stirred awake and one rose from the coconut fibre matting and moved down the hut, prodding those still slumbering with his foot.

"Up, up now," he called.

As they started fully awake the hut-master reached the doorway and stared through the branches overhead into the dawning sky.

Behind him, the others lurched to their feet. A macaw parrot tethered by one clawing foot to a bamboo rail outside screeched a greeting.

Tumbling from the hut the men formed an untidy group in the clearing as a short stocky figure emerged from another smaller sleeping hut to one side of the longhouse. Dark-skinned, his head balding, he wore a faded camouflage jacket. A cotton sarong around his hips was secured by a webbing belt from which hung a vicious-looking machete.

Clapping his hands, the guerrilla leader called his men together. "We pray," he shouted, and launched into a monotone.

The Muslim morning litany silenced the sounds from the trees encircling the encampment. At the cookhouse, three women emerged from the shadowed interior and stood quietly.

The group in the clearing wore a motley collection of clothing, native sarongs, blue jeans or shorts with the one common denominator a red bandana around each head.

The short prayer over, the camp commander called out names from a list and five men peeled off from the broken ranks, pausing for parcels of food at the cook-house, before heading in different directions into the surrounding forest to replace the graveyard shift on sentry duty.

An old woman called the rest over and she and her companions tended large steaming metal pots as the men were handed rattan platters heaped with rice laced with green vegetables and scraps of dried fish. They ate with their fingers.

Bagyo Cruz joined Calo beneath a papaya tree at the edge of the clearing. In the four years since sailing south from Manila, the boy and the man had coarsened, losing the patina of the city. Bagyo was now almost a physical match for Calo, lean, fit and hard.

They and the others in the group formed the Abu Zaid Unit of the Moro National Liberation Front, a revolutionary cadre devoutly Muslim in the otherwise Catholic Philippines, refusing to accept the religious doctrine brought to the islands by Spanish conquerors four hundred years before.

The MNLF had emerged as the spearhead of opposition to the government and Bagyo and Calo soon came into contact with the dissidents in the fertile recruiting ground of the shantytown slums the pair frequented when they arrived.

Religious convictions meant nothing to them when a recruiter approached them where they eked out a living unloading fishing bancas on the Davao waterfront.

Politics didn't matter. They were young, fit, tough, cunning and hungry for adventure. That was enough in their new world of opportunity for the recruiter to talk them into a way to strike out at a society they'd been born to reject.

In the year he'd been in the hills, Bagyo learned too there was profit in revolution.

A recent raid on a small provincial town netted proceeds from ransacking the mayors' house. Now secreted in Bagyo's spare clothing was money in a cashbox he found in a bedroom closet. The death of the mayor and his family, as well as six guests at the daughter's wedding feast during the guerrilla grenade attack, was just the result of what the Abu Zaid unit was trained to do. Something to be thought about with pride.

While Bagyo had not thrown a grenade, he'd fired his AKS with the others as wedding guests fled in panic into the rice fields.

Roman Catholic landholders, descended from immigrant colonists from the north two centuries earlier gloried in their plantation profits, their lucrative income from lumber and gold and tin mining. But the indigenous Muslims of Zamboanga remained serfs, employed for a pittance to serve the *mestisas*, the northerners with a touch of Conquistador blood in their veins.

So the ruling class became legitimate targets in the all-too-often bloody Muslim campaign for independence

With the morning meal finished, the men in the

clearing returned to their sleeping hut where weapons were distributed, a firearm and a machete for each man.

Bagyo shouldered a Chinese made AKS, close cousin to the more formidable Russian AK47 and joined nine other guerrillas. Leaving the rest of the men relaxing in camp to perform routine duties, Calo led his stick of men into the jungle.

They'd cover the foothills below to guard against the Philippine Army patrols that constantly probed the area, maybe call for supplies, dried fish and rice at a supporting village on the coast.

When they encountered the soldiers they'd always found it easy to fall back and lead them away from their base camp which had escaped discovery for more than a year.

As the file threaded through the bamboo, careful to avoid the razor-sharp stakes where a machete had sliced a 70 degree spike on a growing stalk just inches from the ground as a brutal booby trap, Bagyo looked forward to the day ahead, remembering a girl he met when an earlier patrol was welcomed by sympathisers at a fishing village.

While the political ideals of the MNLF mean little he'd found he enjoyed the power he wielded with his automatic rifle. And perhaps more importantly he had camaraderie, a family almost, one of a band of proud brothers.

Chapter Forty-five

NEWLY GRADUATED FROM the Philippines Military Academy in Manila, First Lieutenant Ernesto Evangalista had been posted to the main military base in Davao City earlier that month.

With little time for orientation he was swiftly sent into the field.

Now his 30-strong platoon crouched in a midday halt beside a muddy stream gurgling from the upper slopes of the range hiding the Abu Zaid jungle camp, the soldiers brewing-up after an early morning slog into the hills in the cooler part of the day.

"We've been getting into rebel territory too damn late," Ernesto's commander had raged at the briefing the day before.

"By the time we make contact up there we've been foot-slogging in the mud and slush for three or four hours. When we meet fresh bush fighters they run rings around us. We have to get in there as fresh as the guerrillas."

Evangalista had paraded his men in the hour before dawn at the forward camp he set up after trucks dropped them off five hours out from Davao the day before.

It meant marching in the twilight of stars and the half-moon hanging in the western quadrant of the sky, just enough light to see by. When they reached the heavily jungled lower slopes it was daylight.

They'd made good time and were now some 30 kilometres out from their base. The heat of the day was peaking and Evangalista ordered his men to take what shelter they could find under the huge ferns lining the riverbank, after first stamping out their bivouacs to send reptiles and insects to alternative shelter.

The lieutenant had passed out top of his class at the academy and his favourite subject was the study of guerrilla warfare tactics. He'd researched reports on previous patrols into the cordillera.

"With your permission sir," he'd told his commander, "I'd like to bring the enemy to us. The policy of hot pursuit just plays into their hands, leaving our men exhausted and vulnerable. If we're to have any chance of shutting the Abu Zaid unit down, then we must play them at their own game."

The commander had appraised the clean-cut young man before him. The file on his desk told him that here was one who was heading for the top of the military ladder, potential underlined by the fact Evangalista's uncle was on the general staff in Manila.

"I suggest that's an excellent operational plan, lieutenant. You will enter our approval of it in your patrol report."

Evangalista had ignored the commander's ill-disguised move to share credit should the patrol succeed, saluted and left the room.

Now in the field against his enemy he called his two sergeants to him and opened the canvas map case.

"We are here," indicating a map reference. "If you look at the area, in the four contacts we have had with the Zaids, our patrols have all been led roughly south, west and twice to the east. What do you make of that?"

For a moment the two veteran soldiers stared at the young officer. They were used to college boys leading them and normally remaining aloof and formal. But Evangalista had proved he could march and they appreciated his timing in the dawn. Basing themselves here instead of tearing gung-ho around the jungle had also weighed in his favour.

"Sir," said the senior of the two men, "the only way the Zaids have not led us is north, higher into the ranges. All the other directions involved moving over falling ground. It's easier for the guerrillas to strike and run. To the north, the country rises and the terrain is more difficult. The men have always suspected this is where the base camp must be but in the past our officers have not agreed."

The sergeant was being somewhat undiplomatic but Evangalista ignored the fact.

"Exactly sergeant. The guerrillas always lead us away when they make contact. I suggest that, if we do find them, when they pull out we continue northwards anyway. Let the hunted do the hunting," he smiled.

"I want the men fresh. We'll remain here and move out in the late afternoon when it's cooler. See they get what sleep they can."

Dismissed, the sergeants went to pass on their orders. One glanced back at Evangalista with a look of grudging respect.

"This puppy, he might turn out to be a good one," he said. His companion grunted in agreement.

Chapter Forty-six

The Zaid patrol could smell the village along with the sound of surf crumping against white sand, wafting into the copra plantation bordering the beach.

Dogs barked, children screamed and cried at their play, men called to each other and to their wives as a fishing *banca* thrust into shore. The pungent odour of dried fish, hanging from racks like translucent amber jewels in the sun, reminded the guerrillas they were on a replenishment mission.

On the edge of the coconut plantation, Calo dropped prone and covered the last few yards to the village compound on his stomach. The others copied his movements.

Bagyo gritted his teeth and swore under his breath as a coconut husk hidden under the surface of the fine white sand dug cruelly into his groin.

Calo, just ahead of him suddenly got to his feet, his body language seeping from tension to relaxation.

"It's clear." He motioned his followers to their feet. "The headman's signal is there."

The hamlet was Muslim and supported the guerrillas. The headman, a haji wearing the white crocheted skull cap of one who'd made the pilgrimage to Mecca, had a son serving in another unit to the south of the Abu Zaid territory.

If there'd been signs of a government patrol in the region there'd have been a net folded over the bamboo railing on the small deck that jutted from the headman's *nipa* hut.

It's absence declared the area safe and Calo led his band out from the coconut palms. Their appearance brought a sudden silence to the small village until the red head-cloths signalled their identity and then there was a mass swarm towards them. Children and dogs led the rush while the adults followed more sedately, women branching off to their individual huts to see to boiling rice and steaming fish as a meal for their guests.

The headman, a grey-haired, wizened figure in a pair of torn cast-off jeans faded by salt-water, his skinny torso bare, stepped forward and clasped both of Calo's hands.

"*Salaam, aleikum,*" he intoned and received the response *aleikum salaam,* as he greeted the other guerrillas.

After the exchange, he led Calo to his hut and the others in the band moved through the village compound and down to the shade of more coconut trees that rustled in an onshore breeze above the white strip of beach.

"We have had a good fishing," the headman said as Calo settled in a corner of the hut and accepted a pipe of rank native tobacco from his host's equally wizened wife.

"We can give you two sacks of fish and two of rice. Any more would leave no reserve for us. Of course you help yourselves to the coconuts."

Calo screwed his eyes against the acrid smoke and passed the pipe to the old man.

"It is plenty and we thank you for the food," he said. "Your friendship is greatly regarded."

The two began discussing the other details of supply, word of other bands in the area and of government troop patrols.

"A fisherman from the south says there is a patrol in the hills as we speak," said the *haji*.

"It is as well to be warned," Calo replied.

There was movement at the back of the hut and a young girl aged about fourteen came diffidently forward with a tray made of split bamboo. On it steamed a whole fish with a bowl of rice and side dishes of fiery chillis and dark soy sauce.

The two men fell silent as they reached for the food, using the fingers of the right hand to serve themselves. The left hand was reserved for bodily cleansing and never touched what reached their mouths. Calo had adopted the Muslim code of eating simply for its good sense.

The girl returned to the rear of the hut and then emerged again leading a procession of women from the headman's kitchen behind his home, making their way down to the sand to where the Zaid guerrillas lounged on the foreshore.

Bagyo was dozing, his back against the bole of a palm that swept out over the water, bent in some forgotten storm.

A shadow fell across him and he snapped his eyes open. The dark shape against the sun softened into the face of a young girl who held a bowl toward him.

He could smell the fried fish as he reached for it and became aware of his companions hungrily eating. Chewing on a mouthful he looked quizzically up at the girl who remained standing above him, pretty with long black hair to her waist and dressed in a red sarong trimmed with a wide white border. In her ears hung golden hoops of brass wire.

"Hannat," he said. "I hoped you would still be here."

The girl bent her knees and squatted before him on her haunches, pulling her sarong modestly around her lower legs, her eyes smiling.

"I stayed behind when the others went to Davao," she said. "Grandfather says he needs me here until my mother and aunts come back from the marketing."

Every three months, a group of village women travelled by banca and then rickety bus to the port city to sell dried and salted fish, dried prawns, small red bananas and coconuts either for cash or as barter for cloth and other manufactured necessities of life.

"I'm glad," says Bagyo. "I wondered if I would see you."

She smiled. "I too wondered if you would return before the rains." The monsoon season was approaching and with it the threat of typhoons.

"Grandfather says I have to go back to school at the end of this week, when mother and the others return."

She lowered a hip to the sand and sat, separated by a metre or so in the interests of modesty. While he continued to eat he was aware of an embarrassed glow as heads turned in their direction, some of his companions with sly grins.

He raised himself up against the palm trunk and looked down at Hannat. The smooth brown skin of her cheeks were like silken mirrors catching the light from the sparkling sea just a few metres away. The crumpling wavelets were reflected in the fathomless darkness of her eyes. He felt a yearning, a tightness that he experienced the first time they met. He shifted uncomfortably and crossed one leg over the other to assure himself the firming between his legs might not be apparent to anyone else.

He longed to touch her, to hold her hand in his. But to do so would invite attention from an elder in the village. There was always one watching when strangers came and mindful that he was a village guest he kept his distance.

Hannat smiled, aware of his discomfort with a feminine wisdom as old as time.

She glanced around her, at the eating men, the children clustered around them admiring the wood and metal of their weapons, at the villagers who were slowly returning to the chores of the day.

"Do you still think you can come to Davao?" she asked suddenly.

Swallowing the last morsel of fish Bagyo coughed to hide a momentary confusion. When last they'd talked on the beach he'd made a show of bravado, suggesting they could meet in Davao where Hannat studied at a Muslim school three terms a year.

They'd be away from watchful adult eyes. He wasn't really sure why, but in late night talks with Calo he'd become aware that any furthering of his friendship to Hannat would depend on being alone with her. Calo's words were street crude, but expressive.

"If she's hot for you, you gotta get her on her own, and from what I've seen, she's bloody steaming for you."

After such exchanges in the long hut in which they slept Bagyo had slid his hand to his penis at the thought, constrained from the natural urge by the proximity of sleeping companions. But the thought of being alone with Hannat burned within him and when she raised the prospect of just that, here on the beach, his mind raced.

"Do you want me to come," he said to give himself time to think. Hannat smiled again and suddenly reached towards him to pick up his food bowl, getting to her feet. As she did so she dropped something from her closed hand then snatched up the bowl and moved off to clear away after the other fighters.

Bagyo stooped and covered the scrap of paper, watching her. With a last smile in his direction Hannat hurried away to her grandfather's hut.

Bagyo wandered down to the water where he peered at it. In a child-like scrawl Hannat had written 'Davao City, 11 Bolivar Street, I stay with my married sister. She knows about you. You can come and see me there.'

A surge of excitement. She wanted to see him, away from the village, away from prying eyes. Her sister was in on it. She was hot for him!

Bagyo turned away along the beach as though to walk off his lunch and go for a pee beyond the village. His mind raced as he considered what had been so easily said. How to get into Davao City? He'd get help from Calo to go in on an Abu Zaid unit job. From time to time there was mail to send or messages to collect. A day-long journey by bus from a pickup point on the coastal road meant he could spend two or three nights in Davao before getting the twice weekly return bus back.

He skipped a few steps and his heart swelled in excitement. Hannat liked him! He had a girl!

He turned to walk back to the village feeling virile and light, his feet barely seeming to touch the white sand, to skim through the water where it feathered the beach. He had the Abu Zaid unit, he had Calo, he had a home. He had a girl! He was a man!

Chapter Forty-seven

THE LIEUTENANT DOZED in the shade of a groundsheet draped over poles cut from the bush when he felt himself shaken fully awake.

"Sir, wake up," came the whisper again. Evangalista opened his eyes to find a trooper crouching over him. A few metres away another trooper had roused the sergeants who were clambering to their feet.

Fully awake now, Evangalista stood.

"We have a contact sir," said the trooper. He'd been posted a mile upstream from the bivouac, with others in a similar perimeter around the main body.

"I was on the ridge sir. I saw a group of men cross on the skyline of the next ridge to the north. They're heading southeast towards us. I estimate they're about three miles away with the valley they have to come through."

"Well done trooper," said Evangalista, clapping him on the shoulder. "Get some food. Sergeants!" The two veterans stepped up.

"You heard that?" the lieutenant asked. "Upstream for a mile to the ridge. Let's see if we can provide a reception committee!"

Quickly, the patrol was quietly called to order and the camp cleared. The men started moving up to the ridge, checking their weapons as they went.

* * *

Five men in Calo's group went down in the first fusillade that swept the trail where it wound up towards the ridge about three hundred metres from the top. Evangalista had wanted them closer into his net but a scared trooper jumped the gun and his shot triggered an echoing response from the other soldiers.

Two bodies lay inert on the track below the soldiers together with a number of hessian bags. A cloud of white burst from one, obviously food supplies, rice.

Evangalista spotted a wounded man crawling to cover. The others had escaped into the jungle.

"Sergeant, put the man who fired that first shot on a charge!" The young lieutenant was livid, his rage barely controlled. "Now the positions are reversed. They're in the jungle and waiting for us."

Through his binoculars only the brown dirt of the green jungle-edged trail, spilled rice, bags and the two bodies were now visible.

Suddenly from the jungle came a heart-chilling scream of agony, rising and falling, sending a shock of sympathetic horror through the members of the patrol.

A quarter-mile below their position on the ridge, a few metres off the trail at the base of an ironwood tree, Bagyo Cruz lay with his back supported by the sweeping root complex.

Above him knelt Calo, fear whitewashing his face as he tore off his red scarf and began winding it round Bagyo's right leg. Blood, scarlet-black in the dim light of the rainforest pumped steadily from an ugly hole below the knee. Calo grabbed a stick from the jungle floor and threaded it through the loop of scarf he'd made, twisting it tightly.

Bagyo made short, gasping sobs of pain as he tried to get his shocked system under control. His hands clutched his upper thigh in agony, his brain trying by brute force to keep the fire in his lower leg at bay. Then Calo finally tightened the tourniquet and as the blood flow lessened, Bagyo fainted.

But the horrific screams continued. Two other guerrillas nursed wounds. A bullet had merely clipped one's hand and the top joint of his index finger had been blown away. But from the other man, the agony issued. A bullet expressly designed to maim and kill had tumbled at 2,800 feet a second into his stomach. The fighter with the hand wound dragged him off the track and two other survivors carried him to the tree. Calo knew immediately there was no hope for him. He'd been virtually gutted and as the dreadful screams tore at their nerves he nodded to his second in command standing to one side.

The young man, a veteran of the MNLF campaign had fought before. There was a swiftly muted crack as he fired his AKS from an inch away into the dying man's head.

Calo turned back to Bagyo. "We'll have to get out of here," he addressed the group at large. "That's a full patrol. Our only hope is to get back to camp. With luck they'll wait before moving up, expecting us to be in ambush. But they're too strong. Come on."

He and another fighter lifted Bagyo's inert form and stealthily they picked their way through the jungle on a line to regain the track lower down in the valley and out of sight of the troops still waiting on the ridge.

There was no sound of pursuit when they stopped to listen at vantage points in the familiar terrain.

If the soldiers had moved out after them, they'd be moving carefully and slowly, expecting a rear-guard action at every bend in the trail.

But Calo's men had one thought in mind, to get back to the camp and safe haven. Getting treatment for Bagyo's leg was Calo's paramount concern. The wound had brought home the fact that he was the only family he had, their union born, tempered and strengthened by mean survival.

Burdened with Bagyo's weight it took two hours for the survivors to cover the distance back to the camp.

Alerted by a runner, the remainder of the Zaid Unit hurried out to meet them.

Transferring their wounded comrade to a rude litter of

fibre and bamboo they carried him to the sleeping hut.

The unit commander hurried in with a white tin with a Red Cross on the lid. From it he took a packet and quickly sprinkled a sulphur drug liberally into the wound. Bagyo stirred and groaned. The glass ampoule of a disposable morphine syringe was snapped off and the commander injected him. After a few minutes, as his groans began to subside, he finally drew Calo aside to hear what happened. Then, dispatching one of his men down the trail, he warned the rest of his men to be on full alert.

He examined the youth who's finger was shot away and treated it with an antibiotic salve before bandaging the stump and doling out a small package of di-gesic painkillers.

Two kilometres down the trail, the young man dispatched to keep guard sat in the crook of a tree branch over the trail, looking out through the branches to where the ground fell away towards the foothills. At a subtle change in the forest noise, only evident to one keenly attuned to his surroundings, he cocked his head to listen. Where all around him there was a pattern of noise from birds, small wildlife and the hum of a million insects he became aware of a patch of uncanny quiet. Like a ghost moving through the jungle from the south, a patch of silence swirled as the life of the jungle died in suspicion and threat flowed towards him. The soldiers were coming.

The guerrilla leapt to the jungle floor and began running back to camp, fear spurring a barefooted dance through the sharpened fascines of the booby-trapped bamboo.

Chapter Forty-eight

THE BLOOD TRAIL was easy to follow, spotting the spongy forest floor every few yards. The soldiers came onto the camp after hours of cautious stalking approach.

Smoke drifted from one of the huts as they fanned out around the clearing. There was no sign of life and the area seemed deserted.

Then there was movement on the far side of the clearing and an old woman stepped forward from the forest fringe. As the soldiers perceived no threat and swung their weapons back to cover each other as they moved swiftly now from building to building in the camp, she walked slowly to where Lt. Evangalista stood. After his sergeants emerged from behind the longhouse to signal that the camp was securely in his hands, he turned to her, too old and frail to flee with the others ahead of his overwhelming strength.

"Sir," she quavered. "Sir?"

Even as she spoke there was a shout from the longhouse. "Lieutenant," called one of the sergeants. "There's one in here. He's hit. They've left him behind."

"Old mother, you have nothing to fear from us," Evangalista said to the woman. "Go about your business." He hurried across to the longhouse and stooped through the entrance.

Bagyo lay on a bamboo sleeping mat, pain-wracked eyes tracking the lieutenant's approach. Noting the pistol at the officer's belt he closed his eyes, his fevered mind trying to bring some order to his thoughts. His last clear memory was one of a beach, the village, of the girl Hannat. The departure from the village is a blank. Then the shattering pain and blackness.

* * *

He opened his eyes, his brain somehow facing his new circumstances. *Government troops. The firefight. He's been caught. Will it come now?*

He knew from the Abu Zaid unit's own history, re-told around the evening fires, that MNLF rebels received a swift and brutal retribution at the hands of the soldiers.

But the Abu Zaid commander had assured him as two of the guerrillas dragged a struggling, protesting Calo out of the hut, that badly wounded as he was, he'd get medical treatment from the army. To flee through the jungle would slow the unit and eventually lead to Bagyo's being abandoned or his death at the hands of one of the unit. He must take his chances with the soldiers.

Strangely, he felt no fear. It was an alien emotion in a life without expectation. Then he thought of Hannat again and a keen sorrow grew where fear had not.

Opening his eyes again he found the lieutenant on one knee, lifting the field dressing on his wound.

Was it worth bringing this one out of the hills for questioning? Evangalista turned to find Bagyo watching him and gazed in surprise at the bloodshot but otherwise unmistakably green eyes fixed on his, the tousled auburn hair. Eurasian, European? But fighting with Muslims?

Lt. Evangalista looked to where the sergeant waited. "Look at him sergeant. What kind of Muslim rebel is he?"

The sergeant said grimly, "If you want me to find out sir, leave him with me for a few minutes."

But the officer quickly shook his head. "Get a medic in here." he commanded. "This one's coming back with us. We'll see what he knows when we get back to camp."

The sergeant knew his officer well enough by now to see he was a little different from the norm. "Yes sir," he muttered and left to find the patrol medical orderly.

Evangalista turned to Bagyo. "I don't know where you're from my young friend. But we'll get that wound seen to and then perhaps we'll find out."

As he spoke there was a commotion outside; a series of shouts, a shrill scream and then a fusillade of shots which ended abruptly.

The lieutenant raced for the doorway pulling out his pistol. To his right, beside what appeared to be a cookhouse, his men were grouped in a circle.

"What is it," he called as he hurried across.

He stepped through the circle. The sergeant he'd sent for the medic lay face down. Across his lifeless form was the old woman who'd remained in the camp, the carnage of her wizened flesh testimony to the bullets that were fired. A few feet away lay a bloody machete.

"What the fuck happened here?" demanded Evangalista in shock.

"Sir the old woman... the sergeant was passing the cookhouse and she came out with that!" The trooper who answered pointed to the weapon on the ground. "She must have been crazy. She hit him in the back of the neck before he could move. We opened fire but we were too late."

Evangalista looked down at the gaping wound that had parted the vertebrae at the top of the sergeant's spine.

He called to a radioman and within minutes was in touch with his base. After a short discussion, he handed back the microphone and turned to his men.

"We're getting a ride home. The slicks will be up in an hour. Set out a smoke-flare pattern in the clearing to guide them in. We'll take the sergeant's body with us."

He prodded the woman's body clear of the fallen soldier with his foot. "Bury the bitch."

The loss of the veteran sergeant was a professional and personal blow that took the gloss of what had been a very successful patrol.

The flight of six Iroquois helicopters found them just before dusk began to reclaim the jungle from the day.

An hour after Bagyo Cruz was loaded aboard the leading chopper in the custody of the lieutenant, he was carried into a small hospital facility at the military base in Davao City.

Under the eyes of an armed guard in an emergency ward, a Roman Catholic nursing sister, having cleaned and bound his wound, stood at his bed with a form.

"I must have your name, young man." She spoke kindly. Drowsy from the narcotics in his system Bagyo complied.

"I am called Bagyo Cruz," he said simply. "That is all I know." He turned his head on the pillow to look at the wall, clutching the amulet on its cord around his neck as the strong dose of morphine transported him mercifully to sleep.

He slept still when a tired doctor arrived, took one look at the wound in his leg and ordered an operating theatre prepared for an amputation.

Chapter Forty-nine

Great Barrier Island, New Zealand: December 1998

THE RISE AND fall racket of a revving chainsaw rose around Okupu Bay. Behind the family home above the wharf, young Peter Brian stepped back from a saw-horse, pressed a button into silence and flicking the sweat from his face with his free hand began pushing the wood he'd cut for the stove into a pile with his feet.

A strong well-built boy turning eleven, he'd been charged with responsibilities in return for weekly pocket money, Maria was at first horrified when Sean began teaching him to handle the small Stihl chainsaw.

"But he's too young Sean," she cried when she found her son cutting through lengths of dry ti-tree dragged from the acres of scrub at the back of their property.

"I'd rather he does it properly and under supervision than experiment himself when we're not around," was Sean's reply.

"Anyway," he'd said fondly, ruffling his son's head and noting again the intelligent grey-green eyes. "Peter's already a master fisherman. He's responsible and that should be recognised."

Maria soon realised her son was quite capable of carrying out the task and ceased to worry. In fact she soon had seven-year-old Jan helping out in the kitchen, garden and with the hens. The latter have in fact had been 'deeded' to the girl as her special preserve and she carried out the daily task of finding the eggs and feeding her charges with serious dedication, recording her daily activities and egg production in a special notebook.

In the kitchen below the slope where Peter worked, Maria rinsed the dough from a dessert pie from her hands, reflecting on how her life had settled into a routine she would never have dreamt of a decade before.

Each day she saw the children aboard the bus for the school on the east coast of the island and at times when Sean was busy up the coast with the crayfishing, she'll sit a while in the sun on the terrace with a last cup of coffee before beginning the chores of the day and muse over her happiness, occasionally touched by a shadow as she thought about Peter and then later Jan having to leave the island for high school. But a committee of local women, herself among them, was drawing up a plan to have a high school opened on the island as its population continued to grow.

With the business going well, she and Sean were becoming more involved in the local community and there'd been a number of suggestions that Sean should stand for election to the local council.

Until now he'd demurred, citing his workload, but recently had been heard to expound at some length on what the island really needed and Maria suspected another approach from his friends and neighbours would meet with a more receptive ear.

Peter interrupted her thoughts from the back door of the house as he dropped an armload of firewood into the basket by the stove. He moved over and gave her an impulsive hug.

"Love you mum," he said and Maria flushed with pleasure. Her two children had been brought up in a cocoon of love and security. Surely they could get a high school on the island. She didn't think she could bear to have them sent away to school, to only return at weekends and holidays. She vowed to put some subtle pressure on Sean that evening to take more seriously the council suggestion. He'd then be in a position of influence when the time came to get the education ministry to recognise the islanders' needs.

Maria trimmed the last of the pastry on the fruit pie and was opening the oven when the telephone rang. Wiping her hands on her jeans she glanced to the sideboard above the ringing phone where the first of the year's Christmas cards are displayed. How time's flown she thought, lifting the receiver.

"Maria Brian," she said. There was a slight pause and then a crackle of static.

"This is the overseas operator in the Philippines," came a familiar lilting *Tagalog* accent. "Please we have a reverse charges call from a Sister Jan for Mr Sean Brian or Maria Brian. Will you pay the charges please ma'am?" Maria, stunned, quickly assented.

Moments later Sister Jan's voice came on the line.

"Sister! How are you? It's good to hear your voice. And we already got your Christmas card. The mail service is much faster than in the old days."

Maria chattered to cover a growing feeling of anxiety. Why was Sister Jan calling?

Suddenly she wished Sean was home. Then Sister Jan spoke.

"I'm sorry to call collect but I'm at the convent and there's a toll bar here. Because of the local staff," she added hastily. "Maria, his name has surfaced again. I know it sounds incredible but there's a Bagyo Cruz in a military hospital staffed by us in Davao City. It's way down south on Mindanao."

"Whatever could our Bagyo be doing so far away?" Maria was stunned by the news, replying by rote.

Sister Jan had written some time ago about crossing paths with a Bagyo Cruz in Manila, just a few hours too late to make a positive connection.

"That's hundreds of miles away. If it's him he can't be that much older than Peter." Then she corrected herself realising Bagyo would now be well into his teens.

"Maria," said Sister Jan quickly, "this young man fits in age and in general description. But there's more. He has a bullet wound. He was picked up by the army in a patrol against some rebel groups down there. This Bagyo is under arrest in a military hospital.

"We still have a little money in our account here so I'm flying to Davao City this evening to see if it is really him and to see if I can help. I just had to let you both know in the meantime."

"Thank you sister. Thank you. Please call us collect at once if there's anything we can do. And please call immediately you've seen him."

After a few more words, Sister Jan said goodbye and broke the connection. Maria walked shakily onto the terrace and sat at the table there. Sean would not be back for a couple of hours at least.

She made a decision. "Peter," she called. "Peter, take the Zodiac please and fetch your father. Tell him Sister Jan rang with some news. He should be off Whangaparapara harbour, maybe just around at Black Reef."

Peter hurried towards the wharf and the inflatable and fibreglass tender tied to it, thrilled at any opportunity to skipper the 15-horsepower Zodiac the family used for transport around the bay.

Maria saw her own Jan walking back up the drive from feeding the chickens. She waved with a smile before moving back to the kitchen, a thoughtful expression settling on her face.

That night the Brian's held a family conference. It was only a week before Christmas but Sean by some strange premonition knew he had to go.

"I can get a flight in the morning and make a same-day connection from Sydney to Manila then on to Davao City. Of course I won't go if Sister Jan has doubts and she should be able to call us tonight. But I'll make the bookings just in case and I promise I'll be back by Christmas Eve."

At midnight they were awoken from sleep by Sister Jan on

the telephone from her hotel room in Davao City. The boy in the military hospital was indeed the Bagyo Cruz she'd lost so long ago in fire-ravaged Tondo.

Chapter Fifty

Davao City, Mindanao, Philippines: December 1998

SISTER JAN WAS at the airport to meet him, hurrying forward through the throng in the crowded arrivals hall and they briefly embraced.

"Always trouble Sean, isn't it? We always meet in times of trouble." As she turned and led the way slowly towards the exit Sean touched her shoulder.

"The boy, how is he?"

"Please Sean, a moment, let's get clear of this crowd. I have a van and driver from the convent." Sister Jan was once again in the nun's habit she preferred when away from her official duties.

"We'll talk on the way. I'm afraid you can't see Bagyo tonight. We have to deal with some red tape because he's officially in custody, a prisoner."

They pushed their way slowly through the arrivals shed that still bore the utility stamp of the United States Airforce which constructed it as an aircraft hangar in World War Two.

With Christmas week gaining momentum it's was packed with travellers bent on celebrating Christ's birthday at home with their families. Bing Crosby's *Silent Night* poured hollowly from the public address system, interspersed by staccato *Tagalog* flight information, repeated in English.

The doors into the terminal had been sprayed with fake snow and daubed with green holly leaves in a festive gesture that Sean found slightly ludicrous in the 30 degree Celsius oven he stepped into on the concrete outside.

As always the crowd melted before Sister Jan's habit and moments later he pulled closed the sliding door of a white Nissan van.

Sean and Sister Jan sat in the back seat away from the driver who wove slowly towards downtown Davao through the heavy traffic from the airport. The rutted roadway was packed and they made slow progress.

"Now," said Sister Jan. "Yes it's definitely the boy we knew so long ago from Caritas. His medical records, inoculations and suchlike, including blood type were all kept at one of the medical centres we took him to as a baby. There's also a snapshot of him at about three years of age with the records. You can see the likeness. And the name alone is unusual enough to make it certain. Anyway I was allowed briefly to see him, as I'm senior enough in the order to check on the condition of patients who are in custody. I'd recognise him anywhere." She paused, staring out the window at the hurrying figures, the street stalls and rude shops where naked bulbs from pirated electricity lines are beginning to wink on in the dusk.

"But there's some very bad news, Sean."

He looked at her with a frown.

"Let's hear it Sister. The sooner it's dealt with the better." Sister Jan turned from the window.

"Bagyo has had part of his right leg amputated," the nun says quietly.

"Oh bloody hell," said Sean softly. "Oh my God, the poor little bugger."

He checked the flow of language but did not think to apologise.

They sat in silence for a few minutes and then Sean said "We've got to get him out of there. He's only a kid. What interest can the army have in holding a kid?"

Sister Jan laid a hand on his arm, leaning against him as the van swerved to miss a girl weaving erratically on a motor-scooter along the pot-holed road.

"Rebellion is a serious business here," she said.

"The army considers teenage guerrillas just as capable

of pulling a trigger as an adult and they're treated the same. Bagyo was injured in a clash with a government patrol and he was wearing the red scarf of the Moro National Liberation Front fighters.

"Under military law, and that's martial law here, he'll be tried and sentenced. And that usually means a long prison sentence. If they prove he's killed any government troopers, it will probably be death.

"But the boy knows this and it is as if he doesn't care at all. When I spoke with him he was, well, very depressed but also sort of fatalistic. He looked at his missing leg and just muttered 'I won't be like him. I won't be like him.'

"When I asked what he meant and he simply said a name. Rick or Rigg, something like that, and then he said 'He shut the door. I don't want to be like him.'

"That was all. His state of mind worries me as much as anything. He speaks the language of the streets, although he did get some sort of education in an urban refugee camp. Obviously his life has been dreadfully hard."

"God what a mess," said Sean. This time Sister Jan looked at him with eyebrows arched and he had the grace to apologise. "I'm sorry Sister. I guess I'm tired and a little upset." He gave a wry smile. "I must remember who I'm talking to."

They reached a small Spanish Mission hotel near the military garrison headquarters. It reflected the red tiled roofs and the yellow stucco exterior of the military buildings and many of the nearby stores and houses in this older section of the city.

"We'll both stay here," said the nun as Sean tipped the driver and retrieved his bag from the front seat.

"Tomorrow we have an appointment at 11 o'clock with the local area commander to see if they'll allow you, as a foreigner and a journalist, to see the boy."

Sean realised with some relief that he was still listed as a journalist in his passport and as such the intelligence wire in

Manila would have been humming since he passed through passport control at Benigno Aquino airport.

He stopped at a sudden thought and then, following Sister Jan into the hotel, he registered and collected a key.

Later, over a simple dinner of fried rice in the hotel dining room Sean gave voice to his thoughts.

"Sister, I have an idea. Do you remember a man called Pedro Wright, the former National Police Bureau chief?"

"Yes he's now a senator and a fairly respected one too."

"Well," said Sean, "I knew him pretty well years ago. I'm going to call him to see if he can cut through some of the bull…the ah, red tape…?" He paused expectantly.

"It's possible he could help I suppose," she replied.

After coffee and plans to meet in the morning, Sean became aware of the fatigue from his three-stage flight from Auckland and he excused himself. They bid each other goodnight and went to their rooms.

Sean called and asked the hotel switchboard operator for a connection to Manila, glancing at his black and silver Omega diving watch, a gift from Maria. It was nine o'clock, hopefully a good time to catch Wright.

From his bag he took a battered green contact book which lists names in a dozen countries. Giving Wright's unlisted phone number in the capital to the operator he waited and after several rings and a short exchange with a servant, Wright was on the line.

After exchanging greetings and briefly covering their respective histories, Sean explained the reason for his call.

Wright was sympathetic, but said: "While I'll make some inquiries for you Sean, I have to warn you, the military have a pretty free hand down there. The local commander is handling assassinations, grenade attacks, hell they even bombed a village wedding for God's sake. There are no rules. It's a dirty war. But in your case at least, I'll make some calls and try and get you access to him."

Saying goodnight, Wright promised to call next morning with any news. "Before your 11 o'clock appointment at the garrison," he finished.

It's was not until Sean hung up that he realised he's not mentioned the time of his meeting with the military commander.

He rummaged again in his travel bag for a bottle of Glenfiddich from Auckland airport's duty-free shop. Finding a scratched glass in the bathroom he poured a couple of fingers and sipped it neat in preference to adding dubious mains water from the tap.

The drink took some of the tension out of him and sitting on the edge of the bed, he re-ran the day in his head, the end of his precipitate dash from Great Barrier Island. Was it only yesterday?

Why had he come so far for a foundling he once shelled out a few dollars for? Was it for Maria? But he sensed there was something much deeper behind his dash across the Pacific and pouring another small Scotch he leaned against the headboard. Perhaps a hangover from the old days, the need to up and go, the adrenaline rush of international flight and a different country after the days of being essentially island-bound. Or then again, was it something more? Was his news instinct behind this? Throughout his career, Sean had developed a 'nose for news' that was the envy of many of his colleagues. Somehow, he'd managed to be a step ahead of the pack, sensing a story, an event, before it became overt and attracted widespread attention.

Was there an event here that he still does not see? A turning point, a catalyst, a watershed?

Sean wearily closed his eyes. Tomorrow was still to unfold and right now the toll of travel needed payment. He finished the drink and felt utter weariness replace curiosity and speculation. He undressed to shorts and T-shirt and climbed into the single bed.

Chapter Fifty-one

Wright hadn't called by the time Sean and Sister Jan left the hotel for the short walk to the military camp which sprawled over several blocks near the city centre.

They passed through a guardhouse fairly promptly, but not before a thorough body search for Sean, a female soldier ushering Sister Jan into another room for, in her case, a symbolic and cursory indignity.

They are then kept waiting for a full hour in the wood-panelled anteroom of an office, which bore the name of Colonel Geronimo Honasan, Commander, Southern Philippines Military Region.

Despite the business-like atmosphere as they watched a constant flow of uniformed men and the occasional woman in and out of the double doors, a surprisingly robust Christmas pine tree, covered in winking red lights, stood in the corner of the room. Sean walked across and discovered it was made of wire and nylon, probably, he mused, government issue; military commanders, for the use of.

Eventually a smartly uniformed sergeant with the braid of an aide de camp approached them.

"The colonel will see you now." He ushered them towards Hosanan's office.

The Colonel looked up and motioned them to comfortable seats in front of his wide cane-topped desk. He was a swarthy long-faced Filipino with hair that reminded Sean of a silent movie star, slicked back with oil. A cheroot propped in an ashtray on the desk lazily swirled smoke towards a fan that hummed in the corner of the room.

The colonel picked up a file as his aide left, closing the doors behind him.

"So, you have an interest in one Bagyo Cruz, one of our

murderous so-called freedom fighters?" he said with a thin smile.

"Just exactly why does a foreign journalist want to see an imprisoned guerrilla?"

The question threw Sean completely off balance and he struggled to think of an appropriate response, his mind racing as he discarded thoughts such as 'my wife wants me to' 'we think it's someone who went missing and we have always felt a loss…' Before he could formulate a reply, Sister Jan spoke softly.

"Colonel, we believe the youth you are holding is a foundling that my religious order cared for in Manila. This gentleman sponsored the child and provided money for his support until he went missing many years back. Thus both Mr Brian and myself have a natural as well as a vested interest in the wellbeing of the boy. We feel a bond and want to do what we can to help him."

The colonel listened, his face softening fractionally at the nun's reasoned tone.

"I greatly regret there will not be much you can do to help him," he said.

"Our instructions in dealing with this armed insurgency are very hard and fast. In this case, we recovered among his effects, a cashbox taken during the massacre of a wedding party for a local official. The evidence is therefore quite damning."

He stopped as the telephone on his desk rang. He picked up the receiver and listened.

"Yes sir," he said, and again "Yes sir," before hanging up.

Looking quizzically at Sean he let out a long breath.

"It seems you have friends in high places Mr Brian. You are to be allowed to see this youth but not to meet with him."

"The hospital prisoners will be exercising in an hour. Until then, my sergeant will escort you to our canteen where he will see that you're given some lunch."

They were led out of the office by the colonel's aide who showed them down a flight of stairs to a half-empty ground floor canteen where they toyed with a plate of soggy sandwiches, both nervous of the encounter Sean was about to face.

Sister Jan spoke again of her brief meeting with Bagyo.

"He's a lad beyond his years Sean. He's intelligent but there's an undercurrent of cunning that must've been instilled into him through the need for survival. And there's a haunted look in his eyes. Perhaps it was losing the leg. But there's something somehow empty there too." She paused. "It's like an old man's eyes in a child's face, wisdom and pain all mixed up together."

She was interrupted by the arrival of the sergeant at their table. He motioned Sean to accompany him, asking Sister Jan to remain behind. "Only Mr Brian, Sister. I'm sorry, the colonel's orders."

Outside there was a waiting jeep and after driving across the spartan parade ground they turned down a tar-sealed side road lined with white-painted rocks placed with military precision. At the end was a small compound enclosed on two sides by ancient stone walls, on the others by high fencing topped with ribbons of razor wire.

A small group of men was gathered in one corner of the concrete yard near an open doorway. One was in a wheelchair, others displayed bandages, plaster casts and slings.

They looked disinterestedly across as the jeep pulled up.

But a pyjama clad-youth on crutches moved awkwardly away from the group, lifting his hand to shade his eyes.

Moving slowly he hobbled toward them, stumbling once or twice. He had one complete leg. The other ended just below the knee in a heavily bandaged stump. Unconsciously Sean lifted a hand as if to steady the crippled prisoner. Then the youth was leaning heavily on his supports at what Sean realised was an inner fence, a low wire a dozen metres from where he stood.

Man and boy stared at each other, eyes locked. The same electricity that thrilled through Sean one Christmas morning in Manila was in him again as the boy looked steadily at him.

"Bagyo, I've come to, Sister Jan and I…" Sean spoke as the sergeant loudly intervened "No words sir, you cannot communicate with the prisoner. Now we must go. Come!"

There is no mistaking the order and Sean backed away from the fence still holding Bagyo's gaze as if mesmerised, unwilling to break the contact until he stumbled as he backed into the jeep.

Turning to climb into the vehicle he looked back again but the young man had turned away, slowly swinging his crippled body towards the others in the compound, his head bowed.

Watching him go, Sean felt hot tears stinging his eyes and again wondered at the emotion evoked by the foundling who was now almost a man.

Chapter Fifty-two

BAGYO AWOKE AN hour before dawn on the narrow cot that served as his hospital bed. His first sight was the slowly revolving fan swinging on loose screws from the concrete ceiling. His missing foot throbbed right to the non-existent toes and gripping the edge of the cot he managed to roll onto his side. Beside him and across the small prison ward were three other beds, all occupied by sleeping forms lit by the feeble light from a low wattage bulb burning in the passage outside the open doorway. From it hung a faded cardboard cutout bell covered in silver stars, a gesture of festivity from the nurses.

Bagyo was housed in minimum security with free access on his crutches to the latrine down the hallway and even the prison courtyard where the high razor-wired fence was a sufficient deterrent for the maimed and sick in the hospital wing.

Counting his heartbeats with the pulse of his missing foot an ache swelled inside him as his gaze alighted on the cheap wooden crutches leaning against the locker beside his bed.

A whirl of memories flooded through his mind, coalescing, fragmenting images chasing each other through his head, a girl with black hair, a fire, tears in the street, a man lying in a room, a crutch raised and threatening, a door slamming over and over.

Other images. A footless cripple hobbling through the crowds on a busy street, importuning, crying 'Sir, you help me, Sir.'

He was then waking in another place, rolling away from his friend Calo on the dried grass of a park, walking along Roxhas Boulevard in Manila with a girl called Riti.

Images of traffic and crowded jeepneys, memories of

noise. A taxi at traffic lights, a man in the back seat looking at him then giving him money. The man getting out of the taxi. Bagyo scared, poised to flee. The man taking something from his neck and placing it in his hand. White and smooth.

Bagyo imagines himself back in Camp Crame where the refugees of Ermita found refuge. Here is order, security and he learns to read, his imagination soaring beyond the confines of the camp as he grows. And always the tooth the man gave him. Now it's around his neck as always. It's become a talisman and without it he's scared to move.

Even prowling the murky streets of MP Burgos for his human prey he'd kept it with him, pocketed because Calo forbade the waxed cord around his neck.

'If you have to run and someone grabs it they'll saw through your bloody throat,' he'd said.

Well he won't be running anymore. Looking back to the ceiling fan as it spins he forms a picture in his mind of yesterday's encounter in the courtyard. The man standing outside the wire, staring.

Bagyo recalls the face, his wondering as the figure spoke before being turned away from the wire by a guard.

Then Bagyo the child, hovering on the median strip of four lane lines of snarling traffic, receiving an offering he didn't understand. The money too he remembers and its swift passing into other hands.

He recalls tears and deep emptiness. He has the same feeling now, a sense of futility, loneliness and the bleakness of a crippled life reaching before him, a future to nowhere.

He's on a beach. The flavour of fish, the taste of salt. A girl's eyes reflecting the flickering magic of the sea, her hair swirling in the breeze. Skin warm but not for his touch. Calo's voice 'Your girl eh? Your girl!' Hannat. His lonely reverie interrupted by a figure in the doorway.

One of the Filipina nursing nuns. She's always been kind to him and he raises himself on his elbow, calling softly across the room. Rising further he swings his good leg from the cot, reaching to the thong around his neck.

"Please Sister, take this." The nun moved to his bedside and Bagyo pressed something into her hand. Their whispered conversation was brief before Bagyo asked her to pass his crutches.

"I need to go," indicating the passageway to the latrines near the entrance to the courtyard.

The nun tucked the crutches into his armpits and the crippled youth swung himself from the bed.

Chapter Fifty-three

THE NEXT DAY at noon, Sean received a summons to come alone to Colonel Honasan's office.

Sister Jan was in her room making contact with any and all members of the church in Davao City who might possibly bring some influence to bear in helping Bagyo Cruz.

Both she and Sean are by now resigned to the young man's incarceration but are determined to do all they possibly can to ease his term and make what plans they can for his eventual release.

Sean was speaking long distance with Pedro Wright in Manila when the messenger arrived from the colonel. He motioned the boy to wait and listened as the senator spoke.

"Sean, getting you, as a foreigner and a journalist at that, in even only to see him, took a lot of political favours. As I warned you, the gloves are off down there. My best advice to you is go home. You can do nothing but let justice take its course. Your friend Sister Jan can keep contact with him in prison. Go home Sean." Pedro Wright broke the connection. Sean sat on his bed, his mind casting about for another avenue of help when the messenger tapped again at his open door. He handed Sean an envelope and left without waiting for a reply.

Twenty minutes later Sean was again seated before Colonel Honasan. The officer was dressed in an immaculate uniform, his hat and swagger stick placed neatly on the clean and polished desk.

For several moments he was silent, studying the man before him. Then he spoke.

"Mr Sean Brian, I am to inform you that the prisoner Bagyo Cruz, a terrorist member of the so-called Moro National Liberation Front was shot trying to climb the wire outside the security ward during the night. My guards are under orders to shoot all escapees. He was young, I know. But he was a prisoner at the wire and he was shot, killed. His body will be buried within the prison."

Sean was frozen, unable to fully take in what he heard, his mind reeling, his arms wrapped across his body, a futile barricade against the enormity of the colonel's message.

The officer continued less formally "*Pare*, the prisoner left something. He knew what would happen to him. He deliberately put himself under fire from his guards."

He took an envelope from his desk and tipped it. From it fell a curved, white object.

The colonel picked it up suspended on a leather thong as Sean still struggled for composure, his whole being seething in shock and despair.

The pale ivory cast ghostly circles in the air, turning slowly.

The colonel said softly "He asked a nun to give this to the father – *bigyan ito sa ama, ang mga tao gamit ang mga mata*. I'm sorry – I must translate for you: give this to the father, the man with the eyes."

Epilogue

ON CHRISTMAS EVE in the house above the bay at Okupu, Sean, Maria, Jan and Peter all gaze at the tree cut from the hill behind the house. Fairy lights twinkle from its branches and gaily wrapped gifts are placed below it. The scent of freshly cut pine mingles with the warm aromas of food from the wood stove in the kitchen.

Sean holds Maria in his arms. She's beautiful. He notices the wings of silver hinting in her hair.

Looking down to where Peter and Jan crouch to contemplate the contents of the packages under the tree they've festooned with decorations Sean says quietly "I love you all very much," before taking Maria's hand and leading her through the open doors onto the terrace.

They walk on slowly down the path of crushed scallop shells leading to the beach, into a warm clear night holding the promise of another hot island summer's day to follow.

Standing at the water's edge Sean lifts from around his neck the whale's tooth on its leather thong.

He holds it to his lips for a long moment and in a sudden mental metamorphosis he's in the street outside the prison walking through crowds, not seeing, not hearing.

Shock, despair and an aching inside. He has been unable to talk to the youth yet he can feel him, see clearly those eyes that once mirrored his own. The loss is one of an infinity of time and hopelessness inherent in the filthy streets of Tondo the night a storm was rising.

Somehow Sean found his way home from Davao to Great Barrier Island, forever branded with an image of a grubby brown face, an arm outstretched, a whispered plea.

Then he shakes the thoughts from his head as a wavelet crumples at their feet. One arm holding Maria tightly, he swings the other.

With an easy underarm throw he releases the talisman on its cord high into the path of the moonlight carving across the bay, star-capped sentinel hills mute witness to a homecoming.

Across the bay the oily essence of a long-dead whale still seeps through sand from an ancient deep grave on the beach. The dark stain is licked by an ebb tide as the ivory flickers once high in the soft light before slipping silently back into the sea.

That instant there's a pulse in the night, the unseen beat of a wing on warm air. Sean is momentarily giddy and his heart seems to swell within him. He can't breathe and he reaches anxiously for Maria's hand. The feeling slowly subsides.

They turn and walk together along the sand and Maria slips an arm around him.

"Tomorrow," says Sean, "I must start to write..."

Lightning Source UK Ltd.
Milton Keynes UK
UKHW011028091221
395376UK00001B/290